**"Christmas is here, Merry old Christmas,
Gift-bearing, heart-touching,
Joy-bringing Christmas, Day of grand memories,
King of the Year!"**
—Washington Irving

Most holidays last only a short while, but the romance of Christmas lingers on. It's the season for mistletoe and crackling fires, for stolen kisses and ecstatic reunions, for blushing glances and the heart-pounding magic of love.

Many of us have a secret picture of Christmas Past, each one filled with nostalgic yearning for a simpler time when windows shimmered with candlelight, skirts swirled and skimmed the floors, and gentlemen were gallant and true. These four sparkling novellas by Kay Cornelius, Rebecca Germany, Darlene Mindrup, and Colleen Reece will whisk your heart away to those days gone by and their timeless enchantment of romance.

You'll follow a headstrong young woman across the Kentucky frontier, then join a small-town couple in their struggle to adjust to the changes of life. You'll ache with the longing of a woman alone on the Dakota prairie, and triumph with an Irish lass seeking her true love in the cold Canadian wilderness. Let the dreams come softly shining—come along for a *Nostalgic Noel!*

A Nostalgic Noel

Kay Cornelius

Rebecca Germany

Darlene Mindrup

Colleen Reece

BARBOUR
PUBLISHING, INC.
Uhrichsville, Ohio

Published by Barbour Publishing, Inc., P.O. Box 719, Uhrichsville, Ohio 44683
http://www.barbourbooks.com

 Member of the
Evangelical Christian
Publishers Association

Printed in the United States of America.

A Nostalgic Noel

Cane Creek Christmas

Kay Cornelius

Dedication

For Kathryn Amy Parvin, dedicated teacher,
talented musician, and devoted wife and mother,
my lovely and loving daughter—and my friend.

Chapter 1

On December 24, 1806, Rachel Taylor sat in the small log schoolhouse near Bryan's Station, Kentucky, and tried hard not to stare at Matthew McNaught. Now nineteen, the young schoolmaster was four years older than Rachel, and she had known him all her life. Yet on this day, as she settled the younger children around her to listen to a special story from their schoolmaster, she felt suddenly shy and awkward. She was almost glad when Vinnie Fletcher, at five the next-youngest of Asa Fletcher's motherless brood, plucked at her sleeve and forced Rachel to look away from the dark-eyed, undeniably handsome Matthew McNaught.

"Miss Rachel, when's my papa gonna come home?"

Before Rachel could reply, Vinnie's brother Tom, four years the girl's senior, glared at his sister. "Shush up a—askin' that! He won't get here a bit sooner with you all the time talkin' about it."

"Don't be so hard on her, Tom," Rachel said softly. "She's still just a baby."

Tears filled Vinnie's eyes, but she shook her head at Rachel's words. "I'm not a baby! I'm a big girl."

"Then act like it!" Tom returned to the boys' side of

the one-room schoolhouse, and Rachel felt a stab of pity for this boy of nine. He tried to hide how much he missed his mother, but Rachel knew he must be anxious at his father's long absence, as well.

Aware that Matthew had probably heard the whole exchange, Rachel gave Vinnie a brief hug, then put a warning finger to her lips as a signal for the children to be quiet. Esther Taylor, who was seven, leaned her head against Rachel's shoulder as if jealous of her sister's attention to Vinnie.

"Listen, boys and girls. Master McNaught has a special story to tell us." Rachel's dark eyes met the schoolmaster's.

When his glance lingered on Rachel, she quickly lowered her eyes and hoped he wouldn't notice the sudden blush she felt coloring her cheeks.

"Thank you, Miss Rachel." Matthew had been standing, but now he folded his nearly six-foot-tall frame in a manner that reminded Rachel of the way her father put up his jackknife when he finished using it, pushing first one blade and then another into its place. When he had settled himself and seemed satisfied that he had everyone's attention, Matthew began to speak in the calm, surprisingly deep voice that Rachel had come to admire.

"On this last day before Christmas, I want to tell you a story I heard back home when I was about the age of Tom Fletcher here."

"Where was that, Master McNaught?" asked red-haired Sally Dermott, who spent many hours in the dunce's corner because of an apparent inability to remain silent for more than a few minutes.

"In Virginia, where I lived before I came to Kentucky," Matthew replied. "It is a story so old that no one knows when it first began, and no one knows when its telling will end. And once I start this story, you must all be very quiet and listen and not say a word." Matthew looked directly at Sally. "Does everyone promise to do that?"

When fifteen heads bobbed in unison, the schoolmaster nodded his satisfaction, took a deep breath, and began the story.

"Once upon a long, long time ago, in a land far away, it fell out that a poor old man had to travel a great distance in the bitter cold of winter. This old man had only one cloak, and although he wrapped it as tightly around him as he could, the wind began to blow and soon he started to shiver. It was a bitterly cold night, but the old man was grateful that he could see the stars, for he was using the brightest one to help him find his way home."

"The North Star!" Sally whispered under her breath, then put a hand to her mouth as she realized she'd spoken aloud.

Matthew went on as if he hadn't heard Sally. "This star had guided him for many nights, but on this particular evening, a strong wind blew clouds across the sky, and then a heavy snow began to fall. The old man could no longer see the path in front of him, yet he kept on walking because he knew that it would be dangerous to stop."

Matthew paused and noted the children's unspoken

Why? then nodded as if to acknowledge it.

"You know how it is here in Kentucky in deep winter, when the snow falls and the wind blows. People don't go out in a snowstorm, because it is cold and they might lose their way. Well, at the time of this story, not only was it cold, but many wolves still roamed the deep woods."

The children exhaled suddenly and felt a shiver of fear. They knew that even now in Kentucky, wild animals still came out of the woods when they got hungry, and they'd all heard wolves howling on a clear, windless night.

"Now, as far as the old man knew, not another human being lived within miles of where he passed through these deep woods, and as the night went on and the air became colder, he feared that he had lost the trail. He knew he might be wandering aimlessly, going ever more deeply in the woods. Then he heard a single wolf howl, and then another, and soon the whole night seemed to be filled with fierce cold and stinging snow and the shrieks of the wolves. Not only that, but the sound of the wolves seemed to grow closer with every passing minute. Every time the old man changed his direction to try to get away from the wolves, he heard their howls from that way too, until he knew that they had him surrounded."

When Matthew stopped speaking for a moment, Vinnie drew a sobbing breath, and several of the other children seemed equally affected. Rachel hugged the child and directed a quizzical glance at Matthew. She'd never known him to tell a story like this, almost as if it were designed to upset the children.

"Then the old man remembered that it was Christmas Eve, the night that God sent His Son to earth as a baby. He realized that the star he had been following for so long could be the same one that brought the Wise Men from a far country. He closed his eyes and asked God to move the clouds aside so he could once again see the star and follow the right path. He shivered in the cold wind, but he felt happy in the thought that the wind would take away the clouds and give back his guiding star.

"After a long while, the old man dared to open his eyes again. He looked up and saw that clouds still hid all the stars, and the stinging of icy needles against his skin told him that the snow still fell. And, yes, the wolves still howled, first from one side and then from another.

"But then the old man noticed something else. Off to his right, through some low-hanging, snow-covered branches, he saw a faint gleam of light. He turned toward it, and although at times he almost lost sight of it in the thick snow and the snarl of the trees, the old man kept going toward that light. Once he tripped over a fallen limb and fell to the ground, but he made himself get up and keep going. After a while, the old man realized that as the light grew stronger, he no longer heard the wolves, and he thanked God that they had gone away.

"Then, as he came closer to the light, he saw that it came from a candle set into the lone window of a small cottage. Its soft glow reminded him of the warmth he might find inside, and although his strength was all but

13

spent, the old man managed to keep going. He didn't know how he did it, but he managed the last few steps on feet that were numb from frostbite. By the time he reached the cottage, he was too weak to raise his hand and knock. Instead, he fell forward, against the wooden door."

Matthew paused, just long enough for Sally to blurt out, "Then what happened?"

"Inside the cottage lived a good man and his wife. They were poor, and the winter had been hard. They had only a few crusts of bread and some cheese in their larder, and only one candle-end left. Yet, that night, the husband had lighted their last candle and put it in the window.

" 'Perhaps it will show the way for the Christ Child,' his wife said, for that was a custom in those days. They said their prayers and lay down in front of the embers of the fire, thankful for a warm and safe place to sleep.

"You can imagine how surprised they were when they were awakened from a sound sleep by a thump against their door.

" 'No one would be traveling on such a cold and stormy night,' the wife said. She feared to see what had caused the noise they heard, but she went to the door with her husband and helped him drag inside the old man they found lying there.

"When the traveler opened his eyes and saw that he was safe, he thanked God. 'I saw your candle in the window, and now I live,' he told them.

" 'We put it there to welcome the Christ Child,' the woman said.

" 'But you needed it more,' her husband added.

"The old man could say nothing then, but he never forgot how a candle in the window of a lowly hovel in the deep woods had saved his life. From then on, as long as he lived, he made sure that a light burned in the front window of his house, and every traveler who came into its light received a warm welcome."

For a moment after Matthew stopped speaking, the children remained quiet, then several spoke at once. "And they lived happily ever after!" exclaimed Esther Taylor, who liked for stories to end that way. Elspeth Elliott, at twelve the oldest pupil, asked if the story had any truth in it at all, a question which the schoolmaster either didn't hear or chose to ignore.

Vinnie Fletcher turned to Rachel, her face aglow. "Maybe a candle would help bring Papa home. Can we put one in the window tonight, Rachel?"

"That's not for her to say," Tom reminded his sister, his tone heavy with disapproval.

Rachel stood and stretched her stiff muscles. "Come, children, we should be getting home."

"If you can wait a moment, I'll walk with you," Matthew McNaught said.

Rachel tried to hide her pleasure. "We'll all help put things aright," she said, and set about to match action to her words. Tom and Abby, his seven-year-old sister, along with Rachel and her brother John, who was nearly ten, put out the schoolhouse fire, secured the shutters, and stacked the benches while the youngest, Vinnie and Esther, made a great show of sweeping the floor, but with more giggling than real progress.

15

Gray twilight had begun to streak the winter sky by the time Matthew bolted the schoolhouse door and joined the small procession of pupils moving down the hill toward the settlement called Bryan's Station. With Vinnie holding one of her hands and Esther the other, Rachel had a hard time slowing their pace for Matthew to catch up with them.

"I liked your story, Master McNaught," Esther said when Matthew fell into step beside her.

"Me too," Vinnie echoed.

"I wonder that you've never told it before," Rachel said.

Matthew shrugged. "I've never been a schoolmaster at Christmas before," he said.

"Can Vinnie and me go on ahead, Rachel?" asked Esther. At Rachel's nod of approval, Esther and Vinnie scampered ahead to catch up with the others.

Glad for the opportunity for a rare more or less private moment with Matthew, Rachel cast about for a topic of conversation. "I knew your folks came from Virginia, but I never heard where." Rachel's inflection made it a question.

"Over Staunton way," he said. "I still have a passel of kin there. I've been thinking of going to see them again."

"Your folks came here before the siege, didn't they?" Rachel already knew the answer, but she wanted Matthew McNaught to keep talking to her as long as possible.

"Yes, about the same time as yours, I reckon, but not from North Carolina, like your folks and the Boones

16

and Dermotts." They approached the main part of Bryan's Station, and Matthew's gesture took in the two rows of cabins which faced one another across a crude street some twenty feet wide. "It's hard to imagine what this place looked like, surrounded by palisades and with lookout towers at all four corners," he said.

"Or how it must have been when the people living here had to fight off all those Indians back in 1782."

"Sometimes I wonder if all the stories they tell about that time are gospel truth," Matthew said.

"Like how our mothers went out of the gates for water right under the Indians' noses, knowing the siege was coming."

"Oh, that happened, all right," Matthew said. "The women never had much to say much about it, but my aunt in Virginia still has a letter my father wrote to her about it, naming each and every one of the thirty-seven women. He believed it was only through God's providence that their lives were spared."

"And the Station came out all right too, although the Indians killed a few men and fire arrows burned some of the cabins. My father says it was almost like a miracle."

They slowed their pace near the Taylors' house, one of the original Station cabins that had been greatly enlarged with timbers taken from the palisades when the Indian raids finally ended and such defenses were no longer needed. The children stopped at the doorway and turned to wave a final greeting to Matthew.

"Happy Christmas, Master McNaught!" they called, then disappeared inside.

"I suppose I should go in and help with the children," Rachel said. She was reluctant to leave Matthew, but many eyes watched them, and she knew that tongues would wag if they didn't part company soon.

Matthew looked at Rachel with genuine concern. "I heard Vinnie ask when her father was coming back. It was good of you folks to take the children in when their mother died, but it must be getting a bit crowded at your place by now. Any word on when Asa Fletcher will be back?"

Rachel shook her head. "No, he just said he had to go away for a time to get some business settled. We all thought he'd be back by Christmas, but now with the weather likely to turn bad, we might not see him until spring."

"I hope no misfortune has befallen him."

"So do we," Rachel agreed.

For a moment, she thought Matthew was about to say something else, perhaps something personal. But then Mrs. Elliott came out of her house with a bucket over her arm, apparently bound for the spring, and her curious glance obviously made Matthew uncomfortable.

"I must get home," he said. "Mrs. Eggleston expects me to turn the fireplace spit for her tonight."

Rachel almost envied the stout woman who had moved into the McNaught cabin after Matthew's mother had died within a month of his father's death.

"If you have the chance, come over on Christmas Day. Ma's mincemeat pies are especially good this year."

"Thank you, but I'm taking Mrs. Eggleston to her

sister's in Lexington. We'll no doubt stay there several days."

"Well, Happy Christmas to you, anyway."

"The same to you and your house," Matthew responded. Rachel wanted to stand there and watch until Matthew disappeared from sight on the other side of the hill, but she made herself move on to her own home.

I should chide myself for mooning over Matthew McNaught, she acknowledged, but thinking of him gave her too much pleasure to try very hard to direct her thoughts elsewhere.

Rachel was about to step onto the Taylor doorstep when the front door burst open and Vinnie, her eyes wide with excitement, ran into her.

"Come quick!" she urged.

A sudden fear seized Rachel. "What is it? Is something amiss?"

Impatient at Rachel's lack of speed, Vinnie grabbed Rachel's hand and pulled her toward the door. "No, no," the girl cried. "He's here! Our papa's come back!"

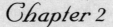

Here she is, Papa," said Vinnie when she and Rachel entered the combination kitchen-sitting room, the largest in the Taylors' rambling frame home.

Asa Fletcher stood in front of the fireplace, the center of attention. He held three-year-old Betty, his youngest, while Abby and Tom stood on either side. Vinnie continued to pull at Rachel's hand until she stood in front of Asa.

"Say hidy to Papa," Vinnie prompted.

Embarrassed, Rachel felt her face warm. The man who stood before her seemed somehow different from the Asa Fletcher who'd been their neighbor for the past few years. His scraggly beard and long hair were neatly trimmed, and instead of the familiar buckskins, he wore a suit made of some kind of dark cloth. But most unsettling of all was the strange way he looked at Rachel.

"Hello, Mr. Fletcher," she managed to say, accompanying her words with a slight curtsy as a sign of respect for an elder.

"Howdy, Miss Rachel. The younguns tell me you and your ma took good care of them whilst I was away."

Seeing her daughter's discomfort, Mrs. Taylor spoke for them both. "We tried to, and that's a fact."

"It wasn't hard," Rachel added. "The children mind pretty well, for the most part."

Asa Fletcher grinned widely, revealing he'd lost several teeth. "Well, I guarantee if'n you use the strap on 'em, they get to mindin' a heap better."

Rachel's father nodded. " 'Spare the rod and spoil the child,' the Good Book says. But the Book also says not to provoke our children to anger."

Mary Taylor looked irritated and glared at her husband before she turned back to her eldest child. "Rachel, I need some help with supper."

"Yes, ma'am." Gladly Rachel took her apron from its peg by the back door and set to work peeling carrots.

Although she never addressed or looked at Asa Fletcher directly, all evening Rachel was aware that he watched her every move. When little Betty fell asleep in her father's arms, Mary Taylor suggested that the Fletcher children should remain with the Taylors until Asa's house could be properly cleaned. Rachel welcomed the excuse to be free from Asa Fletcher's gaze as she took Betty and started upstairs to the loft room where the girls all slept on quilt pallets.

Her relief was short-lived, however, for when the other children had at last said their prayers and fallen asleep, Rachel heard her parents and Asa Fletcher engaged in a conversation which mentioned her name.

More than once in the past few weeks Rachel had overheard her parents talking when they thought all the children were asleep. It was how she had first known, long before her mother mentioned it, that her father was thinking of leaving Bryan's Station.

"The Taylors always had itchy feet, you know," Mary Taylor had told Rachel as they spread quilts out for an airing. "From the time they set foot on the American shore, that bunch of folks never stayed in one place very long."

Rachel knew the story of how the first William Taylor had left England near the end of the 1600s and settled in Delaware. Eventually he moved on to Pennsylvania, and some of his sons went down into North Carolina. It was there her father, namesake of that first William Taylor, had served in the American Revolution before going on to Kentucky, where he had been living for twenty-seven years. It was, Mary Taylor said, an almost unheard-of family record for a Taylor to stay in one place that long.

"What does Pa intend to do?" Rachel asked her mother, as if she hadn't already heard them whispering together late in the night when the wind died down and even the night creatures were quiet.

"He's a mind to pioneer some more. He's due a land grant from Tennessee, and I reckon he thinks he better take it whilst he's still able-bodied."

"I don't want to leave Bryan's Station," Rachel had told her mother then. Even if Matthew McNaught had not recently captured her attention, Rachel would have still felt reluctant to leave the place of her birth. It was home, and she'd never been farther away from it than day trips to Lexington and the few camp meetings where the whole family had been treated to a whole year's worth of sermons, all in a week's time.

"Don't be concerned just yet," Mary Taylor had told Rachel. "Your father talks of more in a day than he'll ever do in a year—that's the way with men. Anyway, you could stay here, even should we move on."

At the time, Rachel had wondered what her mother meant, but try as she could, lying on the floor as near to the loft stair as she dared, Rachel never overheard her parents say just how it would be managed for her to stay in Bryan's Station if they left.

This Christmas Eve, while Rachel was fully aware that she shouldn't try to hear what her parents and Asa Fletcher said about her, her curiosity led her to try. However, since she could only catch a few words here and there, Rachel wound up being more frustrated than enlightened.

". . .a woman grown," Asa Fletcher's rumbling voice said, followed by other words Rachel couldn't make out.

Then her mother spoke. "Rachel has always known her own mind, but. . ."

". . .something needs to be decided soon," Mr. Taylor said. The cadence of their voices continued rising and falling for some time before Rachel heard the scraping of chairs and surmised that the conversation had concluded. As her parents moved toward the door with Asa Fletcher, their voices became clearer.

"She gets on good with the younguns," Asa Fletcher said.

"Loves them like her own kin," Mary Taylor added.

"A sweeter gal would be hard to find in these parts," her father claimed.

"Mercy, look at the time! Since it's past midnight, I

reckon we can bid you a Happy Christmas now, Asa."

"And a happy one it is, indeed, back here with my younguns. I thank you for the supper. And think on what I said."

When Rachel heard the front door close, she quickly crept back to her pallet and feigned sleep. Sometimes Mary Taylor checked on the children before she and William went to their own bed, and although Rachel wasn't sure what they had said about her, she knew she wasn't supposed to hear it.

I'll find out what it's all about tomorrow, she thought drowsily. By the time Mary Taylor climbed into the loft with her candle, Rachel was fast asleep.

Christmas Day traditionally brought family prayers and scripture reading, along with the best dinner they could afford. In addition, family members exchanged simple gifts, usually things they had made themselves. Girls and women often got shawls or dress lengths, while boys and men hoped for new and better knives and ready-made boots and coats.

On this Christmas Day, excitement ran high among the Fletcher children as their father presented them with gifts he had brought back all the way from Pittsburgh, where, he said, he had visited with his late wife's brother, her last living relative. He hadn't forgotten the Taylor children, either; Esther had a real doll, not made of corncobs or straw-stuffed cotton goods, and the boys got tops that spun and skipped like magic over the planked floor.

When Mary and William Taylor were fully absorbed with watching the children enjoy their new playthings, Asa Fletcher motioned for Rachel to follow him into the lean-to where Mary Taylor kept the washing pans and stored household staples.

"I didn't want you to think I'd left you out, Miss Rachel." He handed her a parcel wrapped in oiled paper. "Here—Happy Christmas."

Rachel felt the blood rise in her cheeks. "I—I don't know what to say," she managed at last.

"Don't have to say nothin', just open it," he said. "Go on," he added when she made no move to do so.

From the package's size and weight, Rachel guessed it held a length of material for a dress, but when the folds of the paper parted to reveal the most delicate woolen material she had ever seen, Rachel was too shocked to speak. It wasn't just the softness of the goods that surprised her, but its color—as white as the first winter snowfall, white as a summer cloud. . .

White as a bridal gown.

Rachel regarded Asa Fletcher with a look of near-terror. "I can't take this," she said as firmly as her inner trembling allowed.

"You already did," he pointed out, and Rachel realized she was, indeed, clutching the package to her bodice.

"But—"

From somewhere behind them came the sound of laughter, then a childish voice called out for Rachel, and Vinnie opened the lean-to door and pulled on Rachel's skirt.

"Come back now so's we can eat."

Asa Fletcher put his left arm around Vinnie and his right hand fell lightly on Rachel's shoulder. "We'll talk later," he said.

Rachel closed the parcel and hastened to the loft, where she put it under her pallet.

For no apparent reason, one of her mother's favorite scriptures came to mind, and Rachel murmured it: "Sufficient unto the day is the trouble thereof."

Then she thought of something else, which she expressed as a silent prayer: *God bless Matthew McNaught. And please let him come to see us soon.*

Rachel knew such a visit wasn't likely, but having put her wish into a prayer, she felt better. She took a deep breath and rejoined the others just as her father was ready to begin an especially long Christmas blessing prayer.

". . .and keep us all safe and in Your will in the year to come," William Taylor concluded.

When Rachel opened her eyes, she saw that Asa Fletcher had somehow maneuvered himself to sit beside her. He pointed to Betty, squirming in his arms, who seemed more interested in stroking his beard than trying to feed herself.

"I reckon between the two of us we might can get some food into this youngun," he said.

"No need—I'll help." Tom Fletcher stepped in and straddled the bench between Rachel and his father.

Both surprised and relieved at Tom's intervention, Rachel smiled at the boy, but he quickly turned his back to her without acknowledging her unspoken thanks. "I'll help Ma with the serving," she said, and rose to do so.

We'll talk later, Asa Fletcher had said, but he made no move to do so all the rest of that day, nor the next, when everyone, even the youngest, pitched in to clean the house Asa had abandoned shortly after his wife's death. The preparations took two days, but at last all the Fletchers were back together under the same roof and in their own home.

"It's too quiet around here now," Mary Taylor complained that first night. Esther cried because she missed Vinnie, and although he said nothing, Rachel could tell that her brother John wished he still had Tom around to pass the time with.

"You'll get used to it soon enough," William Taylor said.

"Don't forget we're all supposed to spend New Year's Eve at the Fletchers' house," John reminded his mother when he started off to bed.

"Not likely, with your ma bringing most of the food," William Taylor said. As Rachel rose to leave, he called her back. "Stay a while, Rachel."

Here it comes, Rachel thought. She sat down on the settle between her parents and waited for her father to speak. Instead, her mother asked an unexpected question.

"What did you do with Asa Fletcher's gift?"

"I almost forgot about it, what with everything that's been going on around here," Rachel said, not untruthfully. "It's under my pallet."

"A strange place to leave a gift," her father commented. "I'd like to see it."

"And I, as well," her mother added.

"I'll go fetch it."

The parcel was where she had left it, somewhat flatter but otherwise undamaged. Rachel laid it on her mother's lap without comment. Even in the dim light from the fireplace, Asa Fletcher's gift gleamed softly, unmistakably white.

"Oh, my!" Mary Taylor murmured. She stroked the soft wool almost reverently.

"I've not seen goods like this in all the years I've been in Kentucky," William Taylor said. "That piece of cloth must have cost Asa a pretty penny."

"I'm sure he thought Rachel deserved it. He knows she took on most of the care of the younguns, especially Betty and Vinnie."

"Maybe so, but I didn't expect anything like this," Rachel said. "I tried to give it back."

Her parents exchanged a long, meaningful glance, then her mother nodded, perhaps as a signal that the time had come to let Rachel know what had already been discussed between them.

William Taylor leaned forward and took both his daughter's hands in his own. "Rachel, this material is meant to be made into a wedding dress. Asa Fletcher seeks your hand in marriage."

Although the news was not as unexpected as it might have been, Rachel reacted to it with dismay. Her eyes widened, and she withdrew her hands from her father's and put them to her cheeks. Her mouth felt suddenly dry, and her lips stiff. In a hoarse whisper, Rachel said the first thing that came into her mind.

"But he's so *old*."

Her father frowned, obviously puzzled and perhaps a little annoyed at Rachel's reaction. "Asa Fletcher turned thirty just a few months back. He's a good, steady man, and he needs someone who gets along with his younguns. It's a good match."

Rachel turned imploring eyes to her mother. "What do you say about this?"

Mary Taylor sighed and looked away from Rachel. She gazed into the fire for a long moment, as if its flames might contain some answer. "You've often said you want to stay at Bryan's Station. If that's true, this is your chance to do so."

"Not only that, it'll relieve our minds to have you settled before we go."

Again, her father's words weren't a complete surprise, since her mother had already told Rachel that her father wanted to move on. However, actually hearing it from him sent a chill through her body. "Where do you aim to go?" she asked.

"Down to south Tennessee. You've heard me tell about going there to guard a survey party in 1783. It's a beautiful land, and I'm entitled to a thousand acres of it."

"When will you go?" Rachel asked.

"As soon as the weather lets up and the ground's firm enough for travel."

"But you don't plan to take me."

Her father shook his head and looked exasperated. "Now, did I ever say that? Your mother tells me you don't want to leave Kentucky. Seems to me that you ought to jump at the chance to stay here and get a good man like Asa Fletcher in the bargain."

"Suppose I don't want to marry him? What then?"

William Taylor spoke earnestly. "Rachel, all your life your mother and I have prayed for the Lord to send a mate fit for you. We believe Asa Fletcher's such a man."

Rachel looked back at her mother. "You agree with this?"

"I believe that Asa Fletcher would make you a good husband, Rachel. I know this has all come upon you too fast to take it all in. If the man had time, I'm sure he'd court you all proper-like. But those younguns need a mother's care, and when we leave this place, he'll really have nowhere to turn. At least say you'll pray about it."

"Can you do that?" her father asked.

Rachel nodded, although with obvious reluctance. "I'll pray for God to show me His will in this matter."

Her parents looked relieved, and her mother hugged Rachel. "You're a good girl," she said. "I know you'll do what's right."

You mean that I should agree to marry Asa Fletcher because you've decided that God wants me to.

Rachel dared not give voice to the words, but her heart denied that it was God's will for her to marry a man twice her age, especially when he already had four children and bad teeth, to boot.

She wanted to stay at Bryan's Station, all right, but not at such a high cost.

The thought came to her mind unbidden, but she knew it had been there all along: *If only Matthew McNaught could find it in his heart to marry me, then all would work out well.* Some other woman would come along for Asa Fletcher; Rachel Taylor wasn't the only single female of marriageable age in Kentucky.

No matter what she thought of Asa Fletcher otherwise, Rachel resolved to pray that the man would find someone else to be his wife.

Chapter 3

The day after Christmas, Rachel felt on edge all day, dreading the time when Asa Fletcher would present his formal proposal of marriage. Finally, late in the afternoon her mother asked Rachel to take some food to the elderly Widow Nichols, who lived about a mile in the opposite direction from the Fletchers' cabin.

The weather had turned cold, and not even Rachel's hooded cloak could completely protect her from the fine needles of sleet that stung her face and hands. By the time she reached the widow's door, Rachel was chilled to the bone.

"Bless you, child, for comin' out on such a mean day," the widow greeted Rachel. "I was just sittin' here a-wishin' that someone would happen by."

"Ma sends her best, along with this joint of meat."

"Ah, thank Mary for me. Take off your cloak and pull up a chair to the fire."

Rachel obeyed, doubly glad for the warmth of the fire and the opportunity to stay away from home—and a possible visit from Asa Fletcher—for a little while longer.

"Thank you, Mrs. Nichols. I don't know when I've seen the weather turn bad so fast as this."

"Yes, and isn't it a blessin' that Asa Fletcher got back home when he did? Travelin' on this day would be miserable."

Rachel wondered how Mrs. Nichols knew he had come home. "Have you seen Mr. Fletcher?" she asked.

"No, but Ellie Grant was over yesterday and she said she saw him come a-ridin' in on Christmas Eve. I reckon them younguns was glad to have their papa back."

The last thing Rachel wanted to do was talk about Asa Fletcher, but after she replied, "Yes'm, they all missed him a great deal," she was subjected to a long recital of everything the widow recalled about Asa and his family, which was considerable.

". . .so I said to Ellie, 'That man needs to get him a wife, and that right soon.' Ellie 'lowed as how she thought Asa'd bring him home a wife, he was gone so long."

"Well, he didn't," Rachel said, then stood. "I'd like to stay here by this nice fire longer, but I'd best get home before the path ices up."

"You're right, child. That hill gets terrible slick, and I'd not have you hurt on my account for the world. Tell your ma I'll be around to see her when the weather fairs up."

"I'll do that," Rachel promised.

Rather than take the hilly path that had brought her there, Rachel cut through the piney woods that led to the schoolhouse. The path wasn't so steep, and although it would take longer, Rachel was in no hurry to get back home and face the possibility of a meeting with Asa Fletcher.

Rachel had just emerged from the woods by the

schoolhouse when someone called her name. Startled, she stopped and looked back toward the building.

Could Matthew McNaught have returned and somehow be hailing her from the schoolhouse? Rachel's heart raced, then dropped as she looked back toward the Station and saw Asa Fletcher making his way toward her.

"Miss Rachel! I been lookin' all over for you."

"I was at the Widow Nichols' house," Rachel said.

"So your ma said, but Miz Nichols said you'd just left there a'ready. She was right disturbed that I hadn't seen you on the path."

Now everyone in Bryan's Station will know that Asa Fletcher came looking for me, Rachel thought. They'd probably speculate why soon enough, as well.

"I decided to take the school path instead," Rachel said.

"I would have a word with you," Asa said. "I'll walk you home an' we can talk. This weather's gettin' worse."

"Thank you," Rachel said. Since there seemed no way to prevent it, she would as soon have this interview over with.

A moment later, Asa stopped in front of her under a canopy of branches.

Rachel stood in silence as Asa reached out to take both her hands. His hands were as cold as hers, and she shuddered at their rough touch.

"I reckon it's time we made us some plans, Miss Rachel. You know I want us to get married soon as it can be done proper-like."

"So my folks told me," Rachel said.

"Well, what about it? Name the day, and I'll make sure a preacher gets here to tie the knot."

Rachel made no effort to remove her hands from Asa's, but her expression must have told him how she felt even before she voiced the words.

"I need some time to think about this, Mr. Fletcher."

He regarded her with mixed hurt and surprise. "What for? You'll have plenty of time for that whilst your ma makes up that material and gets your dowry together."

Seeing that he wasn't about to loosen his grip, Rachel freed her hands from Asa's and took a step backward. "I don't think I'm the right one for you to marry, Mr. Fletcher. I'm not much older than your own younguns, and—"

"You get along with them, though, and that's what matters. As for me, I'm not as old as you think, and I'm ready to prove it."

Asa moved toward Rachel as if he intended to embrace her, but she quickly stepped to one side, then turned back to the path. "I have to get home now," she said.

"All right, missy, but before this year's out, I'll look for you to set a date."

"I must have more time than that," Rachel said. Her tone matched the weather, but Asa Fletcher looked as pleased as if she had just promised to wed him the next day.

"I'll wait until Old Christmas, but not a day longer. Now, we'd best get you home afore you catch your death in this cold."

As Rachel feared, the news that Rachel Taylor and Asa Fletcher were courting spread across Bryan's Station like a wildfire. No one said anything to Rachel directly, but through sly winks and knowing smiles, many people indicated they thought something was in the works for her and Asa.

"Everyone seems to think I'm about to get married," Rachel complained to her mother several days after Christmas. "What have you and Pa been saying?"

Mary Taylor's brow furrowed, and she shook her head in denial. "Not a thing, and that's the truth. I 'spect Mr. Asa Fletcher has been doin' the talkin' himself, he's that proud."

"Then I wish you or Pa would tell him not to say such things. I never told the man I was ready to wed him."

Rachel's mother laid a comforting hand on her shoulder. "I fear it's too late for that. What's said can't be taken back. Besides, you might change your mind. All this marryin' business has come upon you suddenlike. I can understand how you might want some time to think on it."

"I've had all the time I need," Rachel said, but her mother merely shook her head and looked at Rachel as if she thought the girl had taken leave of her senses.

On December thirtieth, Rachel had gone to the spring to fetch water when Tom Fletcher joined her. Since he had no bucket, she suspected that Asa's oldest son had probably followed her there.

"Hello, Tom," she said. "I haven't seen you since Christmas Day. I trust you are all well."

Tom's face darkened, and he lifted his chin in defiance. "Oh, I reckon you know how we've all been, Miss Rachel, seein's how you're carryin' on with Pa and all."

Rachel barely suppressed the urge to laugh at the boy's ridiculous charge. "I don't know what you've heard, but I've scarcely seen your father since he came back home," she said.

"Be that as it may, you oughter know that Pa and I don't need you. We can take care of the little ones without anybody else's help."

Rachel kept her voice level. No good would come from telling Tom how heartily she disliked his father's proposal, but she didn't want to leave the boy with the wrong impression, either. "I never said you couldn't take care of yourself, Tom. In fact, since you're here, will you help me with this bucket?"

Tom looked surprised, but he took the nearly full bucket from her hands and carried it all the way to the Taylors' house.

Mary Taylor came out to greet Tom. "Tell your pa we'll be over early to help him redd up for the party," she said as she took the bucket from him.

Tom shot a quick glance at Rachel, and for a moment she thought the boy might say they wouldn't be welcome. Instead, he nodded, then turned away and hastened home.

"What ails that boy?" Mary Taylor asked Rachel.

"Nothing," she replied. Tom's reluctance to the match had nothing to do with her decision not to marry Asa Fletcher, nor would knowing about it make any difference to her parents.

"I'm glad Asa's having this party. It's a nice end to the year."

It would also be a good way to announce our engagement. Rachel shivered in apprehension, then tried to dismiss her fear. Asa had said he wouldn't press her for an answer until January sixth, known in these parts as Old Christmas. *Surely not even Asa Fletcher would say they were going to be married when she hadn't given her consent.* That thought was her only comfort, and once more Rachel prayed that Asa Fletcher would have a change of heart.

Matthew McNaught rode back into Bryan's Station about noon on New Year's Eve, having left Mrs. Eggleston in Lexington, where she intended to spend the rest of the winter with her sister. He hadn't finished unpacking his saddlebags when Asa Fletcher knocked on his door.

"When did you get back?" Matthew asked after the men shook hands.

"On Christmas Eve. There's gonna be a party at my house tonight. I'll be much obliged if you'll come and play your fiddle."

"I'm out of practice, but maybe I can scrape out a few tunes. What time do you want me there?"

"Come before good dark, and we'll have a bite of supper first."

"All right, I'll be there. I know your children were glad you made it back for Christmas."

"Yessir, they seemed to be. Things'll be different soon, though. You'll see."

Asa Fletcher turned on his heel and left without further explanation, and Matthew shrugged and resumed unpacking.

Dusk was painting the sky pink, promising that the first day of 1807 would be fair, when Rachel and her mother made their way to Asa Fletcher's cabin. Each carried a basket of food, the Taylor family's contribution to the evening's provisions. Rachel nodded to Asa, but quickly busied herself with unloading the basket to discourage further conversation. When her mother saw the need for more table linens, Rachel gladly volunteered to go back home and get them.

She was on her way back when she met Matthew McNaught outside the Fletcher cabin. She hadn't heard that the schoolmaster was back, and her greeting was genuinely warm.

"I didn't know you were back," she said. Then she recognized the sack he carried and clasped her hands together in a gesture of delight. "Oh, good! I'm glad you brought your fiddle."

"I hope you can still say that after you hear a tune or two. As I told Asa, it's been a long time since I've played it."

"You're too modest," Rachel said. "Pa says you're the best fiddler in these parts."

Matthew smiled, his teeth white against the growing dusk. "Seeing's how I'm the only fiddler, I don't take that as such high praise."

"Rachel! Where are you? I need those linens!" Mrs. Taylor's voice sounded from the vicinity of Asa Fletcher's cabin, effectively ending Rachel and Matthew's conversation.

"I'm on my way," she called back.

As soon as they saw him, the Fletcher children swarmed around their schoolmaster, and Rachel knew it was unlikely they'd have any time to be alone together that evening.

After supper, the other guests arrived, filling the Fletcher's keeping room with talk and laughter. At their urging, Matthew finished a set of tunes which most of the party-goers joined in singing.

"Let the man rest for now," Mary Taylor said. Everyone crowded around the table, helping themselves to the fried fruit pies she had brought. "We need some water here, daughter," Mary directed.

When Rachel went into the Fletcher's lean-to to get the bucket and drinking gourd, Matthew followed her.

"I'll take that," he said. He placed the bucket and its gourd dipper on the table, then motioned for Rachel to return with him to the lean-to. "I haven't had any time to talk with you," he said. He didn't close the door, but the lean-to was in the shadows, and everyone else was too busy eating and slaking their thirst to notice them.

"How was your trip?" Rachel asked when Matthew didn't immediately speak.

"Fine. But when I got back, I had a letter from my Aunt Alfreda. She invited me to come to Virginia for a visit after Mother died, but I never took the time to go."

When he paused to take a drink from the water barrel, Rachel felt the need to fill the silence.

"So now you're planning to go there?" she asked. Rachel might not know why Matthew was confiding his plans to her, but she cherished every moment with him.

"Maybe. She wants me to live with her brother and go to William and Mary."

"Oh," Rachel said. "Are they more of your relatives?"

Matthew looked briefly surprised, then chuckled. "You never heard of the College of William and Mary?"

Rachel shook her head, embarrassed by her ignorance.

"It's a good school, a place where I can get a proper education."

His words made Rachel shiver in alarm. *Matthew is going to leave Bryan's Station and I will never see him again,* was all she could think. Aloud, she said, "But you're the smartest man in these parts. You already know so much."

"Maybe I know enough for Bryan's Station, but I won't spend the rest of my life in a one-room schoolhouse."

Rachel felt her heart sinking. "When will you go?" she asked.

Matthew frowned slightly. "Are you so eager to be rid of me? Not for a while. These things could take some time to arrange."

"Bryan's Station can't afford to lose you," Rachel said earnestly. *And neither can I,* she thought.

Matthew shrugged. "Schoolmasters are a dime a

dozen. I want to do something else, something greater—"

"Rachel—are you out there? The water bucket wants filling." Neither she nor Matthew had noticed Asa Fletcher until he spoke, and they turned to see his tall frame filling the doorway.

"I'll attend to it right away," Rachel said quickly.

Asa clapped a friendly hand on Matthew's shoulder. "Let's have a lively tune to keep us all awake," he suggested.

❧

Later, as the hour of midnight approached, the gathered assembly turned solemn. When Asa's mantel clock began to strike twelve, Matthew played the Old Hundred tune on his fiddle. Everyone stood and greeted 1807 by singing the doxology.

Asa Fletcher sought to take Rachel's hand, but she pulled away from him. She hoped no one—especially Matthew—had taken notice of it.

"May we all be together again when the next year rolls around," Asa said when the "Amen" died away.

And may I be with Matthew then, Rachel earnestly prayed. She glanced at Matthew, but he was busy putting his fiddle away and didn't look her way.

"Rachel, wake the younguns and let's be away."

The Taylor children slept in a tangle on pallets in the Fletcher loft, but they came awake almost instantly, scolding her for not waking them in time to see the New Year in.

"You can celebrate tomorrow," she told them.

Soon, with a last chorus of good wishes all around, the Taylors said their farewells and went out together into the frosty night.

Rachel watched Matthew McNaught walk away toward his cabin and said a silent prayer that 1807 would, indeed, be a good year for this man she had grown to love.

Chapter 4

R achel spent the first day of 1807 wishing that she could continue the conversation the schoolmaster had started the night before. Matthew McNaught had seemed to be on the verge of revealing his future plans, and even if they had nothing to do with her, Rachel still wanted to know what they were.

When her father and her brother John announced they were going to help build up the woodpile for the schoolhouse, in which lessons would resume the following day, Rachel briefly considered going with them. However, when she realized that Asa and Tom Fletcher would also be there, she abandoned the idea.

After her husband and son had left, Mary Taylor motioned for Rachel to join her by the fire, where she sat knitting.

"Your pa and I thought Asa Fletcher might have something to announce last night," she said. "How does that matter stand?"

"Mr. Fletcher agreed to wait until Old Christmas for my answer, but the extra time won't make any difference. I won't feel like marrying him any more then than I do now."

Mary Taylor sighed heavily and shook her head. "I'll say it again—Asa Fletcher's a good man, and it's always a great comfort when a daughter makes a wise match. I don't know how you'll fare when we leave this place."

"Pa still intends to go south, then?" Rachel asked.

"Aye, and he's already started makin' some plans. Maybe you'll change your mind about Asa Fletcher when it comes down to wedding him or leaving the Station forever."

"I'd rather stay with my family."

Rachel knew her words were true only to a point. She would really prefer to marry Matthew McNaught and stay at Bryan's Station, but if that couldn't be, then she would brave the wilderness with the rest of the Taylors.

"So be it, then," Mary Taylor said, "but you might be making the worst mistake of your life."

"I pray that I am not."

Rachel felt a bit guilty about her answer. In fact, she had almost been afraid to pray about Asa Fletcher's proposal at all, lest God might tell her she should accept it.

"You have a few more days yet," Mary Taylor said. "Sometimes much can happen in a short time."

Matthew McNaught always came to the schoolhouse at first light to build a fire against the chill. The lone fireplace, large as it was, never completely warmed the schoolhouse, particularly on winter days when the wind whistled around the windows and came in under the ill-fitting door, but it helped some.

The schoolmaster was watching the flames ignite the kindling wood and reach out to the oak logs laid across the andirons when the door opened, and the first pupils entered.

"Mornin', Master McNaught," Tom Fletcher said. "Pa told me to come early an' see if you needed some help with anything."

"That was good of him," Matthew said. "Whilst you're still all bundled up against the cold, perhaps you could bring in some more wood. Don't use what we cut yesterday, though."

Tom spoke with the assurance of a veteran woodsman. "I know better'n that."

"I want to help, too," said Abby, then Betty and Vinnie added in chorus, "Me, too."

"You're *girls*," Tom said scornfully, but the schoolmaster overruled him.

"Vinnie, Betty, I need you two to stay inside and help sweep the floor," Matthew said when they began to follow Tom and their sister outside.

Vinnie picked up the twig broom and began to push it around the floor, with little Betty scattering the debris as she trailed behind her. "I know a secret," Vinnie said after a moment.

The schoolmaster raised his eyebrows. "Oh, do you now?"

"Yes, sir. It's about Pa 'n' Miss Rachel."

Matthew's look of faint amusement faded. "What about them?"

Vinnie glanced around as if to make sure no one else would hear, then she leaned toward the schoolmaster. "They're gonna get married," she whispered.

"Is that so? When?" Matthew asked.

"Soon as her ma can make up the white goods Pa brung her into a weddin' dress."

" 'Brought,' not 'brung,' " Matthew corrected absently.

His mind still reeled from the effects of Vinnie's secret when, a few minutes later, the other Fletcher children returned, struggling under the weight of logs almost as large as themselves.

"Tom, come here a moment." Matthew drew the boy aside.

"Yes, sir? Is something amiss?"

"Not at all. I just wondered—uh, about your pa. Does he—has he said anything about—about Miss Rachel Taylor?"

Tom's face darkened. "Just that they're gettin' married, is all."

"I see," said Matthew, who didn't. *Rachel Taylor accepting a man like Asa Fletcher?* It was hard to take in.

"You want me to bring in any more wood?" Tom asked.

Matthew shook his head. "No, thanks, this will do for the day. You and Abby have been a big help."

When John and Esther Taylor arrived a few minutes later, Matthew looked past them in the vain hope that their older sister might be with them.

It's not likely Rachel will come to the schoolhouse again, now that she has more important things to think about, he told himself.

But, Matthew acknowledged, he had other things to consider too, and the sooner he took care of his own affairs, the better.

⁓

January sixth, "Old Christmas," fell, several days later, on the first Sunday in 1807. Rachel almost dreaded going to the meetinghouse that morning, knowing that this was the day she had promised to give Asa Fletcher his answer. *Yet, doing so in public might be better,* she thought. At least he probably wouldn't try to kiss her with the whole congregation looking on.

On the other hand, Rachel suspected that if the preacher who served the Bryan's Station circuit appeared on schedule, Asa just might ask him to perform their wedding ceremony even before waiting to hear her answer.

I can't let that happen, Rachel thought.

"I think I'll walk on ahead," she said when she was dressed and ready to go before the rest of her family.

"We'll be right along," her mother called after Rachel.

At the meetinghouse, Rachel saw that the preacher had, indeed, arrived, since his horse was already tied to the hitching post. However, to her relief, no one else had arrived.

"Come in out of the cold, Miss Rachel," Abner McHugh called to her when he saw her hesitate at the doorway.

"No, sir. I—I'm waiting for someone."

"Might as well do it inside," the parson said.

Seeing no help for it, Rachel entered. She sat on

the backless bench her family usually occupied and drew her cloak tightly around her. If Asa Fletcher came in now, before the service started, she would tell him she couldn't marry him. Otherwise, that encounter would have to wait until later.

The meetinghouse gradually began to fill, and Rachel's family arrived before the Fletchers. Rachel looked at the bench that Matthew McNaught usually occupied and wondered briefly where he was. Her brother John had come home from school the day before saying the schoolmaster didn't seem to be himself.

"Maybe he's coming down with something," Mary Taylor had said. "With Mrs. Eggleston gone, he doesn't have anyone to take proper care of him."

"If you're worried, you could visit him," Rachel said, trying to sound unconcerned.

Mary Taylor had dismissed Rachel's suggestion with a wave of her hand. "Oh, I'm sure he's all right. If he needs help, we'll hear of it."

The Fletchers finally arrived, just in time for the opening prayer. When the last "Amen" sounded, Rachel heard Asa telling his children to go home without him.

"I must stay and have a word with the preacher," he told them.

Rachel hastened to put herself between Asa and the pulpit. "Mr. Fletcher, will you step outside a moment?"

Although she spoke too softly for anyone else to hear, Rachel knew that her mother, standing off to one side, was waiting to see what might happen next.

"Only if you have good news for me," Asa Fletcher said.

Rachel's face grew uncomfortably warm. She lowered her head briefly, then raised it and looked directly at Asa. "Sir, I'm honored by your proposal of marriage, but after giving the matter much thought, I'm afraid I can't marry you."

The spoken words sounded much harsher to Rachel than when she'd rehearsed them in her mind, but once they were said, she felt greatly relieved.

Asa Fletcher turned his head to one side as if assessing the truth of what he had heard. "Is that so?"

Rachel nodded. "Yes, sir. I won't change my mind."

A fleeting emotion—anger, perhaps, or disappointment—crossed Asa Fletcher's face, but his voice betrayed no emotion. "I'll not ask you to. I just wish you had said this to me sooner."

Rachel would have said he should have taken her first answer, but Asa turned away without waiting for Rachel to make any further comment. She stood alone for a moment before her mother came to her and took Rachel's hand.

"Time we went home now," she said.

They were halfway to their house before Rachel spoke. "Mr. Fletcher didn't seem very upset, did he?"

"Don't take it personal," her mother replied. "Men are strange creatures. Anyhow, I don't doubt that you did right in turnin' this one down."

"Even if none other comes along?" Rachel asked.

Mary Taylor smiled. "I'd not worry about that just yet."

Rachel had feared that her refusal of Asa Fletcher's hand would be the subject of much gossip, but the next day all the Bryan's Station residents could talk about was what had become of the schoolmaster.

"He's gone, Ma," John Taylor said on Monday morning when he and his sister came back only minutes after they had left for school.

"Maybe he's just late," Mary Taylor said. "You all just go back up there and wait for him."

"No, Ma, Mr. McNaught's gone away. He left a note on the door."

"I saw it too," Esther added. "It said, 'Called away on sudden business. No school until further notice.' "

William Taylor frowned. "It's not like Matthew to go off like that without a word to any of the school trustees. I'd better go to his house and see if anything's amiss."

"I'll come with you," Rachel said quickly, but her father would have none of it.

"Stay here, all of you. I'll be back soon."

It seemed a very long time to Rachel until her father returned, bearing the news that Matthew McNaught had indeed left Bryan's Station, apparently taking his clothes and books with him. But that wasn't all of William Taylor's news.

"I met Asa Fletcher over there, and he asked us to look after his younguns for a couple of weeks."

"Whatever for? Don't tell me he's running off to Pennsylvania again!" Mary Taylor exclaimed.

"He didn't say, but I suspect that is the case. Anyway, he'll bring them over tonight and leave tomorrow at first light."

This time, Rachel wanted to see Asa Fletcher. While everyone else was upstairs settling the children for the night, she handed him the parcel he had given her for Christmas.

"I thought you'd want this back," she said.

For a fleeting moment, Asa Fletcher's expression made her feel almost sorry for him. His mouth twisted, then he shook his head and thrust the package back into her hands. "No, Miss Rachel. You deserve somethin' for helpin' your ma take care of my younguns. I want you to keep it."

"Then I thank you for it, Mr. Fletcher, although these goods are far too fine for these parts."

Asa grinned, once more showing the gaps where some of his teeth were missing. "We'll see about that. Why, your ma'll likely be making it up for you before the year's out."

"I doubt that," Rachel said.

"Mark my words—you'll see."

"Rachel! We need the rest of the linens up here now," Mary Taylor called down the stairs, rescuing her from further conversation with Asa Fletcher.

"I must go now. I wish you a good journey, Mr. Fletcher," Rachel said, meaning it.

She had nothing against Asa Fletcher. She just didn't want to marry him.

~~~

Two weeks later, Bryan's Station was once more set abuzz when a middle-aged man came riding into town, saying that Matthew McNaught had asked him to finish out the school term. When the school trustees were hastily assembled, they had many questions.

"Where is Master McNaught?" William Taylor asked, but Elliott Spencer wasn't sure.

"He said he had pressing business in Virginia and sent this letter for the trustees," he said, pulling a letter from his pocket. "That's all I know. He said I could live in his house. Do you all want me to stay? Say the word now, for if you don't, I have a place waiting for me in Crab Orchard."

"No, stay by all means," James Dermott said as he unfolded the letter Spencer had handed him, and the others readily agreed.

"What does the letter say, James?" asked William Taylor.

"Just that he has pressing business and deeply regrets any inconvenience to Bryan's Station. Must be important. This just isn't like Matthew."

"Well, at least he sent a replacement."

The meeting between Master Spencer and the trustees had just broken up when they heard that Asa Fletcher had just returned to Bryan's Station from his mysterious journey. This time, though, he wasn't alone.

The Fletcher and Taylor children came outside to meet the rather short and stout woman that Asa introduced as Annabelle Edgar.

"Mr. Fletcher, you forget yourself," she reminded him in a no-nonsense voice.

Asa looked uncomfortable. "Sorry, my dear. Until three days past, she was Annabelle Edgar, widow of my late cousin in Pittsburgh. Now, she's Mrs. Asa Fletcher."

Although everyone had pretty much figured that out, they all seemed surprised at Asa's choice of this woman, who seemed to be some years older than her new husband.

"Which of you are Mr. Fletcher's younguns?" she asked the assembled children. Unsmiling, Tom and his sisters raised their hands as if requesting permission to recite a lesson.

"I'll sort out your names later. I reckon you'd best get your things and come back to the house. We must decide where you will all sleep, now that I've arrived."

"That's quite a woman Asa's gotten himself," Rachel overheard her father say that night when he thought everyone else was asleep.

"It's the children I feel sorry for—Asa can take care of himself."

Amen, thought Rachel. She should be relieved to know that Asa had at last found someone to share his life, but instead she felt only a vague sadness.

Rachel felt even worse when, several weeks later, Tom Fletcher once more followed her to the spring. He stood facing her, his fists balled and his mouth tense, and she knew every word came at a cost.

"Miss Rachel, I'm sorry about those bad things I said to you. If it kept you from marryin' Pa, I'm sorry."

"No, Tom, you had nothing to do with that," Rachel assured him.

"I'd lots rather have you as a stepma than Miz Annabelle, and that's a fact."

Rachel had seen and heard Annabelle Fletcher in action enough to know that, like it or not, Asa's children now received firm discipline from their stepmother. "Oh, I'm sure you'll soon get used to each other," she said.

"I wish you all wasn't leavin' the Station," Tom said after a moment. "John's the best friend I reckon I'll ever have."

"He'll miss you too," Rachel assured him. "You must write and tell us everything that goes on in Bryan's Station, and John will write you about our new home."

"It's a long way off, I hear tell," Tom said. "I hope you won't come to no hurt there."

"So do we. Remember us in your prayers, will you?"

Rachel couldn't be sure, but she thought, through the blur of tears in her own eyes, that she detected an unaccustomed brightness in Tom's eyes, as well.

If I had married Asa Fletcher, I would have been a good stepmother to his children, she thought.

But marriage was between a man and a woman, and Rachel knew in her heart that Asa Fletcher wasn't the man for her.

Who was she didn't yet know, but with Matthew McNaught out of her life, Rachel knew she must resign herself to the fact that whoever he might be, she had not yet met her future husband.

Chapter 5

January gave way to a snowy February, and by the end of the month, William Taylor's plans to move south were well underway. In the first week of March, he returned from one of his frequent trips to Lexington with the news that he had found a buyer for his Kentucky property.

"Robert England's been visitin' friends in Lexington. He's decided he wants to settle down in these parts."

"Can this fellow pay your price?" Mary Taylor asked. She knew her husband had already turned down several others who'd offered less.

William Taylor nodded. "Aye, he just settled his pa's estate in North Carolina, so he has the ready cash."

"When does he want to take possession?"

"As soon as possible. That means we need to get our goods loaded up and on their way down the river right away."

Mary Taylor looked displeased. "With snow still on the ground?"

"The worst of winter is already over. The sooner we get started south, the better. I've talked to a flatboat owner over at Limestone, and he's willin' to take us next week."

"I hadn't thought we'd go so soon." Mary glanced at Rachel, who had put down her sewing to listen to her parents' conversation. "Well, Rachel, it looks like we all have some busy days ahead."

Later, Rachel asked her father if he'd heard any other news of interest in Lexington.

"Not that I recall—oh, there was one thing. Mrs. Eggleston's sister took a bad spell. The woman probably won't live much longer."

"I'm sorry to hear it. Maybe Mrs. Eggleston will come back to the Station and keep house for Mr. Spencer now."

"I much doubt it, since our new schoolmaster's wife will be joining him shortly. What made you think of that?"

"No reason." Rachel made to turn away, then looked back at her father. "I wonder if she's heard anything from the other schoolmaster," she added, afraid that even the mention of Matthew McNaught's name might bring the blood rushing into her cheeks.

"I don't know, since I didn't speak to the woman myself. From what we know, Matthew's settled with his mother's folks in Virginia. I doubt he'll ever come back to Bryan's Station."

And if he does, we won't be here, Rachel silently added. She knew she was foolish to keep hoping to see Matthew McNaught again, but she couldn't keep him out of her daydreams.

In one of Rachel's most favorite imaginings, Matthew would ride into the Station moments before the Taylor family was to leave. He'd jump from his horse and take her in his arms, right there in front of all the people in Bryan's Station who had come out to bid them farewell.

"Don't leave, Rachel. I love you and I want you to marry me," he'd say.

Rachel's actions would be her first answer. She imagined twining her arms around Matthew's neck and raising her face to his to be kissed, while his strong arms held her close.

"Yes, Matthew, I'll marry you," she would say, and all the onlookers, including Asa Fletcher, would cheer. . . .

However, when the day of the Taylors' departure arrived, the actual event was nothing like Rachel's daydreams. The family left their now bare house before dawn, bundled up against the raw cold and fine drizzle that sent a chill to their very bones. Since the residents of Bryan's Station had been saying their good-byes for several days, Rachel was neither surprised nor disappointed that no one had come outside to watch them leave.

Almost no one, that is. Tom Fletcher hailed John, who turned back for a last conversation with his friend.

"John! Time to go," William Taylor said after a moment, and the boys parted with obvious reluctance.

In Rachel's last backward look, Tom Fletcher stood, with no one else in sight, in the crossroads of the path leading to the Bryan's Station schoolhouse, waving good-bye.

If I had married Asa Fletcher, I'd be standing there with Tom instead of leaving with my family.

The thought made Rachel feel even colder. She shivered and turned away, quickly blinking away the tears welling in her eyes.

Rachel knew she must look ahead, not back. Bryan's Station and all the people—including Matthew McNaught—who had filled her life there were now part of the past. Hard as it was not to, Rachel knew she mustn't dwell on what might have been.

God has something even better in store for me, she told herself.

In time, she would know what it was.

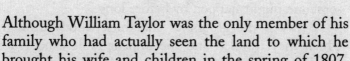

Although William Taylor was the only member of his family who had actually seen the land to which he brought his wife and children in the spring of 1807, even he was surprised by what they found when they finally reached the area.

"This was a true wilderness when I first saw it," William said when it became apparent that the part of Tennessee he sought to claim had already been settled by many others.

However, the few settlements soon thinned, and they saw fewer cabins and signs of civilization as they went.

"This land still looks pretty wild to me," his wife said.

"To me, too," said Esther. Deep woods had always made her feel uncomfortable, and what passed for a road had narrowed to little more than a path through dense forests.

"How much farther do we have to go?" John asked.

His father pulled out the dog-eared map on which his claim was marked, looked at it, then squinted at the pale sun. "The grant runs along Cane Creek. If I'm not mistaken, we've been ridin' alongside it for some time. We're gettin' close."

"Maybe we can ask somebody," Esther suggested.

"Who? We've not even seen a cabin for hours," said Rachel, whose interest in their new adventure had waned with every weary mile they had traveled.

"We'll go on a while longer, then make camp for the night," William Taylor said. "I've a feelin' that someone might happen by before long."

Between the gloom of the thick woods through which they traveled and the impenetrable canebrakes that lined the creek beside them, night would fall early. William Taylor decided to stop before the sun had disappeared behind the westernmost stand of trees to their right.

"I smell smoke—something must be on fire nearby," John said almost immediately.

With his woodsman's skill, William Taylor raised his head and sniffed the air. "It's most likely from a campfire. If there was a hill hereabouts, we might be able to spot where the smoke's comin' from."

"I can climb up that pine tree yonder, Pa," John volunteered.

His father looked in the direction John pointed and nodded. "All right. Stand on my shoulders and you can reach the first branch."

"Be careful, now," his mother added.

"Don't go any higher," William Taylor said after a while, when John was far above their heads.

"I can see the smoke now," John called a moment later. "It's coming from the east. I can't tell how far away."

"Come down now, Son." William Taylor called to John. To his wife, he added, "East—that could mean the smoke's coming from the other side of the creek."

"Maybe not. You ought to see if you can find someone, anyway," his wife urged.

"All right. I'll take my bedroll in case the dark catches me. I'll just stay where I can and come back at first light."

"Be careful," Mary said, and Rachel knew her mother must be a little concerned about being stranded at night in a wilderness without a man's protection.

John's father helped him to the ground again, then he picked up his bedroll and rifle. "I expect I'll be back soon. John, you stay here and take care of your ma and sisters."

"Don't worry, Pa." Pleased to be left in charge, John busied himself making their camp and tending the horses. However, Mary Taylor continued to stand staring down the path long after her husband disappeared from their view.

"Are you all right, Ma?" Rachel asked.

Mary Taylor smiled faintly. "Of course I am. I was thinkin' about the way things used to be, when your pa and I was just wed. This isn't the first time he's traipsed off into the wilderness and left me by myself," Mary Taylor said.

"He'll be all right, and so will we," Rachel said, somehow sure of it.

"I think we should all say a prayer for Pa," Esther declared, and her mother agreed.

"In this place, especially, we daily depend on the mercies of the Lord. We must never forget that. If we put our trust in God, all will be well."

Once the sun went down, the air turned much cooler, and Mary Taylor and her children lay close together beside the campfire, fed periodically from the store of wood John had gathered.

Rachel stayed awake for some time, watching the brilliant display in the heavens and wondering, as she often did, if Matthew McNaught, wherever he was, might also be staring at the same stars. She slept and dreamed he stood beside her on a high hill, naming the constellations. She awoke in the night to the screech of a distant owl, her pleasant dreams of Matthew shattered.

Rachel wasn't worried for her father's safety—he often went out hunting for days at a time, and had never had any harm from it—but she still felt a sense of relief when he returned at sunup.

Esther was the first to spot him. "Look, here comes Pa!"

"Someone's with him," John added.

"Why is that man wearing such funny clothes?" Esther asked.

"You've seen buckskins before," Rachel reminded the girl. Men in Bryan's Station seldom wore them anymore, except to go hunting.

A thick black beard and mustache obscured the man's

features, but his smiling countenance told the Taylors they had nothing to fear from this rough-looking man.

"I trust you all passed a good night," William Taylor greeted Mary rather formally.

"Aye, we did that," Mary said. "I take it that you found the campfire, and with it, this man."

"He found me first," William said. "This is David James, and he's agreed to help us find our land."

Mary nodded politely. "Much obliged. Do you live in these parts, Mr. James?"

"Just call me 'Davy,' ma'am. My place is over to the head of Mulberry Crick, a few miles west, but I hunt all around. This-here land's got just about ever' kind of game any man could want."

In addition to his odd appearance, Davy James' flat twang and sharp vowels didn't sound like the speech of the people around Bryan's Station. Out of the corner of her eye, Rachel saw Esther cover her mouth in an attempt to keep from laughing aloud.

"We had roasted squirrel for supper last night," William Taylor said as if to confirm his companion's words.

"I brung you what was left, ma'am." The man held out a leather pouch to Mary Taylor. "I reckon it'll do to break your fast."

"So it will, Mr.—Davy."

"Davy showed me a good spring just down the way a bit," William Taylor said. "Sweetest water I've tasted since we left ho—I mean, Kentucky."

Rachel noticed her father's near-slip, but no one said anything. Like it or not, Tennessee was now their home, and she knew they should all learn as much about it as they could.

After breakfast, the Taylors' new friend led them a mile or so down the path that passed for a road. "Deer made it first, then the Indians that hunted them made it wider," he explained. As they walked, the young woodsman talked about his wife, Hannah, and their children. He invited the Taylors to come to call as soon as they could. "Hannah gets right lonesome for another woman to talk to. She'll be mighty glad to have another family settle in the county."

Although he had little formal education, Davy James had some knowledge of surveying, and he and William were soon able to locate, with reasonable certainty, the beginning and end of the Taylor grant.

The family walked across the area their father and Davy declared to be theirs, looking for the right spot to build the house.

"Now, if this land belonged to me, I'd use this place right here for my house," Davy said.

The land looked no different from any other to Rachel, but she soon saw that Davy James knew this raw land in a special way. The half-acre to be cleared for the house was ideally situated close to Cane Creek for washing and cleaning, but it was also near an everlasting spring that appeared to spout from the solid rock.

"Limestone water—that's the best drinkin' water a man could want," Davy declared, and after tasting it, the Taylors agreed.

"It's a bit away from the path," Mary Taylor said, but her husband said that was an advantage.

"Those who seek us will find us, and we'll not be bothered with all the rest," he said.

It isn't likely that we'll be bothered by people out here, Rachel thought. She had to admit that the land was beautiful, but she recalled what Davy had said about his wife wanting company. *This land could, indeed, be very lonely.*

After selecting the spot where their house would be built, William decided to return to Nashville with his family and leave them there while their new house was being built.

"I really don't mind living in a log cabin again," Mary Taylor told her husband. "It'll put me in mind of our first home at the Station."

"Aye, but in those days we had no children. They're used to better, and now that I can afford to give it to them, I will."

"I suppose it's just as well. Maybe we can find a place in Nashville with a garden spot, and a school for John and Esther."

William Taylor nodded, pleased with the way things had worked out. "That's what we'll do, then come fall, the Lord willin', we'll be livin' in the grandest house in these parts."

Chapter 6

Even before she left Bryan's Station, Rachel knew she would miss the place where she had been born and lived all her life, but she had no idea just how much. At first, the daily hardship of the journey from northern Kentucky to Tennessee took every ounce of energy she and her family possessed. The trip south to the land on which they would live gave them a better idea of what they would be up against when the time came to settle down at Cane Creek. Rachel felt some relief when they returned to Nashville, the largest town she had yet seen.

As soon as the Taylors had a place to live, their father enrolled John and Esther in a school run by an aged, half-deaf master, who seemed to think that knowledge could literally be beaten into his pupils' heads. The first time John came home with bruised arms, William called on the master to express his disapproval. When Esther received similar treatment soon afterward, he removed both children from the school.

Mary Taylor expressed her doubts at the wisdom of her husband's action. "Master Payne is old-fashioned, I grant, but the children need something to occupy their time. Maybe you should give this schoolmaster another chance."

William shook his head. "He won't change his ways and I'll not change my mind. I didn't send my children to school to be beat half to death. Rachel can help Esther with her schoolin', and I'll see to John's."

As a result, instructing her sister gave Rachel something to occupy her mind for at least a few hours each day. The rest of the time, as she did various chores about their rented house, she tried not to dwell on what had been left behind in Bryan's Station. At night, however, she often found herself thinking of Matthew McNaught.

Rachel couldn't quite visualize him in that unknown place called Virginia, since she didn't know what he was doing there. Time after time, her mind returned to last Christmas at Bryan's Station and Matthew's moving story about a lost traveler and a candle in the window. Although the Taylors had made the journey to their new home in far less severe weather, Rachel drew a comparison between Matthew's story and their present circumstances. For the first time in her life, Rachel found herself to be, like the old man in Matthew's story, a stranger traveling in a strange land. Now that she had actually seen the isolated land where their house would be built, Rachel's lonely heart ached even more.

No one could find them even if they wanted to, she feared.

~⌒~

The week after John and Esther left school, Rachel helped them write a letter to the Fletcher children, and

her father added a rough map of the Cane Creek area.
John labored over a note to Tom Fletcher which related
some of their traveling adventures and mentioned their
new home.

*Our place is on Cane Creek. Pa says that the house will
have lots of glass winders and two storys. It is where the X
is on Pa's map. Come to see us some time ef you can. What
is the news? Tell ever one we are well and hope this fines
you the sam.*

Although Rachel smiled at some of John's spelling,
she didn't correct it. Tom Fletcher wasn't much shakes
at spelling, either, and the boy would have no trouble
understanding John's meaning.

William Taylor addressed the envelope with the
Nashville post office as a return address. The house
wouldn't be finished for some months, and they hoped
the Fletchers would write back before then.

"There's no tellin' where the nearest post office to
Cane Creek will be by the time we get there," William
said.

"That's somethin' else you need to find out," his
wife said.

The list of things they didn't know about their new
home was so long that sometimes Rachel wondered that
Father had been so eager to claim this land. However,
everything had proceeded more or less according to
plan, and unless something unforeseen happened, the
new house should be ready to be occupied in the fall.

"I hope those mechanics you hired know what they're
about," Mary Taylor said. "I'd not want to find the house
built in the wrong place, or the workmanship poor."

"That's why I intend to be there the whole time, workin' alongside them," William said.

"Can I go too, Pa?" John asked. "I'm big enough to help."

William looked at his wife. "I had thought to leave John here with you," he said.

Mary Taylor shrugged. "He's no school to attend, and Rachel and Esther and I can manage without him. Do as you like."

"You can keep up with my schoolin', too," John added.

"Then it's settled—but I expect you to pull your own weight, or back here you'll come."

"I want to go, too," said Esther, who was becoming an accomplished whiner.

"No, missy, you stay here with your ma and Rachel. It won't be long before we'll all be together again."

As a stormy, wet spring gave way to the heat of summer, the Taylors' small vegetable garden began to produce, far earlier than would have been possible in Kentucky.

"We should have an even longer growin' season on Cane Creek, being as it's even farther south," Mary Taylor said.

"I hope it's not as cold as Kentucky in the winter," said Rachel, who had seen little difference between the summer heat and bothersome insects between the two places.

Mary Taylor sighed and swatted at a persistent fly. "At least the new house will have windows we can close. I miss that here."

I've missed lots of things, Rachel thought, but she kept the thought to herself. "Me, too," she said aloud.

The sadness in Rachel's tone made her mother speak words of comfort. "This move's been hard on us all, but soon we'll be settled in the new house, an' things will be better. Your pa says new folks are comin' in all the time. Soon Cane Creek will have a church meetinghouse an' a regular school, just like Bryan's Station."

Rachel attempted a faint smile. "Maybe even better than the Station."

Mary Taylor nodded. "Could be. The Lord has led us here for a reason. Everything will work out for the best—you'll see."

Twice during the summer William and John made the long round-trip from Cane Creek to Nashville. The house was coming along well, he reported, although it had taken much time and even more trouble to get the glass for the windows and find a glazier willing to go so far to install them.

"Did we get a letter from the Fletchers?" John asked each time they came, and he was disappointed when his mother shook her head.

However, two days before the final journey from Nashville to the new house on Cane Creek, William Taylor returned from the Nashville post office bearing the long-awaited letter from the Fletchers.

It had been written in small letters on one side of a

single sheet of paper, which made it hard to read. William read the letter aloud, often pausing as he struggled to make out all of the words. Most of the letter had been poorly penned by Asa Fletcher, with a note from Tom to John at the end. After saying how much he missed his friend, Tom wrote that Sally Dermott had a broken arm and his sister Vinnie had been snakebit, but was now all right. "We get a new baby in October," Tom added, but the next line had been marked through.

William Taylor handed Rachel the letter. "Your young eyes are sharper than mine. See if you can make it out," he said.

No doubt Annabelle Fletcher got hold of it, Rachel thought. "It says 'I hope it's a boy, there are too many females in this family for any use.' "

"Poor Tom!" Mary Taylor exclaimed.

"Now Betty won't be the baby anymore," Esther added.

"No matter—she's not been fussed over since Asa wed that woman," said William.

"Well, at least we know something of what's goin' on at the Station," his wife said.

"I want to write to Tom," John said.

"Nay, wait until we're settled. Then you'll know exactly where to tell them to send their next letter. Nashville's a bit far to come just for mail."

"I can make a sketch of the house for them now," said John.

Mary Taylor nodded. "Master McNaught often remarked on how good a drawin' hand John has. It makes me wonder if he's been heard from since he fetched off to Virginia."

"I'd say not, since Asa Fletcher made no mention of him," William replied.

Rachel turned away, not wanting her parents to see the warm flush that came to her cheeks at the mention of the schoolmaster.

I must stop letting even thinking of Matthew make me blush, Rachel acknowledged. She was painfully aware that such a resolution was far easier to make than to carry out, had she even truly wanted to drive Matthew McNaught from her mind.

Perhaps my heart will forget him someday. But until that time came, her mind would know little peace.

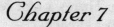

Chapter 7

Summer weather lingered long into the fall of 1807. The sunny October day on which the Taylors finally moved into their house on Cane Creek was as mild as a late May day back at Bryan's Station, which, they surmised, had probably already had their first frost.

"Well, wife, there it is. I hope you like it."

William Taylor had described every feature of the house to his family and shown them rough sketches of the exterior, but seeing it for the first time was an altogether different experience.

Esther clasped her hands in delight. "It's so big!"

"The windows—they're beautiful!" Rachel exclaimed. Two twenty-four light windows flanked the front door, with five more on the second story above them. The whitewashed wooden window frames made a pleasing contrast to the dusty rose-colored brick of the walls.

"A brick house," Mary Taylor said softly. "I never thought to see myself livin' so fine."

"Wait until you see the inside, Ma," John said. "It's bigger'n anything at Bryan's Station, for sure."

"This house will still be here long after we're all gone," William Taylor said. "The foundation's solid, and

73

every wall's plumb. There's a root cellar, and by spring, you'll have a summer kitchen."

"I'm fair amazed," Mary finally managed to say as she wiped happy tears from her eyes.

It took several days, but at last the Taylors were settled into their new home. Since theirs was the grandest dwelling and also the first brick house to be built in the area, people came from miles around to see it.

Most of the male visitors had their own families, either already living in the area or soon to arrive. Rachel's father had met nearly all of them, including the few single males, while the house was being built. Rachel privately thought them to be a rough-looking lot who could use a change of clothes and a bath. When any of the men seemed to regard Rachel with interest, she would look the other way and make an excuse to leave the room. Including the men she had encountered in Nashville, not one she'd seen since leaving Kentucky measured up to Matthew McNaught. Rachel thought it better to risk seeming rude or "uppity" than to appear to encourage their attentions.

Among their first visitors was the James family. Although Davy and Hannah and their children shared a crude, one-room cabin with a dirt floor, they showed no envy over the Taylors' eight rooms.

"I'd not want to scrub all of this," Hannah said when she saw the spacious kitchen. "When Davy brings in fresh meat, the blood just soaks right into the floor. Throw a bit more dirt over it, and that's the end of the cleanin'."

Mary Taylor looked at her wide-planked heart-of-pine floor and shook her head emphatically. "Fresh meat won't be stainin' this floor."

"You hear that, Davy?" William Taylor asked. "I reckon that means my game will have to hang outside."

Davy James laughed and clapped the older man on the back. "I reckon that's so. But any time you get tired of livin' fancy, you'll allus be welcome at my place."

"Thanks, friend. I'll keep that in mind."

In the weeks that followed, William Taylor and Davy James were often in each other's company. When they weren't hunting, Davy helped William and John build a smokehouse so the meat they raised and killed could more easily be preserved.

"Those two make a strange pair," Rachel Taylor said to her mother one morning when William and John rode off with Davy to a honey tree he'd just found.

"Aye, but Davy's been a blessin' to us in many ways. I can't begrudge the time your pa spends with him."

"I just wish—" Rachel began, then stopped, unwilling to finish her thought.

She accepted and was grateful for the blessings of health and prosperity that God had bestowed on them since they left Bryan's Station. But she also wished that some things were different: that she and her mother had the kind of friends they had known in Kentucky; that John and Esther had more companions their own age to play with; that another Matthew McNaught would come along for her—

"Don't wish your life away, Rachel. Each day is a gift from God. Live it as it comes, the best way you know how. All else will take care of itself."

Her mother had said the same thing many times before, but this time the words seemed to mean more. "I know it will," Rachel said, and silently prayed for patience.

By early December, the warmth of October that had continued long into November was but a memory. First, a thick frost traced fantastic forms on the windowpanes and left a rim of crystalline ice on everything. Then dark clouds gathered, and a steady, soaking cold rain fell for several days. After that, a pale sun struggled to shine briefly, only to disappear again into even more ominous clouds.

Still, by the third week of December, the area had yet to see any snow. The worst winter weather would come in late January and February, and December snows were rare in those parts, Davy James had told them.

"I miss the snow we had in Kentucky," Esther said one damp and gloomy afternoon.

John sounded almost wistful. "The Station's probably already had lots of snow by now." He had written Tom Fletcher in October, but so far had no reply.

"I'm just as happy without it, especially since your pa's off huntin'," Mary Taylor said.

John sighed heavily. "I wish they'd let me go with 'em. Pa knows I shoot true."

"Small varmints, maybe, but elk sometimes turn mean. It's just as well that they didn't take you along this time," his mother said.

"Besides, they'll be gone for several days," Rachel added. "You wouldn't want to sleep out in the open in this weather."

"I wish I could take my featherbed and sleep outside," said Esther.

" 'If wishes were horses, beggars would ride,' " Mary Taylor quoted briskly. "We've chores to do before dark. Let's get started."

The hunters were expected to return on December twenty-third, bringing fresh meat for their Christmas dinner. For several days Rachel and her mother had been making pies and preparing other special dishes. They were too busy cooking to notice, but that afternoon, Esther excitedly reported that it was snowing.

Rachel looked outside, but saw only a few sleet needles. "I think you imagined what you wanted to see," she told her sister.

Later, however, Mary Taylor came in from feeding the stock with the news that she, too, had spotted a few snowflakes. "It smells like snow, all right. I wish your pa would hurry up and get back."

"He and Davy must have traveled too far to get back tonight," Rachel said when her father hadn't come home by bedtime.

"We must all pray that God will keep them safe and warm," Mary said.

"I'm sure they'll be all right," Rachel said. She had no reason to think otherwise. After all, William Taylor was an experienced woodsman himself, and Davy James knew every cabin and limestone cave for miles around. If bad weather should overtake them, they'd know what to do.

Even though she wasn't concerned about her father's safety, Rachel found sleep elusive that night. For the last week or so, as the Christmas season approached, she had been increasingly reminded of the pleasant hours she'd spent at the schoolhouse at Bryan's Station the previous Christmas. Since it was almost the last time she had been in Matthew McNaught's company, Rachel found the memory to be bittersweet.

The past was gone forever, Rachel knew. She accepted the truth that life could be fully lived only in the present moment. Yet, especially in the past few days, no matter where she was or what she was doing, Rachel found herself thinking of Matthew McNaught.

Maybe he's in some kind of trouble. The thought brought her from her warm bed to kneel in earnest prayer on the cold floor.

Dear God, guide and protect Pa and Davy and Matthew. Let them not come to harm, she prayed.

With her mind eased, Rachel crept back into bed and slept.

⌒◯⌒

"Come look!" Esther exclaimed from the window in the room they shared.

Rachel looked through the frosty pane and saw that outside, everything had changed. In the night, several inches of snow had fallen, creating a silent, white-wrapped world. Snowflakes, some fat as hen feathers, continued to drift from a uniformly gray sky.

"So we can have snow in Tennessee in December, after all," Rachel said. *Davy James was wrong about that,* she thought to herself.

Esther and John were eager to get outside to play in the snow, but their mother was less enthusiastic.

"I don't like this," Mary Taylor told Rachel as they watched Esther and John toss snowballs at each other.

Rachel spoke with more optimism than she felt. "The snow's not very deep, and the flakes are getting bigger. Maybe that's a sign it'll stop soon."

"Even so, clouds like that can turn mean in a hurry. I wish your pa was here."

"He and Davy can read the skies too, you know. They won't put themselves in any danger."

Although Rachel had spoken with assurance, by late afternoon she couldn't be so sure that all was well with the hunters. The wind shifted to the north, sculpting the frequently heavy snow showers into thick drifts. Rachel and her mother struggled in the face of the ever-rising wind to feed the stock.

At the unnaturally early darkness, Esther became uneasy. "I want Pa to come home," she whined.

"So do we all, but sayin' so won't bring him home," John said, not quite hiding his own concern.

"Your pa's probably snug and warm at Davy's place or somewhere else, waitin' out the storm," Mary Taylor said. "God knows where he is, and He's takin' care of him right now."

Esther sounded anxious. "Suppose Pa can't find us,

like that man in Master McNaught's story."

"What story?" asked her mother.

"The one he told last Christmas Eve," Rachel said. "Esther's right—we should put a light in the window tonight."

"John, fetch the candle lantern. I believe the sill's wide enough to hold it," his mother said.

"I wish I could hear that story again." Esther sighed and climbed into Rachel's lap and regarded her imploringly.

"So do I," said Rachel. *And from Matthew McNaught.*

John returned with the candle lantern, which his mother set on the sill and lighted with a brand from the fireplace. "You tell the story, Rachel," he urged.

"Yes, let's hear it," Mary Taylor said. "It will help pass the time."

"All right. I think I can recall most of it." Rachel stared a long moment into the bright flames that danced in the fireplace, then took a deep breath and began to speak. "Once upon a long, long time ago, in a land far away, it fell out that a poor old man had to travel a long way in the bitter cold."

"Pa's not poor, and he's not old," Esther interrupted.

"This story isn't about him, anyhow," John pointed out.

"Shh! Be quiet or your sister can't tell the story," his mother said.

Rachel started over, telling the story as well as she could recall it. She could almost see Matthew McNaught as he stood in the schoolhouse on that cold day, spinning a tale he said he had learned in faraway Virginia.

". . .When the old man opened his eyes and saw

that he had been saved from certain death, he thanked God. 'I saw your candle in the window, and now I live,' he told the old couple who had taken him in. They said they put it there to welcome the Christ Child. 'But I needed it more,' the man said.

"He never forgot how that candle in the window of a lonely hut in the deep woods had saved his life. From then on, as long as he lived, he made sure that a candle burned in the front window of his house, and every traveler who came into its light received a warm welcome."

No one spoke for a while after Rachel finished. Then her mother wiped the tears from her eyes and sighed. "Thank you for reminding us that this is the season we honor our Savior's birth," she said. "There for a while, I'd forgot it."

<hr>

They remained sitting before the fire in silence for some minutes, until her mother rose and took the sleeping Esther from Rachel's arms. "We can all go to bed now," Mary Taylor said softly. "I have a peace that all is well with your pa. John, light our way."

"I'll stay here and mind the window candle a while longer," Rachel said. She felt wide awake, and she wanted to hold on to the curious joy that telling Matthew's story had given her for as long as she could.

"All right. Make sure to bank the fire before you go to bed."

"I will," Rachel promised.

The fire had already begun to burn low, its blue flames licking the shrinking wood. Rachel stared into its depths and felt a strange exhilaration.

Something good is going to happen, she felt without reason. Rachel wrapped her shawl about her shoulders and knelt before the fire, where she began to pray for her father and Davy and the rest of the family, and as always—and even more so this night, with the memory of his story so fresh—for Matthew McNaught.

Rachel never remembered putting an "Amen" to her prayer, but she knew some time must have passed when she came to herself, lying on the floor in front of the fireplace. The fire had burned even lower, its dying embers casting wavering shadows against the whitewashed walls. However, the candle lantern still burned brightly on the window sill.

Rachel heard a sound, light at first, and then more insistent, and she realized someone must be knocking on the front door.

"Pa's back!" Rachel murmured aloud. She stood and hastened to slide back the bolt and fling open the door.

Rachel gaped in astonishment at the snow-covered figure standing before her. Dazed, she put a hand to her throat. She blinked and swallowed hard, but no words could force themselves past her surprise.

I must be dreaming. This can't be real.

"It's a bit cold out here tonight," the apparition said. "I'd like to come inside."

"Matthew?" Rachel whispered the name, making it a question.

The snowy figure removed the wide-brimmed traveling hat and muffler that covered most of his face and nodded. "Matthew McNaught, at your service, ma'am. I've come a long way. Will you let me in?"

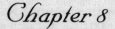

Chapter 8

R achel had never fainted in her life, but she felt close to doing so as she stepped away from the door and gestured for Matthew McNaught, the man she'd thought she'd never see again, to come inside.

Matthew removed his heavy traveling cloak and shook off the snow before he stepped over the threshold. "I don't want to stain your floor," he said.

Rachel wanted to reply that it didn't matter, that nothing mattered except that she was with him again, but the words fled when she tried to say them. To hide her confusion, Rachel turned away and put another stick of wood onto the fire.

She took a long, ragged breath before turning to face Matthew. This time, Rachel managed to stammer a few words, even though they were not at all what she wanted to say. "Wh—what are you doing here?"

Matthew closed the distance between them in one step and took Rachel into his arms. His face felt cold against hers as he pressed her close, but when he kissed her, Matthew's lips felt as warm as her own.

After a while, Matthew pulled back enough to gaze into Rachel's eyes. "Does that answer your question?" he asked softly.

Overcome with emotion, Rachel felt tears of joy well in her eyes. When she said "I hope so," Matthew kissed her again, then indicated that she was to sit beside him on the fireside settle.

"I don't wonder that you're surprised to see me," Matthew said. "Believe me, I'd have been here months ago if things hadn't fallen out as they did."

"What happened? You left Bryan's Station without even saying good-bye."

Matthew shook his head at the memory. "That was my first mistake. I was trying to get up the courage to ask you to be my wife when I heard that you were going to marry Asa Fletcher. I didn't question it—another mistake—and since I had already decided to go to Virginia, I just went sooner rather than later."

Rachel's heart ached at the realization of how close Matthew had come to declaring his love. "I never told Asa Fletcher I'd wed him," she said.

Matthew nodded. "I know that now—and I should have realized it then."

"So did you go to that college in Virginia, like you planned?" Rachel asked.

Matthew nodded. "Yes, but I never got to tell you why. I'd felt a call to the ministry, and I wanted to study as much as I could before being ordained."

"Ordained?" Rachel repeated. "You mean—like a preacher?"

"Yes." Matthew held Rachel's hands tightly. "Does that make any difference in the way you feel about me?"

"Nothing could change that," Rachel said. "I think I must have always loved you—and I always will."

Matthew released Rachel's hands and hugged her close. "Thank God," he whispered. "When I think how close I came to losing you—"

He shook his head, unable to finish the thought.

"When did you find out I didn't marry Asa Fletcher?" Rachel asked.

"Not nearly soon enough. I sent Mrs. Eggleston my aunt's address last spring, but the letter she wrote last summer went astray somehow—I didn't get it until months later. You can't imagine how I felt when I read that Asa had married some woman from Pennsylvania and that your whole family had left the Station."

"What did you do then?" Rachel asked.

"I finished my courses as soon as I could, and I felt obligated to stay on at the little church where I preached Sundays until they got someone else. Then I went back to the Station. Tom Fletcher had a letter from John with a map that showed where you lived. I got outfitted, then started south. I made fair time until the weather turned bad."

"I didn't know John's map was that detailed," Rachel said.

"It wasn't—I had to stop often and ask the way. The last two days, I didn't even come across anyone to ask. I was about to give up and try to find a sheltered place to spend the night when I saw that candle in your window."

"Just like in the story you told us last year," Rachel said.

Matthew smiled and tenderly brushed Rachel's cheek with the back of his hand. "Yes. Your candle led me to you."

Rachel shook her head. "No, more than a candle led you here. Surely God must mean for us to be together."

"Ah, Rachel, I do believe that too."

They kissed again, then drew apart when someone knocked loudly on the door.

"Pa!" Rachel exclaimed, and for the second time that night she opened the door, expecting to see her father.

"I wasn't sure anyone would be up at this hour—" William Taylor began, then stopped to stare at the man who stood beside his daughter, holding her hand.

"Oh, Pa, I'm so glad you're all right. Come warm yourself by the fire. You must be half-frozen."

"I might be all the way so in truth, had I not seen that candle lantern. Is my brain addled from the cold, or is that Matthew McNaught standin' there holdin' onto you?"

Matthew stepped forward and shook William's hand. "Aye, sir, it is. The candle lantern brought me here, as well."

Mary Taylor's voice called down from the stairs. "What's happening? What's all the racket about?"

"Pa's home, and he's all right," Rachel called back.

"Praise the Lord!" Mary entered the room and started toward her husband, then stopped short when she saw Matthew McNaught.

John and Esther followed on their mother's heels. Half-asleep, Esther rubbed her eyes and smiled at her former teacher, apparently unsurprised to see him there. "See, Master McNaught, our candle brought Pa home, just like the one in your story."

Mary Taylor looked from Matthew to her husband. "Will someone please tell me what's going on?"

"All will be sorted out in time, wife. But first, let us thank God for his mercies in bringing us all safely together."

"And in this season, we also thank God for the Christian love that the candle in the window represents. In the end, what really matters is God's gift of His Son," Matthew said.

"Amen," said Rachel. "This is one Christmas none of us will ever forget."

Epilogue

Rachel spoke the truth. No one in the Taylor house on that first Christmas on Cane Creek ever forgot how what could have been a tragedy on a cold, snowy night turned into a miracle of love.

Matthew and Rachel married and moved into a home a half mile up Cane Creek, on land her father deeded to them. For several years Matthew kept a school and preached on Sunday in the same building. Later, others took over the school, leaving Matthew free to devote all his energies ministering to the spiritual needs of an ever-growing population.

Matthew McNaught continued to tell the story of the candle in the window, and year after year, he and Rachel and their children always placed a candle in their front window on Christmas Eve.

Nearly two centuries later, their descendants, scattered far and wide from Cane Creek to California and from Alaska to Florida, still repeat the story and light candles to remind all who might pass by of the true meaning of the season that honors the Light of the World.

Kay Cornelius
Kay lives in Huntsville, Alabama. Her talent for research and detail brings her stories to life. Kay has written several books for Barbour Publishing's **Heartsong Presents** line, including *Sign of the Bow, Sign of the Eagle, Sign of the Dove, Sign of the Spirit, More Than Conquerors, A Matter of Security,* and *Politically Correct.* Each of her inspirational romances is an affirmation of "my own beliefs in the Lordship of Jesus Christ and the love of God that is the source of all human love."

Bittersweet

Rebecca Germany

Dedication

To my mother Wanda Royer for sharing ideas and memories; also to the community of Tappan for historical inspiration.

Prologue

September 23, 1936
Cleveland, Ohio

Gracie, I'm so glad I caught you in."
The phone against her ear, Grace Rudman relaxed against the entryway wall of the boardinghouse and set her handbag down in the telephone nook. Her brother's voice was a soothing balm as she prepared to start another stressful day of job hunting. If anyone could sympathize with her situation, it would be Guy. No matter what, she could always count on her older brother to understand.

Six months ago, when Grace had left Tappan, she had been desperate to escape the small hometown and get to the busy city. After graduation, she had worked hard in a little store on Tappan's sleepy Main Street, saving all her money, until at last she had enough to leave. She'd needed to get away from the people who loved her, especially her father, who couldn't understand that she was no longer a little girl. Everyone had seemed to think that she would simply settle down and be a farmer's wife, something safe and boring.

After her high school graduation, David Matthews,

Guy's best friend, had acted so surprised when she'd said she wouldn't marry him, as though she could have lived the rest of her life on a little farm outside Tappan with someone who had always been like another older brother to her. Marrying David would have been like never leaving home at all. She had desperately needed to get away and find a life of her own, something new and exciting and independent.

Finding that life, though, was proving to be harder than she had anticipated, and she was tired today, tired and a little scared. Hearing Guy's voice made her realize how much she missed him. She loved her brother John, too, of course, but Guy was the one she had always been closest to in the family, and until these last few months he had been the one in whom she had always confided. Tears sprang to her eyes, and she wished he were standing beside her so she could lean her head against his shoulder.

"I know you city gals can be very busy with work and high society," he was saying, "but you haven't called home lately. When will you get home for a visit? We haven't seen you since you left in March." His voice was soft and playfully pleading, one of his endearing qualities.

Grace blinked away her tears and resisted the appeal in her brother's voice. *Long distance calls and train trips are out of the question when you're down to your last dime,* she justified. Instead she said into the heavy black receiver, "I may plan a trip home soon. I miss you, big brother."

"The job keeping you busy. . . ?"

What job? The last three were only temporary positions. She had relied on her substantial savings to get her by until. . .

". . .or maybe some sweet talker has stolen my little sister's heart?"

Oh, if you only knew the half of it. I'm such a fool. Grace couldn't bring herself to tell Guy about Gerald. She glanced around the narrow hallway and frowned. Two boarders entered the ornate front door and were greeted by Mrs. Schumacher. Speaking with the other boarders didn't stop the landlady from continuing to time Grace's phone call. A limit of ten minutes was strictly enforced. Grace sighed. This was not the place or time to go into her troubles.

She spoke in a quiet tone, holding the receiver close to her mouth. "To say the least, I do find myself very busy, but the men of this city have lost their appeal." She sighed again, wishing she could go into more detail. The face of Gerald Renner floated through her mind.

"Well, what I really called to say was that Dad wanted me to let you know—" Guy's voice crackled through the phone wires.

"Wait! I know what he wants to ask me," Grace stubbornly interrupted. Her father was strong and loving, but his overprotective nature balked at giving his daughter the freedom she craved. Grace had fought to prove her independence, yet with every fiber of her being, she longed to go home. But to admit defeat when she had had such large dreams. . .

Grace continued, "I'm sure he wants to know if I

have had enough of city life, if I've blown my savings, if I still go to church, if I'm in any trouble, if I. . ." She ran out of breath.

"Sure he's concerned for you. We all are!" Guy assured her. "He didn't ask anything, but he just wanted me to tell you that Mrs. Miller's dress shop in Dennison is expanding and she is hiring new help with room and board included. I guess he's thinking that you could live closer to home and still have your independence."

Grace hesitated. The job sounded very tempting, but she wanted to make her own choices. Still, the thought of home brought a lump to her throat, especially when she realized that her familiar home and the entire town of Tappan would soon be underwater.

As though he'd read her thoughts, Guy said, "With the water conservancy damming up the valley, things are pretty interesting around here." Guy had his usual positive outlook, but Grace was sure her parents were distraught over the threatened loss of their home. "It would be nice to have you close so you could come home on weekends," Guy added. "Mom and Dad still won't sign the papers that will deed their land to the water conservancy, but more and more of our neighbors have given in. Whatever happens in the end, things here are going to be. . .well, challenging. It might be easier if the family could face it all together."

"Uh. . ." Grace saw Mrs. Shumacher tap the little watch pinned to her lapel. "I'll think about it. Things are busy around here right now. I'll. . .I'll try to call home soon."

Grace hurried her good-byes. She hadn't had a chance to share her own worries with Guy, but she promised herself she would splurge and call him again soon, in another week or two. The next time she and her brother talked, Grace told herself, she would confide in him. She knew Guy would understand. Guy would never say "I told you so."

She smiled to herself, cheered by the thought that her big brother would always be there for her, and then she collected her handbag and marched determinedly for the front door. She still had one hope left if she wanted to be a success in this city—find Gerald Renner and make him give her back her hard-earned money.

Two hours later, she found him in a crowded diner, sitting at the counter in a stylish pin-striped suit and polished leather shoes. She took a deep breath and came up behind him. "I need my money back, Gerald," she ground out, trying to keep her voice low in the crowded diner.

Gerald spun around on his stool. His initial surprise was replaced by a cocky grin on his dazzling handsome face. He stood, towering over her petite frame, and removed his bowler from the next stool.

"Please sit, doll," he droned. "May I order you a coffee or soda?"

Grace stood rigid, holding tight to her resolve. "I have been trying to reach you for over a week. The job at the courthouse turned out to be only a temporary typing position, and I need my savings to pay my rent at the boardinghouse."

"I told you I would get you a car with the money." He sighed. "Please, take a seat, dear. You're drawing attention."

She ignored him. "I don't know how I let you talk me into an automobile. I can't even drive," she spat and crossed her arms tightly in front of her. Of course she had driven the horse-drawn carts across her father's fields, but that hardly counted.

The bell on the door jangled as people streamed in and out on this first day of fall. The waitress jarred Grace on her way past, but Grace remained rooted to her spot by the pie case.

"Even if I owned a car, I would have to sell it." Her voice started to raise. "I couldn't even afford the gasoline."

Gerald gave a pacifying chuckle and took her elbow in an attempt to draw her to the stool. She resisted.

"Grace, you want to make it in this town, don't you?" He turned his piercing gaze on her, and her strength began to waver. He had hit her weakest point. "A young woman like you needs a car and a stylish wardrobe to move up in this town. You'll see. Once you have your own automobile, things will turn around for you."

Grace sighed as she finally slumped to the stool. "Then where's my auto? I know I had more than enough money to get at least a used one."

"Well. . ." Gerald's laugh shook. "It will be another week or so before I can get things worked out. . . Business has been keeping me running. . ."

Grace's anger returned. "Where's my money, Gerald?"

"What do you say we go out and paint the town red tomorrow night?" he suggested, ignoring her outburst.

"My money?"

"Sure—I'll bring it along. If you're really certain you don't want that car." Gerald ducked his head over his cooling plate of meat loaf.

Two weeks later, Grace tossed her hat into the corner of her room and lowered herself to the lumpy armchair. She released her thick brown hair from the clasp at the back of her neck. The room was stuffy with the heat of Indian summer. Her feet ached from a long day of job searching, and she longed for a leisurely soak in a tub. If only the one boardinghouse bathroom didn't have a time limit.

After Gerald had stood her up for their date and couldn't be found, she had given up her private room and had moved in with another girl, who, like Grace, was only a little over a year out of high school. The arrangement was helping Grace afford to stay in the city, but she was desperate for more than temporary work. Her goal to rise to the top of society was going nowhere but downhill—fast.

She felt herself drifting toward sleep when a knock sounded on the thin door.

"I have a wire for you," Mrs. Schumacher started in her thick German clip before Grace had the door opened.

"Thank you."

Mrs. Schumacher held the door open and continued briskly, "Have you seen today's paper? That man you have been seeing since you got here last spring is a wanted criminal."

"Gerald Renner?" A lump formed in her throat.

"Jah, that's the one. He's been robbing good people blind and is now on the run from the law. I could tell he was no saint. I even—" The robust woman broke off her report. "Why, are you ill, child? You look positively sick."

Grace's loose hair curtained her ashen face as her head hung forward.

Mrs. Shumacher grasped the young woman's shoulders. "Do you need to sit?" she asked before a new thought overtook her. "Did that scoundrel take advantage of you? Did he leave you. . .in a compromising state?"

Grace shook her head and murmured, "Only. . .my money." She forced herself to face the realization that she would probably never see her hard-earned money again. It wasn't fair. Even though she hadn't seen Gerald for two weeks, she had held on to the hope that he would eventually bring her the money or a car. She couldn't keep the tears from streaming down her face.

"Oh. . .I should have paid more attention to your money troubles," the large woman moaned as she hugged Grace's slender, petite frame to her ample bosom. "You poor girl."

"Call me if you need someone to talk to. I'll even go with you to make a report to the police." The woman's eyes were unusually moist.

"Thank you, Mrs. Schumacher," Grace finally said as she swiped tears from her streaked cheeks and recollected her rigid composure. She remembered the wire. . . and though her common sense told her otherwise, she couldn't help but hope that it was from Gerald, explaining what he had done. Mrs. Schumacher handed her the message.

Grace tried to smile politely as she closed the door softly behind her landlady.

She retreated to her chair. *I had a feeling that something like this was coming,* she thought. *How could I be so stupid? I even thought he cared for me! How will I ever get back those months of wages? All that time I stayed home and worked in the Tappan store was wasted.* Her blank stare looked past the tiny third-floor window, beyond the four close walls.

I should have married and settled down like any normal young woman. David made a perfectly good offer, but I had to see the world. . .though this is far from what I had in mind.

For some reason, the thought of David Matthews sent more tears streaming down her face. She remembered the way he had looked at her the last time she'd seen him, and she saw again the love and hurt in his eyes. A strange yearning filled her.

She gulped back her tears and slowly unfolded her telegram. And then she simply sat frozen, staring at the words in front of her, unable to make sense out of them.

**Guy in bad accident. STOP. Father is sick.
STOP. Take train home soon. STOP. John**

Grace choked and read her brother's words again. They couldn't be true. Not Guy, who was so dear to her, to her entire family, and to his best friend David—to the whole community, in fact. Nothing could happen to Guy. He was like the ground she walked on, always there, always dependable. Surely God would not let this accident have hurt him too badly, surely he would be fine soon. And Father never got sick. He was so strong, he'd always been strong her whole life. *They'll both be fine,* she tried to tell herself.

But a cold chill settled over her, telling her otherwise. *How can all this be happening at once? Oh God, what are You doing? Please. . .heal my brother and my father.*

Her prayer brought her no comfort. Dread filled her heart, a terrible sense of foreboding. She jumped up and began to pack. As she stuffed her clothing into a trunk, a new thought occurred to her: she would have to admit to her family that she couldn't even afford to buy her own train ticket home.

Grace moved to the bed to weep in despair. *Lord, where are You in times like these?*

Chapter 1

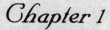

December 18, 1936
Dennison, Ohio

Three months later, Grace walked to the depot to catch a ride home from Dennison to Tappan for the Christmas holidays. After Guy's death and her father's declined health, she had known she could not return to Cleveland; her family needed her to be closer to home. She had taken the job at Mrs. Miller's dress shop, the one Guy had told her about the last time she'd talked to him. The job was not a bad one, but it was boring, and the last months had been a dreary blur of sorrow and discouragement. After her experience with Gerald, she had no desire to return to Cleveland—but she felt no excitement about living the rest of her life in Dennison either.

Going home today brought her no excitement either. Her parents' house was not the same since her father's illness and Guy's death, and she almost dreaded her visits there. Things were too different; Guy's absence was too painful; and soon the entire town would be gone, flooded by the new dam.

Reaching the depot, she stood rigid by the window,

too tense to sit on one of the long benches. She was here to meet Mr. Matthews, her family's neighbor and her only way home today from town. She could see that he had already gone out to the platform to await the train, even though a stiff, cold wind was blowing. The chill had hit with force this past week and Little Stillwater Creek was almost frozen over.

Grace looked now toward the creek, trying to think of something besides the man who would soon be arriving on the train. A train's whistle could be heard as it neared the station from the direction of the neighboring town, and her stomach clenched with nervousness.

This would be the first time in eighteen months that she had seen David Matthews, Mr. Matthews' son, Guy's best friend—and the man who had once asked her to marry him. David could not come home for Guy's funeral, and Grace could only imagine the grief he suffered alone. Her own sorrow had been unbearable and she could barely remember details of the day.

She turned now and looked over the waiting room, thinking perhaps it would be better to sit than be found waiting by the window. But most of the seats had been taken. Being the holiday season, the depot was extremely busy on this Saturday afternoon with shoppers traveling to and from the bigger cities and other people who were already making the journey home for Christmas. Grace could see no comfortable seat available in the small waiting room, so she turned back to the window, pulling her black woolen coat closer as the door opened to receive a new flow of travelers.

The brick-lined platform was full of people, large carts of luggage, and boxes. Grace had to crane her neck to find Mr. Matthews where he waited eagerly for his son to alight the train that could now be seen chugging into the station. Grace imagined David sitting awkwardly on the train, out of place among all the finely dressed people. Of course he wouldn't be wearing the farmer's overalls that he always used to wear, but she could picture him in an ill-fitting suit, his old misshapen hat jammed on his head. She wondered how a farm boy like David had managed all these months in the city. She had been surprised when David had found employment in Detroit.

The last time she and David had spoken, she had been filled with ambition and plans. The memory of her rejection of his marriage proposal was between them now, but she would have been embarrassed to face him even without that, now that all her fine plans had come to nothing.

Working every day with her four roommates in Mrs. Miller's dress shop was getting old for Grace. She was growing to hate the tedium of the stuffy upstairs workroom with its treadle sewing machine that pumped all day long. The widowed Mrs. Miller had been unusually kind, though, at the time of Guy's funeral, advancing Grace the money to move close to home. Grace owed her much and she felt obligated to stay with the position and do a good job.

But it had been a long, busy week at the dress shop, and even if she dreaded facing again the changes in her home, she was glad for the extended holiday. She could have been home by now if only her brother John had picked her up at the dress shop like he usually did for her weekend visit. Then she could have avoided this embarrassing meeting with David, at least for a little longer. But John had said he was occupied today with his own business, and he had made the arrangement for Mr. Matthews to pick her up instead.

Grace frowned as she thought of her brother John. Since Guy's death, he seemed to have distanced himself from the family, spending more and more time with his new girlfriend. His changed attitude toward his family was one of the many disturbing changes that Grace faced each time she went home—but where Guy's loss and her father's illness filled her with sorrow, the change in John made her feel frustrated and angry. *How can John be so selfish? Doesn't he understand that we need him now more than before?*

Grace pushed away her anger with John and scanned the passengers descending from the train. Her eyes were drawn to a handsome young man in a well-tailored navy suit. The brim of his stylish hat had slid to one side and hid his face from her view. He held his head high as he scanned the area, and she wondered if he were in town on business.

She continued to watch as he neared the building, but quickly the young man's hat was sent off with the wind by Mr. Matthews' jovial greeting. Red hair glistened in the winter sunlight. She felt her mouth drop open as she recognized David as the stylish gentleman.

She recalled the last time she had spoken with him. David had been wearing his old overalls, his dull red hair allowed to curl over his ears. He had been well-toned from the years of farmwork, but the same hard work always seemed to give him a tired look. This new David was nothing like she had expected.

David retrieved his hat and followed his father to the door. Grace found herself lifting a hand to check her long hair clasped at the back of her neck, a luxury she afforded herself and chose not to cut to fit new fashion fads. David spotted her even before he stepped up over the threshold and gave her a warm, broad smile.

"Gracie, how are you?"

Grace was surprised by his use of her childhood name. Only Guy had used it in recent years, and the name made her eyes sting.

David's voice was soft and kind. He took his hat in his left hand and gently squeezed her shoulder with his right. "I'm so sorry I couldn't make it home for Guy's funeral." Grace detected moisture in his eyes. "You know he was like a brother to me too, but, praise God, he's with Christ."

Grace couldn't find her voice. This attractive, confident gentleman barely resembled the friend of her childhood. Neither did he appear to have even a flickering memory of their last conversation, when she had flatly rejected his offer of marriage. He seemed to have captured everything she had once sought after—worldly charm and sophistication. His change lacked the pride and haughtiness that many of her friends had displayed, however. But were his show of faith and sympathy honest? Honesty and faith had become very important to Grace.

Grace sat in the rear seat of Mr. Matthews' Ford Phaeton on the ten-mile trip to her home near the village of Tappan. She still had barely said more than hello to David, and now he and his father were enjoying their first reunion in nearly a year.

"That's a nice suit you have there, Son. That Detroit car factory must be treating you pretty good," Mr. Matthews noted.

"It was past time for me to buy a new suit and I could only afford one, so I decided it should be a dandy."

Father and son chuckled over this wisdom.

But strangely, it bothered Grace that David might care so much about appearances. She ran her hand across the lap of her sturdy navy work dress and sighed inaudibly. Was she jealous of David or simply disappointed? After all, hadn't she always secretly scorned his ordinary, worn, farming clothes?

"Have you bought one of those new cars yet?" Mr. Matthews asked his son.

"I don't need a car. The city offers great transportation, and I ride a train to work each day," David stated. "I could get a good deal from the company, though, and may take advantage of it someday."

Grace smothered a cough, thinking of her failed attempt to buy a car.

"I'm up for a promotion," David told his father. "Supervisor. They could let me know by New Year's."

David's father was thrilled, but Gracie wrestled with strangely troubled emotions as the car traveled through the frozen farmland. They crossed the railroad tracks at Station 15, and Grace recalled the awful day when she first learned that her brother Guy had been killed at the crossing. There had been little left of his barely used Chrysler.

"Yes, that's the place," Grace heard Mr. Matthews' soft reply to a question David must have asked. "Such a tragedy."

David turned and looked over the high seat back. "Gracie, I don't know what to say."

"Don't. . .I'm fine. He was your friend, too," Grace said softly and quickly turned to avoid his eyes as she swallowed against the nauseating emptiness in her chest. She kept her defenses firmly in place. The less she talked about such things, the better she could cope.

Within a couple of miles they would be passing through Main Street in Tappan. The town had become a refuge to Grace after her big-city experience last summer. She hated to think that it would all be underwater someday, and she wondered how David would view the village in comparison to Detroit. Would he think that the small town was so little that it would be of little loss to the new lake?

"Look, there it is," David called out, pointing to the new dam. "It's huge. I can't believe it's done." His voice reflected awe. Did she also detect regret, or was it just her wishful thinking? *Misery enjoys company,* Grace realized.

She followed his pointing arm to the massive dirt and cement structure. The dam had been completed in October and was already collecting water that would eventually cover their beautiful valley.

"Has anyone moved yet?" David asked.

Mr. Matthews answered, "Just the Cloughs and the Masons since the dam went right through their properties. Most of the rest will go in the spring, while some will stay 'til the water pushes 'em out."

Grace squirmed on the cold leather seat. Would it take a flood to move her family?

~⟶~

It would have been hard for David not to notice the decline of the Rudmans' once prosperous farm. Tall weeds lined the drive, still harboring traces of the last snow. Tractor and bulldozer tracks from the dam construction made muddy ruts across the western fields and through broken fence lines. The Rudmans' remaining livestock were crowded into a barnyard pen.

Mr. Matthews pulled the car up along the side of the peeling farmhouse as Grace's older brother John rushed out to meet them. "I'm sure glad you're home, Grace," he almost shouted. "Hey, David, welcome back."

David offered Grace a hand out of the backseat, but she seemed to shrink from his slightest touch.

John filled the sudden silence with annoying chatter. "Mother's been like a ruffled hen all day long. She gets so anxious, and none of the church ladies were able to stop in and lend a hand today."

Grace straightened her shoulders and marched through the kitchen door. David grabbed her small suitcase and started to follow her, but John stopped him.

"Let me take that. You'll be wanting to get home."

David stared at John, not understanding his cool welcome, and John ducked his head as if in shame.

David felt his father approach. "Son, I told you Mr. Rudman was sick, but. . .I failed to tell you that he isn't getting better."

"If that's all, then I'll see him now and not wait," David said and sidestepped John to the door.

The kitchen was a jumble of half-finished projects. Biscuit dough was rolled out but not cut. Unwashed dishes were stacked in a sink full of soapy water, and the teakettle whistled on the old coal-fueled water heater. Grace stood in the middle of the room with her coat over her arm and her shoulders sagging.

"Grace," Mrs. Rudman's high-pitched voice preceded her pencil-thin body around the doorway, "your father will be so excited to see his little girl."

She seemed like the same energetic woman David remembered as she fussed over her grown daughter, yet a veil of false gaiety shrouded any feelings of joy.

"Oh, David!" Mrs. Rudman's eyes teared immediately as she reached for the boy she had known in the man before her. "How I have longed to see you again. Guy will. . .well, we all want you to stay to supper."

David ignored her slip. "I would love to, but I must go home to see my mother first."

"Of course, I'm sure she has a whole spread laid out for your return," Mrs. Rudman said.

"Is Mr. Rudman awake?" David asked. "I would like to say hello."

"Well. . .he doesn't take many visitors. He——" Mrs. Rudman stammered.

"I'll just take a minute."

"I wish you would wait until he is better," Mrs. Rudman said sadly.

"Oh, Mother," Grace moaned with impatience, "I'll take him in. You can't keep all of Father's friends away. You just don't know if Father will—" Grace stopped as her mother's face clouded.

Grace motioned for David to follow her and they entered the front parlor. A rocking chair was placed between the fireplace and the piano with a good view out the window toward the town in the east. But Grace's father was leaning dangerously forward in the chair with his head rested against the windowpane so he could look to the west where the new dam hid the setting sun.

David quickly took hold of Mr. Rudman's shoulders and eased him back into the chair. It was obvious that this man was not the robust farmer that David had once known. Grace straightened the quilt on her father's lap as David surveyed the vacant look in the man's eyes and the droop to the left side of his face.

"Hello, Father," Grace soothed. "I brought an old friend."

"Good to see you, Mr. Rudman," David forced around the lump in his throat.

"David will be here for Christmas and will come to visit again." Grace spoke clearly and precisely to her father, then led David back to the kitchen.

She stopped in the hall. "I'm sorry you weren't told," she managed to say without looking at him.

"When did the stroke occur?"

"The day of Guy's death. That was the hardest blow, but he hadn't really been the same since the conservancy first came to take the farm." Her eyes shone, betraying the moisture that had gathered.

David longed to ease her stiff shoulders and comfort her, but it seemed as if she had placed a prickly wall between them. His hand reached for her.

She stepped back. "You'll want to be getting home," she offered and excused herself up the back stairs.

David promised Mrs. Rudman that he would return for a piece of her custard pie the next afternoon, then walked slowly to the car where his own father waited patiently. John's car was gone; he had already taken off to follow his own whims. David wondered why John would leave so soon after his sister's return home.

Oh, Lord, how the Rudmans need Your comforting assurance, he prayed as he settled into the car.

113

Chapter 2

T he waves were deep and numerous. Beams of winter sunlight highlighted their crests, while their troughs were rich in dark color. There would be no containing the waves, and they splashed out in every direction. Though wild, they invited the curious spectator to take a closer look.

David could hear the preacher's voice in the background as he delivered Sunday's message and his Bible lay open on his lap to the book of Luke, but David's gaze was glued to a head of gorgeous mahogany hair two pews in front of him. He had never given Grace's hair much notice before; he remembered her best in braids. Now she styled her hair in becoming waves that reflected the sunlight to its greatest advantage.

When he had left the valley about eighteen months ago, everything about Grace had consumed his thoughts. While living in Detroit, though, he thought he had come to the point that Grace, and marriage in general, were not as important to him. He had found that he had much to offer his job and community, and he still had much to learn about love.

Then why did the slightest tilt of her head catch his attention and the changes of light on her hair fascinate his imagination? Why did he long to understand all that she and her family had been through since their last parting?

David joined the congregation in the closing hymn and prayer, then he moved with his parents toward the center aisle. Many people wished to greet him, and they clogged the center aisle as they offered handshakes and kind words.

From David's side he could see Grace trying to squeeze through the press of bodies. He turned to meet her squarely. "How are you this morning, Gracie?"

"Fine, thanks." She smiled, but continued to inch down the aisle.

"And where is your mother today? I missed her fine piano playing."

"She couldn't leave Father alone and insisted that I come in her place." Grace sounded tired. "I need to get home right away to help her," she sighed, unable to move farther down the aisle.

"Come." David took hold of her elbow and pulled her back toward the front of the church. He was almost surprised that she didn't resist him.

They slipped through a small door at the right and through the pastor's study. Few of the parishioners would think of disturbing this private chamber, but David felt like he was on a mission of mercy to see Grace home with speed. Another small door led to the rear of the church where dead briars clawed at the siding in the biting wind.

"Now," David said, "where did you leave your car?"

"John dropped me off on his way to meet Melissa,

his fiancée, for church up the valley."

"You weren't planning to walk home in this wind, were you?"

"It really won't take long. I walked it almost every day when I worked at the store," Grace flatly stated and started a fast pace down the alley.

David fell in step beside her, skirting nearly frozen mud puddles. They walked in silence, turning onto Rose Street and leaving the village's limits. Two carloads of people from church passed by, waving cheerfully.

Then Grace broke the silence between them. "Your parents will wonder where you went," she stated simply.

"Yes," he acknowledged. "You should have let us drive you home."

She didn't respond, but bowed her head to the force of the wind.

"Gracie. . ." He had many things he would like to ask her, but he didn't know if she would answer. Instead, he found himself saying, "Do you remember how when we were all kids, you, Guy, John, and I would explore the woods on that hill over there?" He pointed to his right and Grace turned to look.

"Sure, but the 'castle' rock with the interesting hiding places is gone—" Her steady voice broke. "They blasted out the side of the hill to get rocks for that dam."

"So many changes that we can't control."

"Be glad you haven't been around to witness the worst of it."

David could hear her bitterness and chose not to speak for several paces. His parents drove slowly up beside them and he waved them on even as the wind whipped around them. Liberated strands of Grace's hair danced around her sad, little face.

David chose a new topic. "How has John been? Where is he working?"

She took a deep breath. "I don't see a whole lot of John. He works for Melissa's father at a county office in Cadiz and spends most of his time with her family. He has very little time for the farm. . .or helping Mother. He can be so juvenile that you would think he was the youngest."

David hid the smile generated by her sibling frustrations. He had never had brothers or sisters to relate to. The Rudman children had been his extended family.

"One could say," David reasoned, "that John has a lot on his mind and is trying to avoid anything stressful or—"

"Then he needs to grow up!" Grace was adamant. "We'll get through this, but. . ."

"Yes, you will make it, and I agree that everyone should do his share. Would you like me to talk to John?"

"Sure, if he'll listen. . ." She slowly changed her mind. "No, it really doesn't have anything to do with you."

"Call me anytime you need a big brother," David offered.

Grace didn't reply and her pace quickened as her driveway neared. She hurried along the rutted lane without looking back.

David stopped, but called, "I promised to stop in

later for some of your mother's pie."

"Fine" was the only answer the wind carried to him, and he turned to the east to follow the road on across the creek to his home.

⌒~

"Can you imagine a place that will seat 36,000 people?" Grace overheard David asking Mr. Rudman. There was no response and David continued with enthusiasm, "I went to a Tigers' baseball game after the additions to the stadium were made and it was fantastic!"

Grace leaned against the wall in the hallway thinking it was nice of David to offer to sit with Mr. Rudman and carry on a one-sided conversation without knowing if anything he said was heard or understood.

David had arrived in time to share a piece of pie with Mrs. Rudman before evening church service. Then he volunteered to sit with Mr. Rudman while Grace and her mother attended church, but Grace felt it was her duty to stay with her father. She straightened the kitchen and found other odd jobs to avoid sitting with the men in the parlor. But when nothing more needed her immediate attention, she found herself drawn to the parlor door by David's rich voice.

Now David had moved on to Detroit car manufacturing and was explaining the attributes of the V-8 engine to Mr. Rudman. Then he extolled the virtues of the brand-new Zephyr that Lincoln had introduced. David worked at Mr. Ford's factory where the Zephyr was made. Grace understood very little of the jargon—she was still waiting to learn how to drive an automobile—

but she enjoyed David's enthusiasm and felt herself relaxing.

"The Lord knew what He was doing when He sent me to Michigan. I wouldn't have believed I could be happy outside the farm. But now my work in Detroit will make it easier to see the farm go," David quietly said.

Grace came to attention and stood stiff. *Lucky you. If I had married you, farming would still be the only thing you knew and you would be faced with losing your liveli- hood. I did you a favor.*

Grace turned to the back stairs and climbed slowly. *Why does it seem that God clearly directed you, David— and not me? If marriage wasn't the right choice for me, neither was going to the big city.*

She entered her bedroom and looked around at this haven that would be gone much sooner than she would like to think about. Her window faced up the valley and she could see David's family farm. Mr. Matthews had already torn down the large barn for lumber, and the house would be moved as soon as possible to a new location on the ridge.

Friends and neighbors were moving on, finding new direction for their lives and starting over. But Grace felt that her life was at a standstill. Her mother refused to make any decision about their farm without Father's direction. John had dealt with it by mentally removing himself from his family and the farming duties. Grace knew her dressmaking job was her future no matter what happened to the farm, though she didn't like it.

"Grace!" her mother shrieked.

Grace jumped up from the edge of the bed where she had been resting and raced down the stairs. Her mother met her in the hall, still wearing her coat. Grace could hear her father coughing intensely.

"Help me get your father in bed, now! So much company has given him a setback," Mrs. Rudman spoke sharply.

David stood over Mr. Rudman rubbing his shoulders and offering soothing words. He met Grace with an apologetic look. Mrs. Rudman refused David's assistance, and she and Grace shouldered the limp man's weight between them.

When Grace returned from settling her father in the downstairs bedroom, David hadn't moved from the parlor. "I'm sorry about that; I didn't mean to excite him," David said.

"It's not your fault," Grace assured him.

"But, Gracie. . ." David tentatively started, "I think your father was trying to say something before the coughing started. Does he ever speak?"

Grace was surprised. "He usually never makes a sound."

"He has this cane." David pointed near the rocking chair. "Does he ever use it?"

"No. . .but. . .I think he could. Though he doesn't seem to have it in him to try."

"Can I come again tomorrow? I would like to try talking to him again."

"I don't think Mother will allow him to be disturbed for a few days. You better not come."

David moved to the back door. "Gracie, I. . ."

"Thank you for coming," she quickly said, not wanting to hear any more apologies—or anything. "We. . .I mean, I think Father enjoyed your company."

A pained expression crossed David's face, but he left without further words.

Chapter 3

D avid stayed away the next day. Grace's father spent most of his hours in his bedroom, and Grace's mother kept her busy creating a magnitude of Christmas delights which included sugar cookies, cherry turnovers, mincemeat pies, braided date bread, and much more.

Tuesday morning, Mrs. Rudman put coal in the little stove that heated the hot water pipes and started the fire going. Grace watched as she moved on to lay wood in the old cookstove. Grace's father had offered to buy a new electric range not long after electricity reached their corner of the world, but Mrs. Rudman remained faithful to her stove even while her kitchen had the conveniences of an electric refrigerator and some small appliances. Today the heat from the old stove would feel good as a chill seeped in around the window frames.

Grace got the recipe box from a window shelf and laid out her grandmother's recipe for Ozark pudding. She read through the instructions.

2 eggs
1 teaspoon baking powder
1 ½ cup sugar
½ cup flour
1 teaspoon salt
1 teaspoon vanilla
2 cups apples, diced
1 cup nuts, chopped

Beat eggs, add dry ingredients. Fold in apples and nuts. Spread in greased 8-inch square pan. Bake in a hot oven (375°) 50-60 minutes.

Then she laid out her ingredients. She could mix up the pudding quickly and it could bake while she took a tin of cookies into town for the widowed Mrs. Douglas. Normally Mrs. Rudman would invite older folks like Mrs. Douglas who had no family to join the Rudmans for Christmas dinner, but she had declared there would be no company this year.

Grace was peeling apples when a crash came from the bedroom. She and her mother raced to the room and found Father sitting on the floor with the bedside table upset beside him.

He looked up at them as they entered the room, and Grace saw something in his eyes, an expression that reminded her of the father who had been gone for a long time. But then he lowered his eyes and moaned, long and loud.

Grace noticed that his cane was clutched in his right hand. She said nothing but pointed her mother's attention to it.

Mrs. Rudman frowned.

They worked together under the strain of lifting Mr. Rudman to the edge of the bed and set to the task of changing him from pajamas to day clothes with little comment about the incident.

Grace was sponging his face clean when a loud popping noise came from the kitchen. She sighed, laid aside her washcloth, and prepared to investigate the noise. Suddenly an explosion rocked the house and filled the bedroom with a gray, acrid smoke.

Mrs. Rudman screamed. Mr. Rudman began making muttering noises. Grace was frozen to her place near the door. She was unsure what could have created the explosion and what she would find outside the room.

There was loud banging on the front door of the house, and finally Grace was able to propel herself into the front parlor. She felt like her body moved in slow motion. The smoke was still thick from the direction of the kitchen as she opened the door.

"Thank God, you are all right! How about your parents?" David rushed past her and toward the smoky kitchen.

Grace was still rooted to the spot.

"The water heater exploded. There's no fire, but a lot of mess." David pulled her outside to the porch. He took her shoulders and drew her to him. Grace took a deep breath of the fresh air mixed with his freshly washed hair and allowed David to hold her. "I was just coming up the drive when the kitchen windows blew out and I saw smoke. Where are your parents?"

Grace came alert and pushed away from David's

warm embrace. "They're in the bedroom," she said, shaking her head and losing hairpins.

David helped Grace move Mr. Rudman to a chair on the front porch. It was a very cold morning and they wrapped him tightly in several blankets and quilts. Mrs. Rudman, who still seemed to be in shock, sat on the top porch step mopping a continuous flow of tears.

"I'll inspect the damage," David announced and headed through the front of the house to the kitchen. This time Grace stayed right on his heels.

The room was swiftly clearing of smoke but everything was black with soot, ashes, and hot coals. Two of the three windows were blown out as well as the glass in the china hutch. The coal water heater lay in a crumbled mass of iron with hot coals spilled around it and steam from broken water pipes clouding it.

"Frozen pipes," was David's only comment.

Grace picked her way over the dirt and coals to where she had been preparing her pudding recipe. Her apples were black with soot and a hot coal sat in the middle of her recipe card, charring her grandmother's script. Red coals were everywhere, smoldering on the floor, table, counter, and almost every other surface.

"We need to pick these up," Grace said and reached for a spoon and large crock.

David opened the remaining window and the door, then took a snow shovel from the back step and started scooping up coals from the floor.

"Look there, Gracie!" David pointed to the ceiling.

In the ceiling, embedded at least two inches deep, was the door from the water heater's fuel bin. Grace thought about how her mother and she had been working near the water heater just minutes before it burst.

"Praise God you weren't in here at the time," David said.

"Father fell out of bed, and mother and I were dressing him when it exploded," Grace said with wonder. If only her father could understand what he saved them from.

"It is good that you happened to be coming this way," Grace commented as she watched David work. She brushed coals from the counter into her crock. "What brought you by?" she casually asked.

David smiled. "I couldn't stay away."

Surely not from me!

"I wanted to try talking to your father again. Maybe his mind is not as paralyzed as it has seemed. Certainly he has every right to be depressed and withdrawn. . ."

Of course, that's all it is, a good deed toward my father . . .but if he thinks he can make a difference. . .

"The water heater," Mrs. Rudman said from the doorway. "Father always thought to check those kinds of things," she continued without emotion. "Can we move him into the parlor now?"

"Certainly," and David hurried to the task.

"I think I'll lie down," Mrs. Rudman told Grace as she trudged up the stairs. "Oh, and the man from the conservancy is headed up the drive. Would you send him away?"

"Uh. . .yes, Mother."

Grace laid her cleaning supplies on the table and

looked around at this latest disaster. So much had happened to her family in the last few months, more than any normal family should have to endure. They were all running out of the strength to deal with new crises. When would this testing end?

She met Mr. Richards at the front door and explained the morning's events, apologizing that neither her father nor mother was available to talk with him.

The man was kind, but he explained, "Miss Rudman, surely your family realizes that the conservancy has made its best offer. We have obtained rights to all the property surrounding this farm—over 2,000 acres total—and the valley will begin to flood as soon as the spring rains come. You can hold out as long as you wish, but it doesn't change the fact that a large lake will begin to form here in less than a year." Mr. Richards stepped off the porch and prepared to leave. "Please have a representative from your family come and see me at my office in town at your earliest convenience. We want to make this change as smooth as possible. Good day. . .and merry Christmas."

He tipped his black hat to Grace as he got into his car. She watched him leave their property and looked to the west. The dam was a large, ugly mound of dirt. Its very presence was choking the life from her family's farm. It had already completely concealed any evidence of two other farms.

Then she looked toward the creek. It still looked innocent enough, though its waters had been allowed to pool downstream at the new gatehouse. She remembered many summer days of wading in the cool stream—and many springs when it spilled over its banks. Grace realized that someday people would boat over this land and pull fish from its waters. Would she even recognize where their farm had been?

A tear slipped down her cold cheek, and she turned to go back inside. David met Grace inside the front door.

"He's right, Gracie. None of us can stop this lake now." He was leaning against the wall, charming in his soot-covered clothes.

Grace was frustrated that his simple words and good looks could stir her emotions. "I know, and I'm sure Mother knows, but I can't make the decision for her."

"I'll continue to pray," he said while his gaze roved her face.

"Perhaps you should pray that God doesn't send us another disaster." Her temper flashed.

A frown creased his gentle brow. "Please, don't blame Him. Your family is still together. You just need to trust Him for your future."

"Don't preach at me, David. My family is a shadow of what it used to be," Grace blurted out before she slowly began to calm down. "I know the Lord can turn out all things for the best—" she took a deep breath "—but I just don't think I can take another ordeal."

David's hand reached for her, but she plodded toward the kitchen, pulling on her last reserve of energy.

Grace and David worked together all afternoon on repairs to the kitchen. David's father came with two men from town to help board up the broken windows and remove the trash. Grace's mother had stayed in her upstairs bedroom all day, and Grace checked her often to see that all was right.

It was past the supper hour before they had a chance to sit down. Mrs. Matthews had sent a warm casserole over in the late afternoon, and Grace was relieved of cooking in the disarrayed kitchen.

David sat with Grace in the parlor while she spooned the noodle casserole into her father's mouth. She had found a tin of undamaged cookies, and David munched them contentedly.

"Thanks for all your help today," she offered without looking at him.

"You're welcome. I'm just glad I was here."

"I'm sure this isn't the restful visit home you had planned."

He chuckled. "At least I have been here among the family and friends who are most dear to me." He meant what he said, and if he had known the extent of the Rudman's troubles, he would have found a way to come home sooner.

He watched Grace wipe her father's face and tuck his quilt around his lap. David marveled at the strength she had shown, not just today but ever since he had returned home. He had always admired her energy, but before it had been demonstrated in her zest for her own life, creativity, and dreams.

Some of her spark might be gone, or buried, but her determination was still strong. *She would have been a good wife for me. . .and she still would be a good wife. But*

I'm past that point in my life. I don't have to marry right away. I can take my time and save money for a home.

He watched the loose curls of her hair bounce with each move and admired the tilt of her pert nose. *Would she wait?* He shook his head, and his cheeks flamed from the ridiculous thoughts he'd been having. *She still sees me as a brother, and that isn't likely to change.*

Chapter 4

Christmas Eve came to the valley on Thursday under the grip of an extended cold spell. A light snow dusted the ground, masking some of the scars from the dam construction. The creek appeared to have frozen solid and some of the youth were excited about a hastily planned skating party for that afternoon.

The morning was very still throughout the house. Grace's mother had not stirred, and like the last two days, Grace didn't expect to see much of her. She had been staying close to her upstairs bedroom.

Grace prepared her father for the day and settled him into his chair near the parlor window. On impulse, she turned the radio on for him, and livestock prices were the topic of the moment.

She anticipated spending her morning in the kitchen working on a new batch of bread. She missed the sunlight the two boarded up windows had given the room. The dirt from the explosion had been cleared away, but the damage was still very obvious.

She was startled when someone came clattering down the staircase.

"John! I didn't even know you were home!"

"I slipped in late last night. I needed to come by for a few things and figured I'd spend the night."

"Well. . .we've missed seeing you. Where have you been staying?"

"I have a friend or two down Cadiz way. I see you've kept pretty busy though," he remarked as he circled the room. "If this house keeps falling apart, we won't have to worry about moving it." He laughed at his joke.

Grace didn't enjoy his humor and her anger rose. His careless attitude sickened her. "Mother and I could have used your help. Luckily David was here and he rounded up some men to haul trash and board up the windows."

"Ah, David, the lost son returned. I'm sure Mother certainly enjoys having him around." John's eyes narrowed with thought. "Though lacking in Guy's flair for pomp and circumstance, he still could do no wrong. I, on the other hand, worry my parents sick about everything—my education, my job, my choice of a wife. . ."

"Nonsense. Why are you so bitter?" Grace couldn't understand his attitude. "We miss you and want to get to know Melissa. Can you bring her over tomorrow?"

"I doubt it." He gathered his coat and a small bag from a corner chair. "Gotta go. See ya later, Sis." He was out the door before Grace got in another word.

With his attitude, she was almost glad to see him leave. She punched her bread dough with vigor.

Midway through the morning as Grace was placing her raised dough in the oven, Mrs. Rudman entered the kitchen for the first time after almost two days of solitude. She wandered around the room, running her hand along the marred countertop and surveying the other changes to her large kitchen.

Grace watched her slow, deliberate movements. Though her hair was sprinkled with silver, she still had a look of youth and refinement about her. Grace had always admired her mother and hated the lines that worry and grief had etched into her face.

"Well, Grace, dear." Her mother finally turned to her with a sweet smile. "I have lived in this same house since the day of my marriage to your father. I shared it with his parents for nearly ten years, and I raised my children here. The property around here has sold and our farm will flood whether or not we sign it over to the conservancy. It will be sad to see the place go, but the conservancy has made a very fair offer." She sat down in a wooden chair that had lost an arm in the blast.

Grace continued to watch her mother in silence, but she noticed a definite peace about her that had not been present for many months.

"The Lord and I have had a long talk. He has made me see that I can't go back to the past, the present is constantly changing, and the future is His alone to determine. Nothing I do can change these facts." She held out her hands to Grace. "My sweet daughter, I think so often of your brother Guy, and finally, I can be happy for him. He is with his Savior." She drew a work-roughened hand along Grace's cheek. "I highly recommend the comfort it brings when you place your trust in the Lord."

Grace hugged her mother and felt she understood the transformation of her attitude. Her mother had grasped onto the faith that Grace had acknowledged but not yet placed her whole trust in.

" '. . .lay up for yourselves treasures in heaven, where neither moth nor rust doth corrupt, and where thieves do not break through nor steal,' " Mrs. Rudman quoted. "We will take what we can with us to remember this old place by, but it will forever remain in our hearts."

She patted Grace's cheek as unbidden tears came to the young woman's eyes.

"Your father and I will move in with Aunt Maggie in Bowerston. She is no young thing and could use the company," Mrs. Rudman continued with a voice full of new purpose. "In fact, she offered the idea to your father back in the summer."

"John and Melissa will marry by March and live in Cadiz." She rose from her chair and hooked her arm around her daughter's waist. "As for you my dear, dressmaking is a fine vocation, but I do wish you would marry, too."

Grace swallowed hard. *You sound as if I can just snap my fingers and make it happen.*

"It's sad that things didn't work out with you and David last year, but with him home. . ."

"Mother!" Grace choked. "I hardly think that's an issue anymore. With Guy gone, David is even more like a brother to me."

"Exactly!" Mrs. Rudman smiled and dismissed the topic with a flick of her wrist. "That bread is already starting to smell wonderful. You're a good cook, dear, but why don't you take the afternoon and enjoy yourself with the kids at the skating party? You haven't had any time for socializing since you've been home."

"I. . .I don't need to play when there is so much to do to get ready for Christmas."

"Your skates are in the attic," Mrs. Rudman stated and gave Grace a playful shove toward the stairs.

The ground was cold beneath Grace as she sat on the bank of the stream to lace her skates. She pulled the laces tight and the one in her right hand snapped. It was old and frayed.

"Having trouble?" David's voice boomed from over her head.

A chill tickled her spine, and she hoped it was due to the slight breeze blowing across the frozen landscape.

"I've got it; thanks," Grace smiled up at him. David looked tall and strong from her vantage point. Even under a blue stocking cap, his face was handsome and friendly. She quickly lowered her gaze and knotted her broken lace.

"Can I give you a hand up?"

"It's not necessary—thanks," she blurted, uncomfortable with the emotions churning inside her. She felt like a schoolgirl with a crush, a woman starving for affection, and a stranger come home, all in one. She couldn't comprehend the power he had over her, and it had been like this ever since the day he stepped down from the train.

When Guy was alive, she had thought of David as

merely Guy's shadow. She had always been fond of David, of course, but she had thought of him almost as an extension of her beloved brother, not really important in himself. Suddenly, he had emerged from Guy's shadow, taking her by surprise. She wondered now if all along he hadn't been more important to her than she had ever realized.

"Well. . .okay." His shoulders dropped as Grace watched him move onto the ice-covered creek and into a group of young townsfolk.

She eased to her feet and struggled for a footing on the bank. She wobbled, nearly fell, then balanced herself against a sapling.

She brushed dirt, snow, and dry grass from her pleated plaid skirt and navy stockings and straightened her coat that sported large, hand-carved buttons. The buttons were a luxury that Grace's mother had griped about, but Grace enjoyed the way they made a sensible, sturdy coat feel special.

Finally, she took a tentative step onto the ice and waited for her ankles to adjust to the skates. Her body teetered like an intoxicated idiot before she got the hang of it.

A shoulder bumped into her, upsetting her precarious balance and seating her hard on the ice.

"Oops," Thomas Cord chuckled. "Reality hurts," he sneered. "You Rudmans think you can hold out and make the conservancy pay you a bundle for an ugly strip of used-up farmland? My dad got top dollar for the best farmland in this valley." He towered over her with his gangly teenage frame. "The conservancy doesn't care if your place floods—now that they own everything around it." He glided away, obviously pleased with his performance.

Grace saw David making strides toward her, and she shot him a warning glare. She gingerly got to her feet and worked at establishing her balance once again.

David hung at a short distance from her with a young girl at each elbow trying to gain his attention.

Grace slowly glided upstream away from the majority of skaters. She knew that some people in the valley looked down on her family for holding out on the conservancy. Many thought that the Rudmans were greedy for money, but there were still those who cared enough to understand the family's plight and sympathize.

Soon Grace was joined by the pastor's daughter, Lydia, and her friends. The lighthearted chatter of the girls made a nice diversion for Grace's train of thought.

Often, though, her attention was pulled to David. She found interest in his skating partners. No doubt, David was used to having several young women on his arm in the city. A handsome, young man with a good job was quite an attraction, and it didn't hurt that he had a friendly, clean-cut personality to go with it.

Grace shook her head free from the web of thoughts. *The gal who reels him in will sure be lucky. That is. . .if she's smart enough to say "yes."*

David longed to go to Grace, to defend her and ease her discomfort. Her stubborn show of independence frustrated him. Pain pierced his heart when she made it clear that she didn't need his assistance.

He watched her now as a group formed around her. She smiled easily at the youths and talked freely with them. She tried a figure eight with Lydia and laughed about their crooked lines. Then she clapped and cheered for a child who demonstrated a simple spin. When she glanced at him, though, her face lost its animation, as though she had immediately erected a wall around her emotions. He longed to break through her guarded borders and see her at ease like that with him.

In the past he had seen her as a carefree tomboy, following her brothers and him into the woods on childhood adventures. He had been present as she had talked freely of her dreams and desires with her brother Guy, but always it had been Guy's attention she craved and David was ignored.

David turned his attention to one of the young women at his side. She had an annoying giggle that hurt his ears while the other exaggerated her wobbly footing on the narrow blades and clutched his arm with long, sharp fingernails.

He quickly tired of their prattle and found himself watching Grace more as she skated with the pastor's daughter, warmed her hands by the bonfire on the bank, and wandered upstream alone.

David grew edgy when Grace went beyond a low hanging tree and followed the curve of the stream out of his view. He could no longer manage polite conversation with his companions and soon broke away from the group.

He skirted the clusters of skaters and kept close to the shore as he wound his way upstream. He was putting a good distance between himself and the other skaters when he heard a splash ahead of him. David sped along the frozen creek, sending snow flying out behind him.

Chapter 5

Grace enjoyed the solitude of the upper stream. The arching trees provided a canopied effect with their snow-frosted branches. She could hear the song of an unseen cardinal while the voices of the skaters grew dimmer. She knew some were headed downstream toward the new pond at the gatehouse, while she entertained the thought of continuing her course all the way home.

Here the stream had widened and she moved toward the shore, unsure that the ice in the middle would be solid. The cardinal seemed to be following her as its song came to her loud and clear. She looked up to spot him on an overhanging branch.

The ice cracked beneath her blades and Grace tilted. Snow covered the ice and she couldn't determine the direction of the crack. She inched forward and closer to the shore.

The ice gave way underneath her. She gasped and dropped over two feet to the rocky creek bed. Her left ankle buckled and the frigid water instantly soaked her nearly to the waist.

She wanted to cry, to scream, but she felt stiff as if frozen in place. The water flowed freely under the icy crust.

She heard a strange scraping noise behind her, then David yelled, "Gracie, are you all right?"

She turned to him with relief. "David! Thank the Lord you've come."

David approached her from the shore side and inched toward the break in the ice. He reached out to grasp her under the arms and pull her up. Her feet came out of the water flailing for a solid footing. Her wet skates slipped on the ice, and David gripped her tighter, popping a loose button on her coat.

"My button!" Grace wailed.

"Sorry," David said as he set her on her feet. Then he quickly swept her up into his arms and tight against his chest, nearly knocking the air from her lungs. Grace desperately searched for a place to rest her arms and finally settled them on his rock-hard shoulders. She was strangely thrilled by the strength evoked from his sheltering arms.

He started a swift pace downstream, and suddenly Grace started kicking and wiggling.

"Stop! My button," she cried. "Go back, David. We have to get my button."

"You're about to freeze! What do you want with a button?"

"But I don't have an extra, and they're very unique. . . and expensive. Go back, please," she begged.

David stopped and stared down into her eyes. "Gracie—" His breath caught suddenly as their gazes locked.

She looked away and thrashed her feet again. "Put me down, David. This isn't proper."

"Why ever not?" his voice rose abruptly. "I'm just a *'brother'* helping his kid *'sister'* who happens to be nuts about a stupid button and on the verge of becoming an icicle." He punched his words at her, echoing those she had spoken to him when she had rejected his proposal.

"Now why are you mad at me?" Grace nearly shouted with indignation. "I'm not the one who lost the button." She found that anger clouded the troubling emotions that his embrace and gaze had stirred in her and put distance between them.

All of a sudden he dropped her to her feet and pushed away from her. He shook his head without another word and backtracked toward the break in the ice.

Grace shivered as his warmth left her. Her skirt still dripped and her legs felt numb. Anger had gotten her nowhere and she felt more confused than ever. Those many months ago, she had said she did not want him, but now she desperately wanted to be back in his arms and know he cared.

She brushed clumps of damp snow from her crocheted mittens. The blood in her left ankle began to pound and her legs started to shake with cold. Grace no longer had the will to stand. She sank to the ice with her legs folded beneath her.

It had started to snow. Big, fluffy flakes floated down from the sky, instantly changing the scene. They covered everything they touched with a veil of white.

"Here's the button. Can we go. . .oh, Gracie, you're going to be sick with cold." David knelt before her and held the button out in his palm. "Truce?"

The button was already a forgotten issue for Grace. "Why did you come after me?"

"I. . .well. . ." David's brow furrowed. "Let's get you home."

He gently scooped her into his arms, and she curled herself against his warmth, locking her arms around his neck. He carried her as if without effort and soon the voices of the other skaters grew closer. Someone shouted as they came into view, but Grace was shivering with cold and she no longer had a clear picture of her surroundings. She leaned into David's warmth and surrendered her plight to his will.

"What happened?" Lydia squeaked as David neared the group at the fire.

David stumbled up the bank and was instantly surrounded by curious young people. "She broke through the ice and is soaked," David pointed out the obvious. "Lydia, will you get my shoes from over by that oak?"

Lydia hurried to the tree while David lowered himself to a log.

"Let me drive her home," a young man from town offered.

"Thanks, but I'll see her home." David finally had Grace willingly in his arms. He wasn't in any hurry to give her up.

"Where's your car, man?"

"I—" David forgot that, like Grace, he had walked to the creek.

"Borrow my car—or better yet, I'll drive you both."

"Thanks," David sighed. He would have willingly carried her home if he had to.

Quickly, he traded his skates for shoes, enjoying the solid base on which to plant his feet. Then he gathered Grace close to his heart again and carried her to the young man's car. He held her in his lap and loosened her skates as the car bumped along a pasture road and up Grace's drive.

Grace opened her eyes as the warmth from the kitchen touched her face. She could feel David's chest rumble as he spoke with her mother, but the words were fuzzy. The muscles in David's arms strained as he carried Grace up the stairs to her bedroom and laid her on her bed. She felt his breath tenderly brush her cheek. Then he spoke quietly with Mrs. Rudman at the door and left.

A flood of emotions too jumbled to describe overtook Grace and tears started to flow freely. She wanted David's arms around her once again. She needed his warmth and tender touch. She longed to feel loved and cared for. She yearned for her father to be the pillar of strength he had always been for her. He would tell her how to cope with the present and plan for the future.

Grace longed for John to be part of the family again, to share the joys and sorrows together. She wanted to have the opportunity to know his fiancée and welcome her into their midst.

She cried for Guy and wished her brother back among the living. He would have had cheerful encouragement for her. Perhaps he could have spoken to

David and made him see that she had changed, that she desired to know him as more than a brotherly friend. She needed a second chance for love to grow.

Grace felt her mother's arms fold around her and rock her gently as the tears continued to flow.

Lord, thank You for restoring peace to Mother. I do want to trust You for everything. Please grant me the peace and patience I need so much. If You will guide me, I know I can endure these times of trial.

Grace eased away from her mother's embrace and sniffed, "Thanks."

"Let's get you warmed up."

Mrs. Rudman helped Grace undress and lower herself into a hot tub of water. The water instantly revived her senses.

Before long her mother had her gowned in thick flannel and tucked into bed with a hot water bottle to warm her feet. Grace still didn't feel warm, but sleep came quickly.

When she woke an hour later, she saw her mother in a bedside chair, dozing over a Bible that was opened in her lap. Her attention was abruptly moved, though, to a pounding from downstairs. She swung her legs out of bed, but when her feet hit the rag rug, she gasped. Pain throbbed through her left ankle and Grace gripped the footboard. As she adjusted her weight to her right foot, her mother woke.

"Why are you out of bed?"

"Someone's downstairs."

"I'll go. It's most likely David. He promised to return." Mrs. Rudman set aside her Bible and left the room, but she soon returned. "If you feel up to it, you should dress and come down to visit with David. You—we all—should enjoy every chance to visit with him before he leaves again for Michigan, and he was so worried about your getting sick."

Grace raised her eyebrows at her mother's retreating form. Leave it to her to play matchmaker. Certainly, Grace liked the idea of being matched with David, but she didn't want a romance with him to be because of the efforts of someone else. She wanted to know that David wanted it too.

Oh. . . .Lord, why can't I leave this in the past? She started to change into a clean dress. *Because David Matthews is the best guy who ever showed he cared for me, and I turned him away.* She yanked her dress over her head. *But, I was immature and foolish back then.* Slowly she buttoned the closure. *Have I really changed that much? I still can't deal with my emotions. I melt at the slightest look or touch from him. He would laugh if he only knew.*

"Grace." Mrs. Rudman opened the door with a worried frown. "Has your father come up here?"

"Why, surely not."

"I know. I usually help him walk anywhere he goes, but now I can't seem to find him anywhere." Mrs. Rudman seemed close to tears. "This is so strange."

"He has to be here somewhere. Did you look on the porch?"

"David is looking outside right now. I'll go and see if he found him."

Mrs. Rudman hurried down the stairs. Grace

moved to follow, but her ankle didn't appreciate the weight applied to it, and she had to hobble slowly down the stairs.

"I didn't see any sign of him around the house or the barn," David was telling Mrs. Rudman in the kitchen. "I didn't even see any footprints to follow."

"He has to be in the house somewhere," Grace declared.

"Then I'll check upstairs again," Mrs. Rudman sighed.

"I'll make another circle outside the house," David said.

Grace limped into her father's bedroom, looking in every space and even opening the closet. She shuffled on to the parlor and found her father's rocking chair empty. The quilt that usually rested across his lap was folded haphazardly on the floor nearby.

Grace was looking out the window when David came back in with snow capping his head in white.

"I went ahead and checked the root cellar and springhouse, but found nothing," he reported.

"I don't understand where he could have disappeared to. He can't walk far alone."

"Gracie. . .where is your father's cane?"

"Here—well, usually it rests right here against the wall." Grace met David's wide gaze. "But he never uses it. . ."

"I think I had better extend my search outside."

Grace followed David through the house. Her limp wasn't nearly as pronounced as it had been. They met Mrs. Rudman in the kitchen.

"Nothing upstairs, not even a clue," she moaned.

"I think I'll do more looking outside, maybe talk to some neighbors," David said.

"His cane is gone, Mother," Grace interjected.

Mrs. Rudman shook her head in despair. "Should I ring on the telephone for help?"

"But. . ." Grace couldn't believe it had gone this far.

"Yes," David said, "It may be time to bring in extra people. Tell anyone who answers the ring to start their search here and fan out. But some should also look in town. Someone could have picked him up at the road and given him a ride in."

Grace sank to a kitchen chair, weakened by worry.

David continued to organize details of the search. "Then I suggest you call John and demand that he get here to help. And don't take any excuses."

Mrs. Rudman's face reddened with the shame of already letting her son put so much distance between himself and the family.

"I'll take the car and start looking between here and my home," David said as he buttoned his coat.

"I'm going with you," Grace suddenly announced.

"No," David said firmly. "You've already had a full day, and you don't need to get cold again."

Grace stood and braced herself for a fight. "I'm either going with you, or I'll start my own search."

Chapter 6

D avid stared at Grace. He couldn't believe how vulnerable she could look one minute and how very stubborn the next.

Mrs. Rudman cleared her throat and went to the phone to give the ringer several quick cranks. She was soon announcing the disappearance of Mr. Rudman across the party wires.

David stood rigid, meeting the challenge in Grace's eyes. He would never forgive himself if she went off on her own and caught her death of cold or found another patch of ice to fall through, but this was a fight he hated to back down from. He wrestled with himself, then ordered, "Dress in your warmest clothes and layer up. You'll ride in the car, but if you dare get out and start prancing through the snow, I'll bring you right back here. Do you understand?"

Grace's eyes narrowed at the ultimatum, but the corners of her lips twitched with the joy of even a small victory.

David shook his head at her as she collected her coat, a sweater, and a blanket. He would always thank God that if nothing more, he had been like a brother to this wonderful young woman. They might never have more between them, but as long as he could hold onto her friendship, he would feel blessed.

"At least five families responded to my call." Mrs. Rudman broke through his reveries. "Plus the reverend will start the search in town."

"Good." David led a bundled-up Grace to the back door. "We'll let you know as soon as we find him. Don't forget to call John."

Snow swirled in when they opened the door. They plowed through a good two inches of the white stuff and climbed in the car. The snow was getting heavier and sunset was swiftly approaching. Time was of the essence.

David drove to his home to inform his parents of the situation. His father was on an errand to town, but his mother promised to go to Mrs. Rudman and wait with her for word.

Grace waited patiently while David made a sweep around his farm for any signs. When he returned to the car empty-handed, she met him with a new idea. "I feel like we should check down by the gatehouse."

"Why? There's nothing down there. I think he would have headed to a neighbor's house or to town."

"I know it doesn't make a lot of sense, but I have a gut feeling about it." She shrugged.

"Okay, it can't hurt to look around." He told his mother the direction they were headed and quickly returned to the car.

They followed good road for only a short distance. The road to the new gatehouse was a rough track through old pastureland. The car jolted in and out of ruts. Grace struggled to stay in her place on the leather bench seat.

David turned on the headlights as the shadow cast by the dam deepened, and their beams shone out over the bulldozed land to where it rose sharply at the dam's base. He stopped the car at the foot of the dam and turned to Grace.

She leaped from the car and started a brisk inspection of the snow up to the water's edge. David scrabbled from the car after her.

"I told you to stay in the car or I'd take you straight home," he yelled over the car's engine.

"And I told you I had a feeling we'd find something here." She stooped, picked something up, and held it toward the car lights.

David moved closer. It was a mitten. "It's small. Do you think it is his?"

"I don't recognize it." Her face crumbled in defeat.

"It was likely left by a skater." David surveyed the area and found nothing more.

Grace sat on the stump of a once great tree that had been sawed and hauled away for lumber. Soon silent sobs rocked her frame.

David approached her slowly, wanting to give comfort but afraid of being rejected. He bent his knees and brought his face level with her. Cautiously, he placed his hands on the stump on either side of her. "Gracie, I—"

"You know," she interrupted with a whimper, "this very afternoon, I asked the Lord to grant me peace and patience to weather the storms in my life. I didn't ask

Him for a new trial." She slammed both fists into David's shoulders then left them there as she gripped his coat collar. "I can't lose my father like this." She was adamant as she stared into his face.

"It'll be all right, Gracie."

"But you don't understand what I've been through," she cried. "No one really understands."

"I understand." David tried to hug her to him, but she kept her arms stiff between them and rubbed her fingers along the wool of his coat.

She gave a brittle laugh. "Do you remember the last day I saw you before you left for Detroit?"

"Don't. . ." David didn't want to rehash the past or hear any hollow apologies.

But she continued, "I told you of my inflated dreams to leave this valley and see the world. Do you know how many months it took me to save enough money before I left for Cleveland? And, do you know that within five months I was flat broke, living in a run-down boardinghouse?"

"Gracie, you don't have to. . ."

"I fell for a guy with all the right stuff. . ."

David hung his head. He didn't want to hear that she was in love with someone else.

". . .or so I thought," Grace continued. "He promised to introduce me to fashionable people and teach me how to fit in." She swung her arms out to her sides. "He lavished gifts on me and made me feel like a queen. Then he took my money with a crazy promise to buy me an automobile. According to him, the right kind of car would give me a foot up in the world."

She brought her arms in with a shiver. "I was so foolish—naïve—that I handed my whole savings over to a handsome cad and never saw it again. I couldn't even pay my own way home for Guy's funeral. I took a loan. . .now I'm stuck in this job. . .no reason to dream—" Her voice broke.

"Oh, honey, I'm sorry."

"See, you were better off without me," she continued. "Failure follows me on every side."

"What?" David cupped her face in his hands. "Everyone learns by mistakes. Mistakes don't make failures." His thumbs massaged along her jawline. He had never desired to kiss Grace Rudman more than this moment.

She still glowed with the sweet blush of innocence, but now a maturity and touch of wisdom also adorned her. She radiated with winter's touch on her cheeks, and her eyes, staring back at him, glistened with. . . Could he dare to call it hope? A hope for them? Hadn't they put that in the past and settled for friends?

He felt himself drawn to her. Her lips shined like a fresh ripened apple. Their breaths mingled in a frosty cloud.

Unexpectedly, a shot rang out and echoed through the valley. They jumped to their feet as one, craning to determine the direction of the shot. Could it be one of the searchers?

Soon another shot followed.

"It sounds almost like it came from the top of the dam," David said. "I'll go check it out while you get back in the car."

Immediately, David started the steep ascent up the embankment. He slipped several times as he attacked the dam wall from an angle.

"Umph!" came from behind him. He turned to see Grace sliding down to the foot of the dam, her arms flailing out to steady her descent.

"Gracie, please, go back to the car." He tried to keep his voice gentle but strong.

She picked herself up and started the climb again. Her face was set with determination as she strained with each new step. He watched as she neared him, puffing for each breath. She flung her hand out to grasp his arm. David reached for her and drew her up to meet him.

"Do you know that you can be very stubborn?" David asked, stifling a chuckle.

"I get it from my father. . .and if he had the will to walk all the way out here. . .I can get myself to the top."

She pulled away from him and dug her toes into the dirt. Her left foot slipped and she cried out. David steadied her.

"My ankle," she gasped. "I twisted it in the creek."

"Oh, Gracie, why didn't you say so?" David sighed.

They were more than halfway up the eastern side of the dam now. David put his arm around her waist and pulled her to the top with him. He kept his arm around her waist to steady her as they looked across the ridge. It was much lighter here and the sinking sun was still visible in the cradle of nearby hills.

A short distance along the leveled top of the dam was a group of five people. Sitting on the ground, looking out over the valley and town of Tappan, were two older men. Standing around them were three teenage boys, one carrying a hunting rifle. David and Grace hurried to them as fast as Grace could manage on her weak ankle.

"Father," Grace called out as they neared the group.

Mr. Rudman turned to his daughter with a very lopsided grin and grunted what could have been her name.

She dropped to her knees and wrapped her arms around his thin shoulders. "Oh, Daddy. . ." Grace whimpered as tears started.

David approached his own father who was seated next to Mr. Rudman. "How did you come to be here, Dad?"

"Well," Mr. Matthews began slowly, "I was headed to town when I met up with an old friend. We hadn't seen each other in a very long time and decided to take a drive. I parked my car along the road at the other end of this giant while we took a little stroll."

David frowned at his father's casual description. He looked to Mr. Rudman and saw a mischievous glint in his tired eyes. "I should paddle you both," David muttered under his breath, but he was overjoyed to see a visible change in Mr. Rudman's spirit.

One of the boys spoke up. "You're right, Mr. Rudman, the shadow of the dam is spreading across the whole valley." It was Thomas Cord. He eyed Grace with an apologetic tip of his head.

Mr. Rudman bobbed his head in agreement.

"One day everything under that shadow will be a

great lake," Mr. Matthews stated. "It will draw hundreds of people for fishing and boating vacations, but better yet, this here dam will save many homes in the outlying areas from being threatened by yearly floods."

"So, it's a case of our sacrifice for the good of the majority?" Thomas asked.

"That's. . .right," Mr. Rudman sputtered. "Be. . . proud."

Grace hugged her father tighter.

Three carloads of people had arrived and were making their way along the ridge to the little group. David recognized his mother and Mrs. Rudman with several folks from the community. Mrs. Rudman ran to her husband and clasped him in a tear-filled reunion.

"Here we have a beautiful view of our valley," Mr. Matthews declared with a sweep of his arm.

The group came to a muted halt as each individual stared across the farms and town that made up the community of Tappan. The shadow of the dam was slowly ending the day for the close-knit community.

Someone started to hum "Silent Night," and soon the voices of friends and neighbors joined in song. Slowly descending snowflakes sparkled in the last rays of the sun.

David touched Grace's shoulder, and she gave him a smile that warmed him clear through.

Chapter 7

Despite their plans to have a quiet Christmas, the Rudmans' house was full of visitors on Christmas Eve. The gathering of friends at the dam had followed the Rudmans home, and Grace served them hot chocolate, cookies, and fresh-baked bread with preserves.

More visitors arrived later to hear the events surrounding Mr. Rudman's disappearance, and soon the house was overflowing with holiday cheer.

It was still unclear what motivated Mr. Rudman to go on his excursion and why he was suddenly able to say some words after months of virtual silence. It was a moment to celebrate, nonetheless, and Grace welcomed the festive atmosphere in the house.

"It's an answer to our prayers," Mr. Matthews told Grace. "God's still doing miracles."

Mrs. Rudman sat down to the piano and started playing carols. Some joined in merry singing, while others continued to visit freely. There seemed to be people everywhere. Grace waded through the masses in the parlor with a tray of sugar cookies, smiling and chatting with old friends.

Someone grabbed her arm and pulled her into the

empty front stairwell.

"David!" She caught her tray as it tilted. "What are you up to?"

"I. . ." He opened his mouth, then grinned like a mischievous child and shrugged. "I guess I wanted to wish you a merry Christmas before I go." In a lightning flash, he bent down and brushed her cheek with a feathery kiss and was gone.

Grace stood transfixed at the bottom of the stairs, her breath caught in her throat. Dreamily, she dropped to one of the wooden steps, balancing her tray on one hand and her rosy cheek in the other. When had a kiss ever been as sweet? What bitter irony that David Matthews now only treated her like a sister.

Christmas morning, Grace trudged down the stairs after stealing almost an hour of extra sleep. The day before had been such a draining day, and they were up late visiting with their unexpected company.

She entered the kitchen to the smell of oven-fresh cinnamon rolls, her favorite.

"Merry Christmas, my sweet," her mother sang, her face wreathed in smiles. "Go get your gifts. We will do an exchange before the 10 A.M. church service."

Grace skipped back upstairs and soon returned with three gaily wrapped packages. In the parlor, her father was sitting straight in his chair and decked in his best Sunday suit.

She kissed his weathered cheek. "Merry Christmas, Daddy!"

A movement in the corner caught her eye, and there stood a small, fresh pine tree.

"Oh!" she gasped.

"Merry Christmas, little sister," John said, popping his head around the little tree.

Grace squealed and captured her brother in a tight hug. John hugged her back and whispered in her ear, "I'm really sorry for being selfish and leaving you here to shoulder all the problems. I came as soon as I got word about Dad, though I missed all the excitement."

"It's forgiven," she smiled up at him.

The family had much to celebrate as they draped the little evergreen in ribbons, glass bulbs, and glittery tinsel. Then they exchanged gifts with each other in expression of their love and thanksgiving. The fact that this would be their last Christmas in the sturdy old farmhouse was far from their minds. Being together was the answer to every wish and prayer. They even openly shared memories of Guy and could laugh together about the past.

The Lord had brought them much healing. The sun reflecting through the window off the fresh-fallen snow couldn't have shone any brighter this morning than the smiles on the faces of the Rudman family.

Grace sat beside her father at the little church on Tappan's main street, ready for Christmas worship. John and his fiancée, Melissa, sat directly behind them. The sanctuary was filled with the low buzz of joyous worshippers as they waited for the special service to start. Mrs. Rudman had taken her traditional place at the piano and was playing a Christmas hymn.

The Matthews arrived and took seats in the pew across the aisle from Grace and her father. David smiled their way and Grace's heart started to thump in response. He was wearing the new suit he had worn home on the train. Its classic style fit him well.

Grace thought of all the things that had happened in the week since their reunion. David had been near her or her family almost every day—often sacrificing precious time with his own family. He was sweet and considerate, a gentleman, and just like a member of her family.

She knew that when he left for Detroit on Monday that parting would pain her greatly. There would be no guarantee when he would return, and with the community's scattering in wake of the dam, it would be less likely that they would visit regularly again.

Lord, she almost chuckled out loud, *if David Matthews is not the man You have designed for me, then You must have someone pretty spectacular in my future. . . because at this point I can't think of anyone better than David.*

Grace had to pull her gaze away from David's brownish red locks, his chiseled features, and his perfectly shaped, strong hand that rested on the back of the pew as he tilted forward to speak with someone. She took a deep, cleansing breath as her father leaned closer, touching her shoulder.

"The best. . .dream. . ." he whispered in a raspy and halting voice, "is usually. . .what God. . .places. . .within reach."

Grace quickly looked at her father. He was settling

back against the pew with a satisfied smile. She glanced around to try and gather what he had been referring to. Across the aisle, David sent her another smile, and instantly her cheeks flushed a rosy Christmas red that matched the new dress she wore. Her father couldn't have guessed what she had been thinking.

The pastor's entrance to the platform saved her from her tortured thoughts. He introduced a group of schoolchildren who reenacted the Christmas story. Then a choral group led the packed congregation in Christmas songs. Grace sang with her whole soul, enjoying the blend of voices.

The second half of the service turned to a time of reflection on the church body and surrounding community. The pastor had a special announcement.

"By Easter Sunday, if all goes according to plan, our church building will have been relocated to a hill six miles east of here. The elders have settled on a fine spot that was donated by a faithful church member."

There was clapping and whoops of joy. No longer did the church people have to worry about tearing down the beloved building.

But when her parents moved to Bowerston, her family would be worshipping at a different church among new friends. Grace would miss the fellowship with these dear people.

She turned her head and found David watching her. His gaze was deep and serious. Were his thoughts similar to hers?

It was slow getting through the lingering church-goers at the end of the service. No one seemed in a hurry to get home to individual holiday celebrations, but preferred to talk about where neighbors were moving to and how many would still be around for Easter.

At home, Mrs. Rudman had a feast prepared. John and Melissa joined the family for the meal along with an older couple from town and the widowed Mrs. Douglas who had been invited at the last minute. Mr. Rudman was also present at the table for the first time in many long weeks. He still needed help managing his food, but it was good to have the family together again.

Grace relished the occasion, eating until she was almost miserably full. Her mother's cooking was always wonderful, and she had made all of the family favorites for the holiday celebration.

Grace also feasted her eyes upon those around the table. She was so pleased that John had decided to join them and bring Melissa. Melissa had a subtle beauty and quiet nature. Her straight blond locks contrasted with John's deep brown ringlets. They made quite a handsome couple, and it was obvious that they were deeply in love.

Mrs. Douglas was a dear soul, reaching her mid-eighties with a mind that was still sharp and energetic. After the death of Grace's own grandmother, Mrs. Douglas had lavished love and attention on the Rudman children, and Grace considered the woman like a grandmother.

Before they were through with dessert, there was a knock at the door. John answered it and ushered David into the dining room. Grace's cheeks warmed at the sight of the young man. She chided herself and tried to continue with her dessert, but all appetite for food had left her.

Mrs. Rudman pulled a chair up to the table for David and placed him between herself and Grace. David casually brushed Grace's shoulder as he sat down to a large bowl of cream-covered date pudding. Lightning struck through Grace and zipped out her toes. Each new encounter with David seemed to awaken startling new awareness within her. At least separation from David should keep her from going on these bumpy emotional rides.

Grace sat back in her chair and sipped from her water goblet. She listened as David conversed with the others around the table. He fit in naturally. He and John teased each other, and Melissa blushed at his charming compliments. Even Mrs. Douglas was not immune to his charms.

"Now, David, dear, I hear you are headed back north to Detroit and you still don't have a wife," Mrs. Douglas stated frankly.

Grace fidgeted in her chair, brushing a hand through the ends of her loose curls.

"Yes, you heard right," David smoothly replied, "but I would gladly take you with me to fill the position."

Everyone around the table burst into humorous laughter. Mrs. Douglas reached across the table and playfully swatted at David's arm.

"I'd go in a second, my dear boy, but the move would be too much on this old one. In fact, I'm staying put until the lake is at my back door. But you young ones have to make a life for yourselves beyond the ghost streets of an old town. Just take an old woman's advice. Remember where you came from and take it with you wherever you go. This town will always, then, be remembered by the wonderful children it produced." Merry chatter continued around the table, and Grace observed with little to contribute. Her mind tumbled as she mulled over Mrs. Douglas' words. *I can always be proud of who I am because of where I came from.*

David leaned toward her, touching his shoulder to hers. "You don't have the Christmas blues, now do you?" he quietly asked Grace.

"No, certainly not. I got everything I wished for."

"Everything?"

"Yes, my father is better, John is home, and Mother has come to a peaceful plan for the future of the farm and their home."

"What about you?" he pried.

"I. . .well. . .uh. . . ." She looked at him with a frown. His eyes showed an honest concern. "What do you want to know?" she almost whispered.

His eyes crinkled with a slow smile. "If you'll take a ride with me later? Dad still has the old sleigh in the barn, we've got a horse that should pull it, and there's a good coating of snow for the runners. Should I bring it over later?"

Grace swallowed hard, a nervous flutter tickling her stomach. "Umm. . .should we invite John and Melissa?"

"I came to see just you today," was his low, rumbling answer that thrilled and scared her at the same time. It was the same thing he had said the day after her high school graduation when he came to propose. That day had ended with her flat rejection. How would today end?

Chapter 8

The chill air nipped at their cheeks as the sleigh cut through the snow. Grace burrowed farther under the quilt while David encouraged the horse to a faster trot. Grace's sudden giggle delighted his ears and he spurred the horse even faster.

It was a picture-perfect Christmas day. Sunlight glistened on the snow and their breath hung suspended in the still air. Smoke from the occasional chimney drifted straight up to meet the clear blue sky.

David guided the sleigh around the perimeter of the valley's bottom then through the main part of town. They waved to a family that was hurrying in out of the cold. Then, David slowed the horse as they started the incline up Mill Hill Road. He halted the horse at the bottom of the path to a hillside cemetery and stepped out of the sleigh.

"Would you like to visit your brother with me?" he lightly suggested as he offered her a hand out of the sleigh.

She gave her hand without a word, and he kept it as they climbed the steep, snow-covered path. Small granite headstones covered the slope before them. They located Guy's plot with little trouble.

"Guy would have loved this day," Grace said into the stillness. "Winter was always his favorite time of the year."

"He loved building snow caves," David said.

"And snow forts," Grace added, "with snowballs."

"And eating snow ice cream," they laughed together.

"A kid couldn't have had a better brother," David reflected more pensively.

Grace slowly brushed snow from the carved stone. David watched her tender ministrations. She pocketed her bare hand for warmth and seemed to search for something within the depths of the deep coat pockets.

"I'm missing a mitten. I had it on when we left the house," Grace said.

"Then it's probably in the sleigh. Here, wear one of mine." David probed his own pocket, and as his hand reached the glove, something hard touched it. He pulled the hard, circular object out and held it toward Grace in the palm of his hand.

"It seems I still have your most precious of buttons, my lady," he said with a bow.

"Wonderful!" she cried. "I have truly missed it. You were so good to rescue it for me."

Her eyes were alight with joy as she turned her face to him and closed her hand over the trinket. David's insides knotted. How he longed to gather her close to him and call Grace his own. He had never been in a better position to make plans for a future—a family of his own. But to be twice rejected could spoil a beautiful friendship. He would have to continue to pray for God's divine guidance.

David turned from Grace and the moment was broken. Grace shivered. She had felt so sure that David was close to saying something. Perhaps something very important. She reached out to steady herself against the stone. It was like ice under her hand.

David abruptly handed her his glove. She slipped her right hand into his large glove, enjoying the soft leather. He continued to scan the view below, and Grace moved to stand beside him.

The town sat directly below them. Bathed in a blanket of white, it was beautiful. To their right rose the wall of the dam, standing sentinel across the mouth of the valley. And to their left the valley stretched long and wide.

David reached down for a broken branch and sent it sailing into the brush. There was a long silence between them, and Grace used it to reflect about life in the valley below. She leaned against a large monument and pulled her coat tight against her slight frame.

All of a sudden, David surprised her by saying, "I may leave for Detroit tomorrow. It shouldn't be hard to change my train ticket. . ."

"What!" Grace came to attention.

"I had a wire from one of my bosses on Wednesday. I meant to tell you about it yesterday. . .but then there was your accident and your father's disappearance. . ."

"Well, what was the telegram about?" she probed, while she tried to look him in the face.

He turned away from her, staring out across the valley below. "I have been offered the supervisor's position that I had wanted."

"That's great!"

He was strangely silent.

"It is great, isn't it?" she asked, suddenly concerned.

"Sure. . .sure. It is a secure position with good pay. I guess I wasn't prepared for the possibilities it opens. The new opportunities." He turned his face heavenward.

Grace sighed, not understanding his hesitancy. "Then you are leaving Saturday so you can accept the position?"

"Yes, they want me to return as soon as possible." He shuffled his feet in the snow, sending tiny snowballs rolling down the slope.

She reached for his arm, touching his sleeve at the elbow. "David, I'm really happy for you. Things seem to be working out for you in Detroit." She paused to focus her thoughts. "You do deserve the best."

He spun to face her and clasped her hand. "Gracie, you. . ." He stopped and closed his eyes. After a moment of quiet he shook his head. "I hear a car coming down the hill. I better tend to the horse. Stay longer if you wish." He turned quickly and bolted down the path to where the horse was tethered.

Grace was shocked by his brisk manner. It was almost like he was fighting some unseen fear. If only he could understand that she was happy for him. He really did deserve the best of everything, even if that meant that his future wouldn't include her.

She walked back to the marker on Guy's grave. *I sure could use some brotherly advice.* But it was the words of her father that came to mind. *The best dream is usually what God places within reach.*

She was already well aware that David Matthews was the best guy she had ever been acquainted with.

Her problem was that she had rejected a perfectly good man. *I just wasn't ready then. I had to do some growing up.* She stared at the motionless gravestone. *I think I'm ready, now, Lord. But what kind of man would want to go through the humiliation of asking a second time?*

Lord, he leaves tomorrow. I'd ask him if I could. It's just too late for us.

A thought struck her with force. How badly did she want David in her life? What was she willing to risk if she really loved him?

She looked down the hill to where David petted the nose of the bay. The car had already passed by and was entering town.

The best dream is usually what God places within reach, vibrated through her mind.

Her feet suddenly took flight. She slipped and skidded down the steep slope and passed David before she was able to stop her forward motion. She limped on her left ankle and stepped back in front of him.

"You can't leave tomorrow," she panted.

"I don't understand."

"Not before we settle something."

He stared at her, undoubtedly thinking she was acting strangely.

"When you asked me to marry you, I had to refuse."

He grimaced and grasped the horse's bridle.

"Wait," she cried and hurried to continue, "I had to see the world to know what I was missing. I needed to do some. . .growing up."

"And. . ." He looked impatient with her speech,

and she almost faltered in her plan.

"I needed time before I could see that," she searched for the right words, "sometimes the best things God has intended for us are right within our reach." She longed for him to understand. "David, what I'm trying to say is, if you would ever ask me again, I would now be more inclined to say 'yes' to your proposal."

He dropped his hold on the horse and took a step toward her. She placed her hands out in front of her in a defensive stance.

"But I will understand if you say you have moved on to new avenues of your life—"

Her words were stalled as David drew her flush against him, and with deliberate slowness, he lowered his mouth to hover above her own. Her breathing caught as she lifted her gaze to meet his dark eyes. What she saw in their depths caused her to relax against him.

Then his lips touched her, the heat searing her wind-chapped skin. She responded to his deepening kiss with all the pent-up longings she had been trying to suppress. It was better than a homecoming; it was as natural as a sunrise.

"Gracie, my love," he moaned as he pulled away, "I have wanted to ask you that particular question ever since I saw you at the train station, but. . ."

"Who wants to ask the same question twice?" she supplied.

"Yes, I guess that's how it was." He smiled and lightly pressed his lips to hers again.

He turned to hand her into the sleigh.

"But. . .where are we going?" She was confused. He hadn't asked "that" question yet.

"Home."

"Home?" Her voice came out flat. Her foot felt weighted as she lifted it into the sleigh.

"I need to talk to your father." He climbed in beside her and smiled at her confused expression. "Yes, even before I ask 'that' question."

With one hand holding the reins and the other holding tight to Grace's hand, David steered the horse and sleigh through the sleepy town of Tappan, along the still pastures of the valley, and to the weathered and worn farmhouse where they would plan their future together. A future made bright by a rich heritage and the goodness of God.

Epilogue

Forty years later

Grace pushed open the sliding glass door and stepped out onto the shaded deck. A cool summer breeze blew across the lake and played with her silver-edged hair. The fresh air felt good to her tired body. She had lugged boxes and scoured cupboards all day long.

Suddenly, David was there, wrapping his arms around her from behind. "The boys and I have all the living room furniture in, but I'm sure you will want to do some rearranging."

"You know me too well," she chuckled.

David hugged her tight.

"Who would have guessed that we would ever buy a retirement home on Tappan Lake?" she mused. "What do you think Mother and Daddy would have to say about it?" She stared across the bay to another area of waterfront homes. "We knew the family that once owned the property under this section of water, and the town is only marked by a much-visited boat launch." She felt close to tears.

David gently encouraged her. "They would say you

have a lovely home on a beautiful lake. It's a far cry from the old farmhouse where you grew up, my love."

"Yes, but does it have the charm of a house that has seen a lot of living?" Grace wanted to know.

"It's home, and we will make many memories with our children and grandchildren," David insisted. "We will tell them of what used to be and teach them how to make the memories live in their own lives."

They watched as their two grown daughters walked out onto the dock, their auburn hair highlighted by the afternoon sun. Julie was just out of graduate school while Karen was a wife and new mother. David and Grace were proud of their beautiful daughters, just as they were of their three older sons, all husbands and fathers.

"God blessed our life in Michigan and now He has brought us full circle," David told Grace as he planted a sweet kiss on her earlobe.

Rebecca Germany
Rebecca is managing editor of **Heartsong Presents,** an inspirational romance book club, and the author of the novella "Evergreen" in Barbour Publishing's *Christmas Dreams*. She has always enjoyed inspirational romances and believes they are a good tool for sharing the Gospel message. Rebecca lives on a small farm in rural eastern Ohio. She is actively involved in her church and enjoys keeping up with numerous family members.

A Christmas Gift of Love

Darlene Mindrup

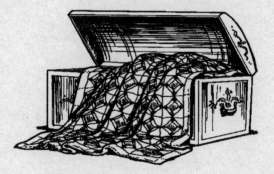

Chapter 1

R ose Johnson clutched the edges of the rough plank table and stared out the window at the bleak November landscape. A brisk, chill rain was pelting rhythmically against the glass pane that was the kitchen's sole source of light. Perhaps she should light the lantern on the table and dispel some of the gloom, but her lethargy wouldn't allow even that much effort.

Sighing, she allowed her thoughts free rein as they pushed insistently against the forced shield of her mind. For the first time in days, the tears came as relentlessly as the precipitation outside.

Papa was gone, and she was alone in the world. What was she to do now? She had nowhere to go, no one to care. If she had any relatives, she didn't know about them. For the last twenty years, it had been just Papa and she; and before that there was Mama.

She smiled as she remembered her mother's gentle face. Mama had died when Rose was just fifteen, and Rose had thought the pain would never go away. But it did. Slowly. Inevitably. Just as this pain would pass, too; but from experience Rose knew it would take time. Lots of time.

She could see her own reflection in the darkness of

the glass. Her wide blue eyes were her only good feature. Her brown hair looked almost black against the darkness of the pane. Papa had named her Rose, but she bore no resemblance to the beautiful flower. She had never had a beau, and she knew now that she never would. At thirty-five years of age, she was well past her prime here on the prairie of the Dakota Territory.

She could hear conversation reverberating from the other room and knew that she would have to return soon. But not just yet. She needed time to herself. Time to grieve.

Since tomorrow was Thanksgiving Day, Rose had decided to forego the more formal wake that would last all night. It was well past four o'clock already and several of the others were preparing to leave, to return to their homes and their lives celebrating a national holiday established in 1863, less than six years ago, by the then president, Abraham Lincoln.

She thought about this Thanksgiving, so different from the past few years that she had spent with her father, and more recently with Ward Taylor, a good friend of her father's. This year there would be no cooked venison with savory stuffing, no wild berry pies, no celebrating of thanks to the Lord.

Well, that was not entirely true. Although Papa was gone, she knew that she still had much to be thankful for. God had given her thirty-five wonderful years with the best papa a girl could have. Now, he was with her mother and she was truly thankful for that. The future without them she refused to consider, for it seemed terribly bleak.

Last night she had lain down to sleep wishing that she could join her parents during the night, but she had awakened this morning before the sun was up, as usual, and knew it was a fruitless wish. God must still have a purpose for her, but right now she couldn't even begin to know what it might be. Her tired mind refused to function properly, and concern for her future continually twisted her mind with worry.

She could hear Ward's deep voice rumbling in the outer room. Rose was always uncomfortable in his presence, even though he and her father had been friends for several years. When he came to visit she usually found an excuse to absent herself. That he knew it was obvious. Still, he hadn't let it affect his friendship with Papa.

Frowning, she tried to think what it was that stirred that sense of panic she felt whenever he was near. He had been only kind to her. Perhaps it was the fact that he was such a large man, and when he spoke she felt he would surely rattle the walls of the small shanty where she lived. He seemed such a powerful man, such a contrast to the other men she had known. Men like her quiet, gentle papa.

And Ward's eyes were the most incredible color of green that she had ever seen, like the shifting prairie grass in the spring, yet they seemed so vacant of any emotion. Almost cold. At least it had always seemed that way to her, but when she mentioned it to Papa, he had vehemently disagreed with her.

She shook her head slightly and tried to banish thoughts of the man from her mind. Going to the cupboard in the corner, she tried to reach the extra mugs she kept stored on the top shelf. Papa usually fetched them for her, but Papa was not here to do so now. Well, at least his body was, but not his spirit. That had been freed from the pain of the last several days.

She closed her eyes against the anguish of that memory. Papa's twisted, broken body that had been brought to her after his horse had spooked and he had been thrown from it. He had lived for three days in excruciating pain before his spirit had finally been put to rest.

She shuddered as she thought of her present company keeping watch on the now cold body of her beloved father. She had always hated the custom of wakes. Why couldn't they just have buried him yesterday and have done with it? If they thought he was merely unconscious and might waken at any moment, she could tell them otherwise.

A small moan escaped her and she leaned her head against the cupboard. She had heard the stories before of people being buried alive, thence the custom of wakes, but nothing would bring her papa back again, no matter how much she might wish it. If only it could be so, she would gladly let the others keep watch forever.

"Here, let me get that for you."

Rose tensed at Ward's voice, the timber of it sending little chills skittering down her spine. He reached around her, pushing against her back as he stretched to the top shelf. Rose stiffened against him, turning slowly when he moved away.

Quietly, he handed her the tray of mugs, his eyes never leaving her face. Rose felt the color spread across her cheeks and unconsciously she lifted a hand to her hair to make sure her bun was still in place. Drawn back from her face so tightly, her hair only added to her wan appearance, but of this she was unaware.

Rose turned away from him and began readying the coffee, pouring the steaming brew from the blue-speckled pot she kept on the back burner of her wood-stove. She pulled some sugar cookies from the jar on the counter and added them to the tray.

Feeling his eyes on her, she grew suddenly clumsy, her fingers failing to do what she required of them. When she snapped a cookie in two, she sighed with exasperation.

"Sugar cookies are my favorite," he told her, his kindness twinkling in those green eyes. A small sound escaped from her throat before she could stop it.

Ward reached to take the tray from her, and set it on the table. When he pulled her gently into his arms she stiffened, and then suddenly she collapsed against him, her tears releasing her of the past hours of stored-up grief. He drew her closer still as he murmured soothing words of comfort.

Rose acknowledged to herself the warmth and security she felt in Ward's arms as he rocked her gently back and forth, and while she longed to remain just where she was, a part of her told her it was not a very good idea. Finally, Rose pulled away, rubbing angrily at the wetness on her cheeks. She refused to look at Ward. "They were Papa's favorite, too," she told him, as though that explained everything. Lifting the coffee tray from the table, she hurried from the kitchen, Ward following close on her heels.

The shanty, though small, still boasted four separate rooms: kitchen, living area, and two bedrooms. For many of the people living here on the prairie, this house would seem palatial. To Rose, it was just home. Other neighbors were seated in the main living area, while Papa was laid out in his own bedroom, awaiting burial the next day.

Rose handed mugs of coffee to those present, passing the cookies among them. When she sat down, she found herself across from Ward. His veiled eyes seemed to be watching every move she made.

Shifting uncomfortably, she dropped her eyes to the black band around his forearm. Every person in the room was wearing such a band, their symbol of respect to her deceased father. Except for a sprinkling of grey throughout his tresses, the color of the band was as dark as the hair on Ward's head. At forty years of age, he was still a striking man where looks were concerned. He had the lean fitness of a man who spent many hours out-of-doors.

Thankfully her attention, and his, was diverted by several people rising to leave. Rose handed them their coats and thanked them for coming. Soon there were only herself, Ward, and Emily Haskins left.

Closing the door against the fast-approaching night, Rose turned to the elderly woman and almost choked at the soft look of sympathy she saw reflected in the older woman's gentle brown eyes.

"I'm not leaving you alone here tonight, Rose. Ward has agreed to stay and take me home after the funeral in the morning."

"That's really not necessary," Rose told her, her own voice tinged with dismay.

Ward gave her a sharp glance. "It's no trouble," he answered her. "Emily and I would be traveling back in the morning anyway, so with the weather being like it is, we thought we would just as well stay." His green eyes roved her features slowly before being caught by the troubled look in her own blue eyes.

Rose was relieved when Ward released her from his mesmerizing gaze and turned instead to Emily. "I am at your command," he told her, his face splitting into a grin.

Emily had a penchant for organizing things, and Rose had no doubt that she was about to do that very thing now. It was quite possible that Ward had suggested it, thinking that Rose would be in no fit state to do much of anything.

Rolling up her sleeves, Emily headed to the kitchen. "Bring me some more wood from the lean-to, and don't forget to feed the livestock. Oh, and Rose, help me find the flour so that I can bake you some bread. I'll not leave you here without the basic necessities."

Rose found Ward smiling at her and couldn't help but smile in return. Shaking her head, she followed Emily into the kitchen. Already the older woman was bustling about finding the items she needed to concoct her famous honey wheat bread.

Rose's eyes fastened on the jar with the honeycomb

smothered in honey. A small smile touched her lips as she thought of Papa and her finding the hive this summer. Together they had managed to smoke the bees and retrieve the sweet liquid, though she had received three stings for her effort and had ached for days. Papa, on the other hand, had not been stung at all. He had laughingly told her that the bees knew she was afraid of them.

"It's amazin' how we women tend to think so much alike."

Rose shifted her wayward thoughts and focused on the woman before her. "What did you say?"

"I said it's amazin' how much women tend to think alike. I could find just about everything in your kitchen 'cause it's pretty much in the same place as mine."

Rose pinched the bridge of her nose, closing her tired eyes. She appreciated Emily's concern, and Ward's, but she would much rather be alone. Papa's body might be lying in the next room, but there was nothing about that to frighten her. If anything, it offered her a slight measure of comfort.

Pulling out a chair at the table, Rose slowly lowered herself into it. She watched Emily working the dough and realized that the older woman had been right. Rose was so tired, she would never have bothered to fix anything for herself to eat.

Ward brought the wood in and dumped it in the bin by the stove. Taking off his dripping sheepskin jacket, he hung it on the hook behind the door. He stretched his muscles tiredly, his grey flannel shirt rippling across his broad shoulders with the movement.

Rose swallowed hard and quickly turned her eyes away.

"What else?" He spoke to Emily, but his eyes were once again centered on Rose.

"The animals taken care of?" Emily asked him.

"I did that earlier." His look swung again to Rose. "You look just about done in. Why don't you get some sleep? Emily and I will see to things here."

Rose was already shaking her head. "I couldn't do that."

Hands placed firmly on her rounded hips, Emily scrutinized Rose with a knowing eye. "Why ever not? You're not much good to us like you are. You're already half asleep on your feet. Good Book says to do unto others as you would have them do unto you. Now, if the shoe were on the other foot, what would *you* say?"

Rose blinked tired eyes up at the elderly woman standing before her. Truth to tell, having someone take charge was a blessing for which she should be thankful. She glanced at Ward and found his lips twitching with amusement. Emily Haskins had always had the last word about anything for as long as Rose could remember. She couldn't think of a time when the spry woman hadn't gotten her own way.

"All right," she relented, rising to her feet. "You've convinced me. I'll go to bed."

Emily's face broke into a broad smile. "I knew you were a woman of good sense."

Ward followed Rose from the kitchen. "I'll just see that the fire in the fireplace is still going strong, then I'll go back and help Emily."

Rose only half-heard Ward placing another log on the still-crackling fire as she sluggishly made her way across the room to her bedroom door. She had her hand on the latch, but stopped just short of lifting it.

When she turned to go to the other door, Ward barely made it there before her. He placed his hand over hers as she was about to pull the latch.

Startled, she jerked her hand back and lifted her face to his in question.

"Don't," he told her softly. "Not tonight. You're too tired. Wait until the morning."

She wanted to argue, but she knew he was right. Still, something about him made her want to do everything opposite to what he suggested. Could it be because everything he said always came out sounding like an order?

As though he could read her mind, he touched her face gently with a curled finger. "Please."

His touch set off an explosion of feelings she had no hope of interpreting. Ward could see the trepidation return to her eyes as she quickly moved away from him. "You're probably right," she told him breathlessly. "I only wanted to see him one more time before the others come again tomorrow. One more time, just he and I alone."

Ward said nothing, merely watching as she quickly crossed to the other door and let herself into her own bedroom.

Closing the door behind her, Rose leaned back against it, pressing a hand to her heart. Never in her life had she been so unsettled by a man's touch. It sent feelings twisting through her that she had never experienced before, made her want things she had long ago considered impossible.

Brows puckering in confusion, she made her way across to her bed and began to disrobe in the dark. The chill temperatures had her hurrying, and quickly climbing beneath the quilts on her bed she curled herself into a ball, shivering against the cold sheets.

How could a man affect her in such a way? A man she barely liked. And now, of all times, with her father lying mere feet away, lost to her for the rest of this lifetime. She was overly tired. That had to be it, for no other explanation offered itself to her fatigued mind.

Huddling beneath the covers, she felt the chill lessen and her eyes grew drowsy. As she drifted off to sleep, she resolved to free herself of Ward's unwanted presence at the earliest opportunity.

"Does she know about the farm yet?"

Ward lifted tired eyes to the woman before him. Slowly, he shook his head. "I didn't want to burden her with that tonight. She'll know soon enough."

Emily pulled out a chair and joined him at the kitchen table. "I agree, of course. It just amazes me that Gabel kept such a thing to himself."

Ward nodded. "He was that kind of man. Willing to help others in any way he could, but not willing to let others do the same for him."

"A lot like someone else I know, Ward Taylor. Maybe that's why you two got along so well."

Grinning, Ward didn't deny it. He lifted the steaming mug to his lips and blew softly. Actually, he hated coffee; but he wouldn't for the world let Emily know that, because to Emily, coffee was a panacea for all kinds of evils. Grimacing when her back was turned, he reached for the sugar bowl and ladled a heavy spoonful into the dark, aromatic brew.

"So what will you do now?"

One dark eyebrow winged its way upwards. "What makes you think I will do anything?"

A very unladylike snort followed his question. "Ward Taylor, you gotta do somethin'. That little girl in there can't take care of herself, you know. She needs a good strong man to look out for her."

Ward had to smile at Emily's reference to a woman of thirty-five years of age being a "little girl." The smile disappeared quickly when he realized what she had said. "Why, you old matchmaker, you! You can just get that notion out of your mind, real quick."

Innocent brown eyes didn't fool Ward for one minute. He knew he had to do something to help Rose, and he didn't need anyone like Emily pointing it out to him. But she was suggesting—no, that couldn't be what she was suggesting. Surely he was being paranoid.

When he looked at her again, his eyes narrowed in suspicion. "What did you have in mind?"

"Well. . ." she drawled. "You could use a good wife and Rose could use a good husband." He rose quickly to his feet, but Emily continued undaunted. "If you had a wife, you wouldn't need to pay me to do your baking, and Maudie to do your laundry, and—"

"Okay, okay," he told her in exasperation, lifting a hand as though to stem the flow of words. "I get the picture. But I thought you enjoyed the extra money, and if it doesn't bother me, why should it bother you?"

"Now don't get ornery," she huffed. "I *do* like the extra money, but I think you could put *yours* to better use."

Ward was shaking his head. "Emily, you never cease to amaze me."

"Did you know Rose ain't got no place to go?"

He collapsed back into the chair. "I know."

"Well?"

Ward stared at Emily several minutes before he realized that he was actually considering what she had suggested. Gritting his teeth, he jumped to his feet, grabbing his coat from the hook on the back of the kitchen door.

"I'll just go check on the animals," he told her.

She gave him a "you don't fool me" look, but she remained quiet as he escaped through the door.

As Ward made his way to the barn he stole a glance at the sky. Clouds blocked out the cold night moon and he knew there would be more rain come morning. What a miserable day for a funeral it was going to be, not that any day was a good one.

Throwing some more hay in the manger, he patted the old milk cow's neck and checked once again to make sure everything was all right. There was very little hay left, but he doubted Rose was even aware of it. He sighed. If only these torrential rains had come this past summer when the farmers needed it instead of now. He hadn't realized just how badly Gabel had been affected by the drought.

Making his way back to the cabin, he made sure he entered through the front door instead of the kitchen. He could hear Emily moving around, humming faintly to herself.

Leaving his muddy boots beside the door, he made his way quietly to Rose's door and pressed an ear against the portal. No sound came from within, so he assumed she was fast asleep. What would she say when he told her everything tomorrow? What would she do? Where would she go? The questions kept circling round and round in his mind. One thing was for certain, Emily's idea was positively out of the question.

Chapter 2

Ward's prediction of rain hadn't materialized as of the time set for the funeral, and he knew Rose was thankful. Hovering clouds to the north spoke of a winter storm approaching and everyone knew that with that storm, winter would set in with a vengeance.

The minister hurried the ceremony, and surrounding neighbors quickly made their way back to their horses and wagons. It wouldn't do to be caught out in a blizzard.

Out of necessity, Gabel's body was buried close to the shanty on the land that he loved. Ward walked beside Rose back to the house, wondering how he could broach the subject of Rose's future. He was relieved of that obligation when Rose spoke first.

"I want to thank you for everything you've done." She glanced at him, but quickly turned away. "Both now and in the past. Papa. . .Papa was grateful for your friendship."

There was a catch in her voice as she said the last and Ward knew she was struggling with tears held tightly in check. He took a deep breath, but before he could say anything she continued.

"It was nice of Pastor Hoover to offer to take Emily home."

He gave her a quick glance, but made no comment.

"I know you must be anxious to get home yourself, but would you like a cup of coffee before you go?"

Ward wrinkled his nose slightly. "That would be nice," he lied.

When they reached the shanty, Rose disappeared into the kitchen to fetch them each a cup of coffee. Ward followed her, watching her without appearing to do so.

He seated himself at the table and Rose pushed a cup in front of him. She sat down across from him and hastily lowered her eyes.

Ward noticed the traces of Rose's tears and felt suddenly very protective towards her. Both she and her father had been good friends to him over the past several years, though he knew that with Rose it was a somewhat reserved friendship. For some reason he seemed to alarm her, but as yet he hadn't found the cause. It had never bothered him overmuch, seeing as how it was her pa he came to see. She had always seemed to just melt into the background whenever he was around.

He had been unfailingly courteous to her whenever they came in contact, but each time he could sense the wall she erected between them. He had never felt as free with her as he had with Gabel, her father. Now, suddenly, he wished it had been different. Then he might know what to say to her now, what comfort he could offer, though from experience he knew there was really nothing you could say to a person who had just lost someone held dearer than life itself. And now he had to give her more bad news.

"Rose, there's something I need to tell you."

When she looked at him with those innocent blue eyes, Ward found himself momentarily rattled. How was he ever going to manage this? It was hard to think straight when confronted by such liquid pools of misery.

"Yes?"

Ward pushed his cup away, rubbing at his face in agitation. "This house—I mean this land—"

"I know what you're going to say. A woman alone can't take care of the land and the crops. I've heard it all before. But other women have staked claims and worked to prove 'em up. I can too."

Pursing his lips, Ward began to draw circles with his finger on the table. He didn't look at her when he said, "There's no claim to prove up."

She frowned across at him. "What's that supposed to mean? Papa has had this claim for over six years now. It's his, free and clear. It was tough, but we did it. We even stayed through the Santee Indian uprisings when most other folks left. This is *our* land."

When Ward captured her look, his eyes were serious. "Your pa mortgaged this land to buy seed for crops. This land isn't yours. It belongs to the Yankton Bank."

Rose's already pale face became even paler. "I don't believe you."

"It's true," he told her. "What's more, I think you know it."

Rose sagged back against her chair. "You're right. I've known something was wrong for a long time now. When the rains failed to come this past spring Papa was more worried than I can ever remember seeing him." Her eyes met his. "Why didn't he tell me?"

"He was hoping to recoup his losses by selling a piece of his land, but—"

"But he died before he could do it," she finished for him tonelessly.

"Yes."

For the first time, Ward noticed a spark of interest in her eyes. "Then I could do the same. Sell some of the land, I mean." The sudden, irrelevant thought occurred to him that her eyes were the very color of a summer sky.

He shook his head slowly. "It's already too late. The bank intends to foreclose by the end of this week."

She rose quickly to her feet. "Then I haven't time to lose. I'll saddle Baron and leave straightway. I should be able to make it to Yankton in two days."

Ward stared up at her in openmouthed amazement. He rose to his own feet, his six-foot-six height towering over her by a good nine inches. "Of all the stupid—don't be ridiculous! For one thing, you'd never outrun that storm." He motioned towards the kitchen window where the morning light already resembled dusk.

"I could try!"

"And for another thing," he went on, "the bank already has a buyer for this property at twice the rate of your father's mortgage. There's no way they're going to give you more time, and especially not to sell off part of the land which would detract from its value."

Rose slowly sank back to her chair. She buried her face in her hands. "There has to be a way," she muttered. "I *have* to keep this property. I have nowhere else to go."

Ward knelt beside her, pulling her hands away from her face. The abject misery in her visage reminded him of a wounded fawn he had come across this past spring.

"There is a way," he told her softly.

Hope brightened her features, and she smiled at him with a smile that seemed to dispel some of the gloom from the darkened interior. "There is?"

Her childish faith disturbed him. He swallowed twice before he could get the words out. "You could marry me."

Her smile disappeared and such a look of horror crossed her face that Ward was momentarily offended.

Rose couldn't have looked more surprised if the floor had opened up beneath her. She stared at Ward with a look that surely doubted his sanity. Neither one spoke for a long moment.

"Just listen to me a minute," he urged. "I'm not suggesting a regular marriage. I know you don't love me, and I don't. . .well, I don't love you either. But we *need* each other."

If she could have gotten past him, Ward had no doubt Rose would have left him kneeling there. She really had no option but to listen to everything he had to say.

"I can't promise you love. All of that died in me

seven years ago. But I can promise you that I will care for you. All I ask in return is someone to meet my needs. I know you're a fine cook, and you have a knack of making even the roughest dwelling seem like home."

The anger seemed to drain from her face as she considered his proposal.

"I need time to think, Ward. Time to sort things through."

"I can't give you that time," he declared roughly. "The minister only stayed for your father's funeral and he intends to leave within the next hour. He's going to try to reach Mitchell before the snow flies, so he would have to marry us now. I can give you five minutes to decide."

With that, he got up and left the room.

❧

Rose sat there, her mind totally blank. Five minutes to decide her future. Of all the nerve! Of course she would decline his offer. In fact she would take perverse delight in doing so. But what *would* she do with her future?

Her mind wandered round and round in circles until Rose thought she would scream, but no matter which way her thoughts turned, she always came back to the same conclusion. She had *nowhere* to go. Marrying Ward offered her a solution, but what kind of woman would she be if she accepted such an arrangement?

Of course, others before her had accepted such a proposal, but that certainly didn't justify Rose's doing the same. Still, Ward had said that he *needed* her. A man alone on the prairie was about as useless as a woman alone on the prairie.

For the first time Rose considered the sacrifice Ward was willing to make for her. After several moments of such reasoning, Rose finally convinced herself that she would be doing Ward just as big a favor as he was doing her.

Not willing to be found waiting for him, Rose got up and went in search of Ward. He was kneeling next to the fire slowly stirring the hot coals with the fire iron. His brow was furrowed in thought and from that distance he seemed quite unapproachable. Rose had to take her courage firmly in hand before she could get her feet to move.

He glanced up as she stopped beside him. Green eyes studied her thoughtfully, their look inscrutable.

"Why?"

He didn't pretend to misunderstand her. "I owe you and your father a lot. It's the least I could do."

Rose blew out through tightly clenched lips. "We owe you just as much, if not more."

He stood and crossed the room, returning the iron to its place by the fire. When he turned back to Rose his expression was carefully veiled. He took her by the shoulders, studying her face carefully. "I need a wife. You need a husband. It's as simple as that. Don't look for something more when there *is* nothing more."

Rose struggled with the desire to say no, but she held herself in check. She needed more time to decide what to do, but her time was rapidly running out. It was clear Ward expected an answer.

"What do you want from me?" she asked in an unsteady voice.

"Only what you're willing to give."

"If I say yes. . .will you. . .do you want. . . ?" Her tongue tripped over the words.

"I expect nothing from you except to care for my home, cook my meals, and possibly help with the land. In time. . .in time, maybe we could learn to care for each other. I don't know. As I said, my heart died a long time ago. I don't know if I have any heart left to give."

Rose lay a hand against his grey flannel sleeve. "You have a heart, Ward. You proved that just now."

She walked away from him and went to the window. Rose knew putting in glass panes was an extravagance, but Papa had wanted it so much for Rose. He had tried to make everything easier for her.

Ward cleared his throat. "Rose, there's something else you need to know."

She glanced over her shoulder, waiting for him to continue.

"My place is nothing like this." He motioned with his hand, indicating the shanty's interior. "I had no need to fix my place up special since. . .since I had no woman to care."

Rose saw the brief look of grief that crossed his features. Ward had lost his wife on the trip out to the Dakota Territory, that much she knew. Something to do with fever. How he must have loved her to feel the pain of loss even after seven years.

"Please don't tell me you live in a soddie," she whispered.

Surprised, he blinked at her before breaking into a soft chuckle, his eyes suddenly alive with devilment. "Nothing like that. I just want you to know that I only have a one-room cabin with a dirt floor. If you decide to marry me, I will immediately begin to change that."

"Only one room?" If anything, her voice was fainter than before.

He nodded. "After the storm passes I can begin to bring logs from the river to add on. It'll take time, but I have nothing else pressing since winter has set in."

Rose turned back to study the outside and saw the first soft flakes begin to fall against the panes. Snow!

Ward noticed too. He came to stand beside her, his attention focused outside. "You have to give me your answer now, Rose."

It seemed an eternity before Rose could bring herself to answer him. She sent up a quick prayer for the Almighty's blessings on this seemingly unholy contract. She couldn't get the words past the lump in her throat, so she settled for nodding her head.

She felt more than saw Ward relax. "You'll have to get your coat and come with me to the Haskins'. Pastor Hoover is waiting for us there."

"You were so sure I'd say yes?" she asked quietly.

"Let's just say I *hoped* the answer would be yes," he answered just as quietly.

～～～

Ward watched Rose cross the shanty to her room. When she disappeared from sight his shoulders slumped, and he let out a long breath. What on earth had he gotten himself into now? Of all the stupid notions, this had to top them all. When Emily had first suggested he marry Rose, he had thought it ludicrous, but after a fitful night with no sleep and images of Rose's less than rosy future, the idea had seemed not only possible, but necessary.

Rose returned and Ward helped her into her coat. He took the blanket she handed him and followed her outside to his waiting wagon. A fine layer of white covered the horses from head to tail.

After tucking the blanket securely around her, Ward climbed into the wagon beside her and taking up the reins clucked to the horses. The silence hung between them, almost deafening in its completeness.

Emily was waiting for them when they arrived. Although the trip was only two miles, snow now covered the ground to a depth of several inches. If the wind should pick up, it would become a full-out blizzard.

Pastor Hoover hurriedly performed the service, smiling at them both when he gave his blessing. In a short time Ward and Rose found themselves on their way back to Rose's shanty. Emily had wanted them to stay for a celebration supper, but prudence dictated otherwise. There were animals to attend to. Besides, neither Ward nor Rose felt that there was anything much to celebrate.

Rose climbed down from the wagon and hurried inside while Ward took the horses to the barn. Her hands were shaking so badly she could hardly undo the buttons on her coat.

She threw the coat on the hook behind the front door and slowly made her way into the kitchen. She went to the window and looked out, not even bothering to light the lamp. Anguished blue eyes reflected back to her from the darkened panes. *Oh Papa! What now? Would you have wanted this?*

There was no answer, only the keening howl of the wind as it began its trip across the prairie.

Chapter 3

The morning dawned bright and clear, almost as though the previous night's storm had never been. It had left behind a reminder, however, and the flat prairie was covered in white for as far as the eye could see.

For Rose, the past twenty-four hours had seemed like a surrealistic dream or, depending on one's opinion, a nightmare. She twisted the gold band Ward had placed on her left hand only last night. Where he had obtained it she had no idea, nor was she about to ask. She had this horrible feeling that it might have belonged to his first wife, Elise, and that he had carried it around with him for the past seven years. Such morbid thoughts made her shiver with distaste.

Now Ward was hitching his team of horses to the wagon in preparation for returning to his own cabin. She could see the frown furrowing his brow and realized that he was concerned for his livestock since he had been unable to make it back last night, the storm having effectively stranded them here. Her own milk cow and Papa's horse were tied securely to the back of the wagon.

She drifted to the front door, opening it and leaning against the jamb. Ward glanced up briefly but continued with what he was doing. The winter landscape shone so brightly it stung the eyes just to look at it. The wind had scattered the snow, piling it up against small obstructions until there were little hills all around.

"I'll be back by sundown. It would help if you had the place cleaned out and your things ready to be moved." He retraced his steps to the other side of the team and began tightening the harness on Big Ben, Old Blue's teammate. "You can leave the bedding since it will be too late to make it back to my. . .*our* place this evening. We'll stay the night here again."

Would she ever feel comfortable around this man? She certainly didn't feel married, though never having experienced that state before, she wasn't quite sure what "feeling married" entailed. "I'll. . .I'll have supper ready when you get back."

Nodding his head, Ward climbed into the wagon. He gave Rose a long, searching look before lifting the reins and clucking to the team. As the wagon moved forward, Rose heard the cackling of the chickens that Ward had crated up to take back with him. They seemed as unhappy with the situation as she was.

Closing the door, she began wandering from room to room, lifting a pot here, moving a blanket there. She stood in Papa's room a long time before shaking her head, and finally pulling herself together. This was getting her nowhere. She knew what she had to do, so it was best to pull herself out of the doldrums and get the job done.

Since she had no crates or barrels, she used her clothes and blankets to pile dishes and supplies into, leaving only those blankets and sheets necessary for their sojourn here tonight. She gathered her breakables next to her storage chest beside her bed and lifting the cover peered inside.

Her heart seemed to lodge somewhere in her throat when she spotted the colorful quilt to one side. She had forgotten. Now, she carefully lifted it out, spreading it across her lap. Tears began to pool in her eyes as she moved her hand softly over the covering.

This quilt had been a labor of love, worked on for months now. She had taken materials left over from worn-out clothes belonging to Papa and Mama, and even her own, and fashioned them into this beautiful spread.

That blue piece was from a shirt she had made for Papa when she was but fifteen, shortly after Mama had died. Mama had taught her to sew, but the shirt had proven trickier than she had expected and somehow she could not get the sleeves to set right. Still, Papa had worn it proudly.

There were pieces from the dresses her mother had made for her as a child. There was even a beautiful piece of faded white satin from Mama's wedding gown.

Rose had been saving these pieces for ages, and it was the one thing Papa had not left behind them when they had come west. Most people would have considered a crate of material pieces a foolish waste of space, but not Papa. He had known just how much they meant to her.

It had only been this past summer that the thought

of making a special quilt for him had occurred to her. She had created her own intricate pattern and worked long hours to complete it in time for Christmas. The tiny, even stitches spoke well of Rose's ability with a needle and she felt a little thrill of pride in herself and her mother who had taken such pains to teach her the finer art of quilting.

Since she had finished the quilt before Thanksgiving, she had put it away until later to give to Papa. It had been all she could do to keep it from him until Christmas. Now, it was too late. He would never see it.

Tears crowded close in her throat and she gently lay the covering back in the chest, arranging her breakables among its soft folds. She shut the lid firmly.

Well, the quilt was hers now. All that was left of Papa and Mama. Even the farm was no longer hers, but no one could take away her memory quilt, especially not some greedy bank. Let them have the land, the shanty, and even the livestock if they so desired, but the quilt belonged to her, and her alone.

It didn't take long for her to empty the shanty of their few possessions. She hadn't realized just how much trifles added to the warmth of a home, but now, with the barrenness, the shanty seemed less friendly somehow. Again she experienced that feeling of living in a dream. She moved listlessly about, unable to set her mind to anything.

Finally, she made her way into the kitchen and checked on the stew she had started earlier. Thanks to Emily, there was bread to go with it, but little else. Still, it would have to do.

The day seemed to drag, and although she was unaware of it, Rose sighed with relief when she heard the returning wagon.

Ward opened the door, stopping on the threshold to scrape off the mud and ice caked to his boots. He glanced briefly at Rose before closing the door behind him and hanging his coat on the peg behind it.

"How were your animals?" she asked him, busying herself with setting the table so that she wouldn't have to look at him. Every time she was in his presence, she felt such acute shyness that it was hard for her to form a coherent thought.

"*Our* animals were fine," he told her, deliberately stressing the pronoun. "Hungry, but none the worse for their unexpected fast."

He joined her at the table, breathing into his cupped hands to free them of their cramping cold. "Smells good," he told her, his nose twitching appreciatively.

Rose ladled him a bowl of stew, adding a buttered slice of bread. She kept wracking her brain trying to think of something to say. Ward seemed equally as uncomfortable.

After fixing her own bowl, she slid into the seat across from him. Giving him a brief look she bowed her head and asked him to say grace.

There was a long silence in the room, and just as she was about to look up to see what the problem was, she heard Ward clear his throat and hesitantly offer thanks for the food.

Rose frowned. Hadn't Papa told her once that Ward was a man of God? If that were so, then why such hesitation over a simple grace?

She kept her gaze focused on her own plate and decided not to worry about it. Let the Good Lord handle Mr. Ward Taylor; she had enough troubles of her own.

After supper, it didn't take Rose long to wash the few dishes and pack them away in one of the crates Ward had brought back with him. She made one more check through the house to assure herself that nothing had been left behind. Ward had told her that the furniture could be stored in the barn temporarily, but otherwise there was no room for it right now in his—their cabin. She was beginning to really fret about this cabin that was soon to be her new home.

When she closed her eyes that night, Rose tried hard to pray and leave things in God's hands, but no clear thoughts would come. Her mind seemed to have gone blank. Finally, she allowed her musings to roam in a wordless appeal that she knew the Lord would be able to untangle and set right. Only He could possibly have any idea of what she was really trying to say. She only knew one thing. God had been with her all of her life, and she was sure He wouldn't abandon her now.

⌒⌒⌒

Conversation was nonexistent for the first two miles of the trek to Ward's cabin. Both he and Rose were busy with their own thoughts, both trying to adjust themselves to their sudden change of circumstances.

Rose wondered just how far the cabin was. She couldn't remember ever discussing it with Papa, but it must be quite a distance since it took the better part of a day for him to reach their place. She really wanted to know, but she was too nervous to ask and draw his attention to her.

"Our place is about ten more miles that way," he told her, motioning to the northeast. His look swung briefly her way. "Are you sure you're warm enough?"

She nodded. Now was the time to strike up a conversation and relieve them both of this tense situation, but her tongue was simply too tied.

As though he read her thoughts, Ward began a rambling monologue of the countryside around, how he thought it was going to be a long hard winter, and what to expect when they reached his place. Rose was trying to prepare herself for the worst.

About halfway to their destination, they rounded a bend in the road which was little more than dug-in wagon tracks. Rose assumed that most of them must have come from Ward and his frequent trips to her cabin.

There was a house nestled back from the road, if one could call it a house. In actuality, it was nothing but a small soddie. Probably the occupants were either too lazy to haul logs from the Missouri River close by, or they had been here too short a time to make other arrangements.

She was surprised when a man hurried out to intercept them on the road. He had a short, neatly clipped beard and although his clothes were little more than patched rags, he was clean.

Ward pulled the wagon to a stop, setting the

brake. He reached down to the man, a smile lighting his features.

"Howdy, Adam. I'd like you to meet my wife, Rose." Ward nodded towards the other man. "The Comptons are our nearest neighbors."

Brown eyes sparkled with friendliness as the man reached out a hand. "Howdy, ma'am."

Rose returned his smile. "Mr. Compton."

"How's the family?" Ward asked him.

"See for yourself."

Over his shoulder, Rose could see a woman and two children hurrying their way. The woman stopped beside the wagon and shyly handed Rose a bundle. "For you. A wedding present."

Rose was stunned. She knew that news here on the prairie traveled as fast as a wildfire, so she shouldn't have been surprised. But she was.

Taking the bundle, Rose unwrapped it, revealing a small loaf of bread. She could feel Ward's eyes on her. When she looked his way, there was something indefinable in his eyes.

"Thank you." She acknowledged the woman's friendliness with a smile that brought a quick one in return.

"This here's Alice," Adam told her, the pride evident in his voice. "She's my missus. And this here's Alicia and Andrew. Twins." He ruffled the boy's hair good-naturedly, but Andrew pulled away.

"Aw, Pa!"

Adam grinned at his son. "Thinks he's too growed up, now that he's turned six."

Rose smiled at the play between father and son. It was obvious that this was a very close and loving family. Her gaze settled on little Alicia, a perfect replica of her mother. Blond ringlets cascaded down the child's back in abundance, and her periwinkle blue eyes smiled timidly at Rose.

"Won't you come in and have a bite to eat? You must be hungry after traveling so far."

Rose was about to answer the woman when she felt a sudden pressure on her knee. Turning startled eyes on Ward, she found his hand gripping her knee but his look was fixed on Alice.

"We can't today, Alice. We still have a long way to go. Besides, Rose fixed us something to eat for the trip."

That was certainly true, Rose thought, *but Ward was being unneighborly to say the least.* Everyone on the prairie shared with each other, helped each other and looked forward to each other's company.

She opened her mouth to disagree with his statement, but he suddenly fixed her with a steely eye. She snapped her lips together, turning back to Alice and smiling with regret.

Ward made as if to leave, but suddenly stopped as though he had just thought of something. He turned to Adam.

"Adam, I was wondering if you might be willing to help me gather some logs from the river. My cabin is much too small now that I'm a married man." Both men exchanged amused glances. "I thought since it was winter and all, you might have some free time to help me. If so, I thought since we would be cutting and hauling logs for my cabin, we might just as well do so for you, too. Now, I can't pay you, but I figured if you helped me, I could help you and we could call it even."

A sudden light entered Adam's eyes and he straightened his shoulders. When Rose looked at Alice she saw the same shine reflected in her eyes.

"I reckon that'd be a fair trade," Adam agreed. "When do you want to start?"

"Is tomorrow too soon?"

Adam grinned. "I'll be there at first light."

Nodding, Ward lifted the reins again and clucked to the horses. They hadn't traveled far when Rose rounded on Ward.

"I can speak for myself, you know. It would have been nice to share a meal with the Comptons."

Ward's lips lifted slightly in an amused smirk. "I wondered how long it would take before you launched your attack."

"I'm not attacking," she huffed, "but you weren't being very neighborly."

When he turned her way, his green eyes were serious. "You're right. I wasn't being very neighborly, but for good reason." He motioned to the loaf of bread that Alice Compton had handed her. "That bread was probably their allotment for the week. Since the drought this past summer and the grasshoppers the year before, Adam hasn't fared very well. He still has three years left to prove up, and if things don't change, he'll lose his claim. You saw the condition of their clothes. They can barely afford to feed themselves, much less clothe themselves. But they're a very proud family. Adam feels if he can't make things work, then they just weren't meant to be. He won't accept 'charity.'"

Rose considered the loaf of bread in her lap. What a sacrifice! "Why didn't you say something? I wouldn't have accepted this."

He turned away from her, studying the white prairie around them. Puffs of frost billowed out of his mouth and nostrils and he pulled his hat lower on his head to ward off the cold. "I wouldn't hurt Alice for the world. I'll find a way to make it up to them."

He remained quiet after that, and Rose observed him silently. Ward, it would seem, had a far larger heart than he gave himself credit for. Her first thought had been to condemn. She dropped her chin and stared at her fingers. If the Lord had wanted to teach her humility, He had certainly found an effective way of doing it.

She had never known hunger herself. Papa had brought money with him when he first settled here on the prairie, so when the crops were scarce, the money had been there. It only now occurred to her that he must have been using that money little by little to make her life more comfortable. She felt ashamed of herself for not seeing it sooner.

She wrapped the loaf of bread gently, as though it were some great treasure, as in a sense, it was.

Chapter 4

Adam showed up as he said he would, at first light. Ward had been awake for hours and had already taken care of the chores and fed the livestock.

The cabin itself hadn't been nearly as unsatisfactory as Rose was expecting, but it was only one large room with very little in the way of furniture. The fact that there was only one bed had caused her serious qualms until Ward began making himself a pallet on the floor next to the fireplace.

Feeling guilty, but relieved nonetheless, Rose had prepared an elaborate supper to make amends. The whole evening had been an ordeal in itself, but one light-hearted moment had occurred at supper time that had relieved Rose of much of her dread of her husband, though at the time it had caused her a moment of panic.

She had poured him his third cup of coffee and was just turning away when he cleared his throat. Turning back, one eyebrow raised in question, she noticed Ward's nervousness. Suddenly, she began to feel rather nervous herself.

"Rose, there's something I need. . .I have to. . .well, we're going to be married a long time, God willing, and you just gotta know."

When he stopped, Rose waited expectantly, not realizing that she was holding her breath.

His chin lifted in determination, his eyes intent. "I'm sorry, Rose, but I just can't abide coffee."

Her breath rushed out of her in a gasp. Is that what this was all about? And here she had been expecting. . . what? She wasn't quite sure, but suddenly her relief lent a sparkle to her eyes, and she grinned at him.

"I'm not offended, Ward," she told him lightly. "Fact is, I can't stand the stuff myself."

His shoulders relaxed, and his mouth curled slowly into a heart-stopping smile. "The way you continually fed me the stuff, I never would have guessed." He shook his head, grinning. "Well, we should save a good deal of money on *that* commodity, then," he finally told her.

Rose shook her own head as she began clearing the table. "And all this time you've been forcing yourself to drink it whenever you came to our place. You should have told me. I thought all men drank coffee. Papa certainly loved it."

His smile was sheepish. "My pa taught me to *never* say anything against a woman's cookin'."

Rose shook her head again, just thinking about it now as she watched Ward hitching the team to the wagon. With Adam's wagon, they would be able to haul twice as much wood and wouldn't have to make as many return trips. It should save time all around, and the sooner the other rooms were added, the better it would be in her opinion. She hated the fact that Ward had to sleep on the cold, dirt floor.

Ward returned to the cabin to retrieve his leather gloves. He paused beside Rose on his way back out the door. "You sure you're gonna be all right here by yourself?"

She nodded. "I'll just unpack some of my things, if that's okay with you."

He lifted a hand and pushed a stray lock of hair behind her ear. His voice was so soft, it sent shivers of awareness throughout her entire being. "This is your place now, too. Remember?" When he bent and kissed her cheek softly, Rose thought her heart would surely come to a standstill. "Make it into a home," he continued. "I haven't had a real one in a long while, and I know you have the knack."

With that, he left her standing there gaping at his retreating back.

By the time Ward had returned, Rose had unpacked most of her possessions, though there was little room in the small cabin to accommodate them. On the mantle above his fireplace, she placed her parents' anniversary clock, surrounding it with her own pair of silver candlesticks that Papa had bought for her twentieth birthday.

She had thought of adding her memory quilt to Ward's spartan bed, not only for the warmth but to add some cheerful color to this otherwise drab cabin. In the end, she had thought better of it. Perhaps there would be a time when she could look at the coverlet without feeling so much pain, but now was not that time. So she had carefully folded the quilt and returned it to her chest.

Over the next few days, Ward and Rose grew accustomed to each other's presence. Their conversation became less stilted, more natural, and before long they were conversing together as though they had been friends a long time, as indeed they really had, though they had not considered it so at the time.

In the evenings when Rose would pull out her Bible for her daily devotions, Ward would continue with his own work. He would clean the halters and oil them against the weather, or sharpen the tools he would need come planting time. Eventually he asked her to read aloud, and though she was surprised, she nonetheless readily agreed. It became an evening ritual that Rose looked forward to.

Ward still slept on his pallet by the fire, and Rose felt guiltier and guiltier about making him do so, especially when he spent such long, hard hours felling trees and she did so little. But when she had suggested switching beds, she had been met with such a cold look of outrage that she didn't dare suggest it again.

It was now a week into December, and suddenly Christmas loomed largely on Rose's horizon. The holiday didn't strike the same chord of joy that it usually did, however, and she wondered just how she and Ward should spend it. It was the day set aside to remember Christ's birth, but Rose didn't think her Lord would really mind if she didn't celebrate just this once. After fretting about it several more days, she decided that she would just ignore Christmas this year. She was fairly certain Ward would agree with her.

In this she was wrong. When she suggested it to

him, Ward told her that he had already invited the Comptons to spend Christmas with them. "I'm sorry," he told her, although he didn't look it. "I didn't know you felt that way."

Peeved, Rose told herself that he had no way of knowing *how* she felt since he was never around to talk about such things. She stopped in her tracks, realizing just how much she had been missing him when he was away. Of course, that was logical. It was lonely out here on the prairie, she reasoned, ignoring her heart when it tried to presume otherwise.

As she was preparing for bed that night, she happened to catch Ward's regard fixed intently on her as she brushed her long hair her usual one hundred strokes. Her fingers grew clumsy as they always did when he looked at her in such a way, and she dropped the brush.

Cheeks filling with color, she lifted it from the dirt and shook it out. Reluctantly, she looked at her husband again only to find him stirring the logs in the fire in preparation for the night. She curled down among her covers and tried to get her heart to steady into its normal rhythm. It was a long time before sleep found her.

The cold breeze from the cabin door closing roused Rose in the middle of the night. Sitting up, she tried to rub the sleep from her eyes, wondering what time it was and what had disturbed her.

She could barely make out the hands on the anniversary clock in the dying light from the fire. Twelve-twenty. Ward's covers were thrown back and his bed was empty. Heart jumping in alarm, she hastily climbed from her own warm cocoon and slid into her robe.

Opening the door, she scanned the area to see where Ward could have gone. A light glimmered faintly from the barn, and closing the door behind her, Rose headed in that direction.

By the time she reached the barn she was shivering with cold. She opened the door, swiftly closing it behind her. When she turned around she found Ward staring at her in surprise.

"What are you doing out here? Get back to the house! You'll freeze in that getup."

Ignoring him, she moved forward to where he was kneeling. "I thought something might be wrong."

He shifted his position next to his mare, Beauty, who was lying on her side, her flanks heaving. Rose's eyes widened in surprise. "Is she foaling?"

The look Ward focused on the mare was grim. "Yes," he told her shortly. "Now go back to the house."

"Is something wrong with her?"

"She's breech," he told her through gritted teeth. "Now, for heaven's sake, get out of here."

Rose looked from the heaving mare back to Ward. She could sense his desperation. Not only was the foal valuable, Ward truly cared for his animals.

"No," she answered him firmly, moving closer to his side. "I want to help. Just tell me what to do."

He looked as though he were about to argue when Beauty whinnied in pain. Giving Rose brief instructions, he turned his full attention back to the mare.

They worked together, side by side, until the first

220

fingers of dawn were spreading across the sky. Just when she thought all hope was lost, Ward managed to turn the foal slightly, enough to allow it to pass through the birth canal.

Only moments later, a wet and bloody but triumphant colt struggled to get to his feet.

"It's a boy!" Rose exulted. "A beautiful baby boy!"

Ward shook his head slightly as he wiped his hands on a rag, his lips turning up into a reluctant smile.

Now that the excitement was over, Rose found herself trembling with the below-freezing temperatures. Although the barn was relatively warm compared to the great outdoors, it was much too cold for someone standing in her nightgown and robe.

Ward noticed her shivering and came quickly to her side. Pulling his own sheepskin jacket from the stall where he had left it, he wrapped it securely around her. His eyes found hers and held. "Thanks for your help. I couldn't have done it without you," he told her softly.

Rose swallowed hard against his fingers where they clutched his jacket together at her throat. Her eyes were drawn to his as they darkened in response to hers. He leaned forward and lifting her chin with his thumbs he pressed his lips warmly against hers.

Rose went from freezing to feeling as though her entire being were on fire. When Ward wrapped his strong arms around her, she leaned her full weight against him, knowing that her own legs would be useless as support.

She thought the moment would never end, in fact hoped that it wouldn't, but Ward pulled away when he heard Adam's wagon entering their yard.

He dropped his arms, stepping back from her, something undefined in his eyes. Rose shivered against the returning cold, her mind filled with a mixture of wonder and confusion, and turning, she fled back to the cabin.

For the next several days Ward took pains to avoid being alone with Rose as much as possible. She jumped whenever he entered a room, and she sensed he knew it had to do with that moment in the barn. The friendly rapport they had established had vanished, but she realized that what was done couldn't be undone. She would have to do something to make him comfortable again.

Ward was clearly surprised when Rose followed him out to the wagon the next day.

"Do you think I can ride with you to Alice's today?"

Since he and Adam had accumulated enough logs to build a cabin, Ward had insisted that Adam have first priority. Pride battled stubbornness, and stubbornness had won out. Rose had had no doubt of the outcome. Ward had a tendency to have his own way, one way or another.

The two men working together should have most of the cabin raised by that evening, barring unforeseen circumstances. Alice would be ecstatic.

Ward studied Rose a moment as she quietly awaited his answer. Her coat was buttoned tightly against the bitter cold and she was clutching a bundle in her arms.

He hesitated, but she knew he really had no reason to refuse her.

"Sure. Climb up."

He helped her into the wagon, reaching into the back to grab the blanket he kept there. He dropped it over her knees, fitting it snugly against her sides. When his eyes met hers, Rose felt there was a moment when it seemed as if the entire earth held its breath.

Turning quickly away, Ward picked up the reins and snapped them against the horses' flanks.

When they reached the Comptons' soddie, Alice met them outside, her face wreathed in smiles of welcome.

"Howdy! I'm so glad you came," she told Rose, her voice filled with pleased expectation. Little Alicia stood shyly watching from the doorway, but her brother Andrew pushed his way forward to stand beside the wagon.

Climbing down from her seat beside Ward, Rose followed Alice inside while Ward went to find Adam.

Alice's soddie was small as it was, but when Rose's presence was added along with the two children it became quite cramped. How could she stand it? The claustrophobic feeling such a tight space engendered would make even the sturdiest soul run mad.

"Can't I go outside and help Pa, Ma?" little Andrew whined.

Alice glanced quickly at Rose, her face filling with color. "It's too cold son, and you haven't a warm enough coat," she told him quietly. Sighing in disgust, Andrew flung himself down next to his sister and began playing with the wooden blocks their father had made for them.

Surveying the room, Rose noticed only one bed in the soddie and wondered where the children slept. Her question must have been reflected on her face because Alice hastily assured Rose that they all slept together since it was warmer that way. There was only one thin, faded quilt on the bed and Rose's heart went out to this family. They tried so hard to give the impression that all was well. No wonder Ward had invited them for Christmas.

Settling her pack on the table, Rose addressed Alice. "I hope you don't mind, Alice, but I brought some things to add for lunch. I so wanted to have some company today, but it hardly seemed fair for me to just wish myself on you and your family without bringing something along to feed that giant of mine."

Tears came to Alice's eyes as Rose unloaded her pack. "I fixed too much chicken last night, 'cause Ward found a bunch of prairie chickens and brought them home for me to cook. I guess he forgets there's just the two of us."

Alice didn't bother to suggest that Rose could have put them in her cooler pit and frozen them, and Rose was certainly not about to mention it herself.

"I also tried a new recipe for cookies that Emily Haskins gave me, but I don't think they turned out as well as Emily's, so I think I'll try again. Do you think Alicia and Andrew might like some?"

Rose wore such a woebegone look, her voice tinged with just the right shade of anxiety, that Alice hastened to assure her that Andrew and Alicia would be pleased to try some. As for the children, although their manners kept them from saying much, their eyes spoke volumes.

When the men came in for lunch, they both stopped short at sight of the heavily laden table. Besides the chicken and cookies, Rose had brought potatoes, squash, and bread. If Ward was surprised by the great quantity of food, he didn't say so. His eyes rested thoughtfully on his wife, and when she chanced a look at him he smiled at her. Her cheeks filled with guilty color and his smile widened into a full grin.

Adam said nothing, but there was a suspicious sheen in his solemn brown eyes. When he said grace, Rose felt a lump rise in her throat at his fervent thanks.

When they were on their way home that evening Ward was unusually silent. He stopped the wagon suddenly and turned to Rose. Circles of frost puffed around his face almost hiding him from view.

"That was a wonderful thing you done. I'm right proud of you for thinking of it." He landed a kiss on her surprised mouth, and lifting the reins, clucked to the horses.

Rose's astonishment turned to a pleased feeling of accomplishment. She felt warm all over, but of course that had nothing to do with Ward's kiss. Nothing at all.

Chapter 5

T hat's a mighty fine woman you got there, Ward."

Ward glanced up from notching the log between his feet and smiled at Adam. "That she is, Adam." He thought again of how Rose had come with him again, bringing an old coat of hers for Andrew. She had made it sound like Alice would do her a favor by taking it since it was too small for her, and could Alice manage to use it? Yes, Rose was a manipulator all right, but she always did it in such a nice way.

"How'd someone as ornery and cantankerous as you get such a fine woman out here so far from civilization, anyway?" Adam teased.

Ward lifted the log, motioning for Adam to take the other end. "Same way a *pigheaded* old coot like you managed to get someone like Alice, I reckon."

Adam laughed, lifting his end of the log. They moved as one, hoisting it and dropping it into place. Adam stepped back, brushing his hands together. He nodded his head in satisfaction.

"Looks like one more should do," he told Ward. They moved towards the logs still piled a few feet away. Lifting one away from the others, each man began to notch his own end.

"Truth to tell," Adam continued, "I think it must have been the Good Lord looking out for me. Seems He's been lookin' out for me right well."

Ward stopped chopping, resting the head of the ax against the ground and leaning on its handle. "You can say that after all that's gone wrong the past two summers? You may lose your claim."

Adam snorted. "Pshaw, that ain't nothin'. I still have my family, and good friends like you. Didn't God send you to me just when I was about at the end of my rope? Now I won't have to worry about my family this winter. They'll be snug as a bug in a rug."

Smiling, Ward continued notching the log. "Adam, you've given me something to think about."

Yes, he did have something to think about. It was amazing how much had happened in so little time. It was almost as though the Almighty had allowed Gabel Johnson to die so that Ward could step in to take care of Rose, so that Rose could in turn help the Comptons. Of course it was foolish to suppose that one knew the mind of God, but sometimes it was simple to see how things might have been arranged.

He knew Rose, though sad, had no worries about her father's death. She was absolutely certain where he would be in his afterlife.

And what about Ward, himself? He hadn't had nearly as strong a faith as Rose, because when Elise had died he had turned his back on God. Before her death, he and Elise had talked often about the possibility of one of them being taken from this life. Elise had showed him in the book of Hebrews that Satan had the power of death. He knew that to be so, then why had he blamed God?

Because God was stronger than Satan; he knew that, too. Yet he was angry with God for allowing his beloved Elise to die. Thinking back on it now, he realized that it had been *his* idea to move to Dakota Territory. Elise was one of those women who would follow her man anywhere, but he knew she would never have survived for long on the prairie. The solitude alone would have killed her. Guilt over his own selfishness shuddered through him. A thought crossed his mind that deepened his guilt. Where would Rose be now if Elise hadn't died?

To shake away such gruesome thoughts, he threw himself into his work so that by the end of the day, the Comptons' cabin was finished except for the caulking that Adam could do on his own.

The women came out to admire the men's work and the children ran excitedly in and out of the open space that would be used as the door. The structure stood solidly against the ever-present prairie wind.

"Oh, Adam." It was all Alice could say as tears pooled in her eyes. They worked so hard trying to make a home out of this inhospitable territory. For Alice to have lived in a soddie as long as she had gave credence to the woman's remarkable ability to adapt. Ward knew it came from the great love Alice had for Adam, wanting nothing but to assure her man's happiness, just as Elise had for him. And now Rose was doing her best to adapt to his harsh life.

As Ward began gathering his supplies together, Adam came up and slapped him on the back. "We can start on your place tomorrow."

"If you don't mind," Ward told him, keeping his face averted, "I'd just as soon wait a day. I need to figure where I want to build, and how many logs it'll take. Why don't you go ahead and chink your cabin and make your door?" He lifted his head enough to catch Rose's eye and give her a wink.

Dawning comprehension brought a quick smile to her lips. "What a great idea! That means I can have you all to myself for one whole day."

Ward's heart jumped at this pronouncement. If he didn't know better, he'd think she actually meant it.

Alice and Adam exchanged knowing smiles.

"Well, if you're sure," Adam told Ward. He turned to his wife. "Then, woman, you should be snug in your own house by tomorrow evening."

❧

On the ride home, Rose suddenly turned to Ward. "Ward, how come you haven't been affected by the drought and the grasshoppers?" She had seen the barn and knew that it was full of supplies for both the animals and himself.

He glanced at her briefly. He took a long time answering, almost as though he had to choose his words with care. "When I lived back East I had a good paying job, a nice home and a pretty good nest egg in the bank. After we decided to come out here, I sold the house for a fair price and added to my nest egg. Elise and

I decided not to bring too much with us. We figured that since it was easy enough for boats to travel up the Missouri, it should be easy enough to get goods from the East by way of Yankton."

He stopped, his thoughts obviously far away. "I still have most of that money. After Elise. . .after Elise died, I didn't need much for myself. I've tried to use some of my money to help others, but it's hard. These are a proud people."

His look returned to her, one dark eyebrow lifting high. He nodded to her hand. "Even your ring."

Rose felt her heart drop. "My ring?"

"Didn't you ever wonder where I got it?"

Her face turned so red, Ward's other eyebrow rose to match its counterpart. He grinned, but turned his attention back to the road. "Someday, you'll have to tell me just exactly what you did think. I got it from Emily. The Haskins have had almost as hard a time as everyone else. Emily mentioned to me a long time ago that she had her grandmother's wedding ring, and if she could find a way she'd sell it. I remembered."

Rose wasn't exactly sure how she felt about this revelation, but it made her glad that Ward had been able to help the Haskins. Secretly, she was also relieved that the ring hadn't belonged to Elise, though why it should matter so much she wasn't sure.

They rode the rest of the way in thoughtful silence.

 ⌒⌒⌒

It was just two weeks until Christmas and Rose began to fret about what to serve for Christmas dinner. She was growing more excited just thinking about sharing with the Comptons. It had been so much fun to make them happy with just the little she and Ward had done. The Bible was right. It *was* more blessed to give than to receive.

Ward had absented himself from the house in the evenings, not coming in till long after dark. It bothered her that he spent all day chopping logs for their cabin and then spent so much time doing she knew not what out in the cold barn.

It was below freezing tonight and still he hadn't come in except for a quick bite to eat. Lips setting into a firm line, she pulled on her coat and went in search of him.

When she first opened the barn door, she couldn't see Ward anywhere. Thinking he might be someplace else, she was about to close the door when she heard a faint scraping in the corner. Following the direction of the sound, she found Ward in the end stall surrounded by shavings of wood. He glanced up in surprise.

"What on earth are you doing?" she asked warily.

Ward went back to carving on the piece of wood he held in his hand. Rose could see the beginnings of a rifle barrel forming from the wood he was shaving.

"I'm making a toy for Andrew. For Christmas."

Her mouth dropped open. "A toy?"

Rose's eyes went beyond Ward to the corner of the stall and she could see something covered with a burlap sack.

"What's that?"

"Something for Alicia."

Rose pushed past him and lifted the cover, gasping

in surprise. Color came to Ward's cheeks, but he didn't stop his work.

"Oh, Ward! It's beautiful!" Rose stroked her hand softly over the toy cradle, sliding a finger gently around the intricate design carved into the headboard. "How did you do it?"

He shrugged, lifting the rifle for inspection. Closing one eye, he pulled the toy to his shoulder to check that the barrel was forming in a straight line.

"I used to be a carpenter."

Amazed, Rose could only stare at him. She hadn't known that about him! Of course there was very little about her husband she did know. She watched him work several more moments. Periodically he would stop, blowing into his hands to relieve them of the cold.

"You should come inside. It's much too cold out here," she told him.

He shook his head. "Can't. Gotta get this done by Christmas."

She frowned at him. "Well, bring it inside then. It's warmer by the fire."

He glanced up at her in astonishment. "It would make too much of a mess. Elise hated having wood shavings all over the house."

Rose felt a slight pang at mention of his first wife. "Well, I'm sure she didn't have a dirt floor either. How's a few shavings of wood going to hurt that? Besides," she reasoned. "You can always sweep them up."

He studied her pensively. "You sure?"

She nodded. "Course I'm sure. Come inside now."

It was two days later as she watched Ward whittling away at the wood that she came up with an idea. From what she could see, Alicia had no doll to play with. Being a man, Ward had probably never considered that fact.

After supper, she hesitantly approached him. "Ward, do you think Alicia would like a new doll to go with her cradle?"

His eyes brightened at the suggestion. "Why, I think that'd be a great idea. I never thought about a doll." Rose hid a smile.

"Do you have the stuff to do it?"

"I still have some scraps left. . .left from before. I think I have enough for a doll and a small quilt."

"Well, if you don't, give me a list. I plan on going into Yankton tomorrow." He went back to his whittling. Surprised, Rose continued to stare at his down-bent head.

"But, that will take you four days!"

He scrutinized her tense face, his eyes unfathomable. "You scared to stay alone?"

She pressed her lips tightly together. "Course not, but this isn't exactly the time of year to be making such trips. What if you get caught in a blizzard?"

He rose to his feet, placing his hands on her shoulders and staring solemnly into her worried eyes. "There's settlers between here and there. If I have to, I can take shelter."

Hearing the determination in his voice, Rose knew it would do no good to argue. When Ward made up his mind to do something, nothing could sway him from his purpose.

Sighing, Rose turned away. "I'll make the list."

Ward studied the sky along the northern horizon. This didn't look good. He was caught on the open prairie and a storm was rapidly approaching. He knew it had been foolish to try and make the trip to Yankton at such a time, but he wanted to pick up something special for Rose as a Christmas present.

He knew how much she loved to read, and her own books were already dog-eared from use. Probably she could recite the books verbatim.

He glanced at the crate behind the wagon seat. It had been unwise perhaps, but it was something he had been determined to do.

As a man, he had a lot to occupy his time. There were barely enough hours in the day to get all his work done, even in the winter. But for a woman, it was different.

Course, he knew women weren't idle. Far from it. They filled their hours with hard work and all the little details that made a house a home. But women felt the solitude more. To Rose, reading was like visiting with a neighbor.

She had been so patient with him, waiting for all the things that would make his cabin more the home she was used to, and never complaining. In fact, she had encouraged him to put the Comptons first.

He shook his head. She was nothing like his Elise. Elise had been like a beautiful fairy, flitting through her life with gay abandon. Rose, now she was different. Rose was more like the wild prairie rose that her name brought to mind. Sturdy, dependable, a spot of beauty in a rugged landscape.

He frowned. Just exactly when had he started thinking of Rose as beautiful? The frown deepened as he tried to reason it out. Maybe when she had first sat cross-legged on the bed combing her long, dark hair with the fire reflecting off of it in shimmering particles of light.

He had wanted to go to her then. It had taken all of his willpower to turn away. Had love been creeping up on him unawares, only he hadn't recognized it as such? Could she tell? Probably if she knew his thoughts and feelings, she would freeze him out as she had after that first kiss in the barn. The cold December landscape had been nothing in comparison.

As the wind picked up and feathery flakes of snow began to fall, he wondered if he would ever have the chance to find out.

Rose watched the huge snowflakes as they drifted to the icy ground. This was the day Ward was supposed to have returned home. She went back inside, praying that the wind would hold off and that this would just be another snowstorm instead of the blizzard the howling wind could make it.

For the first time, she felt frustrated at the dark interior of the cabin. In her own shanty, Papa had placed purchased glass for windows. Ward had not, and now with the shutters closed the dim interior seemed full of foreboding as she heard the soft breath of wind turn into a whirling gale.

So much for prayers. She switched her petitions to asking for Ward's safekeeping. If anything should happen to him, she didn't know what she would do.

Sitting down hard on the chair next to their eating table, Rose put her face in her hands. *How, God? How had this happened? How could I possibly be in love with my husband? When had it even started?*

She had always been a little afraid of him, but not because she thought he would hurt her. No, it had more to do with the way he made her feel. Had she been falling in love all along only hadn't realized it?

She picked up the small sticks lying on the table and began to tie them together with cord. Ward had given her several carved figures: Mary, Joseph, Baby Jesus, several wise men, and several shepherds. There were even tiny sheep, cattle, and a donkey. He had been whittling them over the past several years. His ability to carve such intricate, beautiful things still filled her with awe. What an incredible gift God had given him. Did he recognize it as such?

Her part was in making the crèche where they would sit. Funny, she and Ward seemed to complement each other well as they worked together.

As she worked, she tried to ignore the ever-rising wail of the wind. Placing cut pieces of hay among the crèche, her petitions to the Lord grew more fervent. What would she do if something happened to Ward? To have finally found love and then to have it snatched away so suddenly was incomprehensible. Surely God could not mean for such a thing to happen. She needed time to make Ward love her in return.

Setting Mary next to Joseph, she allowed her thoughts to wander. Did Joseph love Mary, or had Mary had to contend with a marriage such as Rose's? Joseph was a good man, that was evidenced by the fact that he wanted to put Mary away quietly instead of making her face her shame. But did he love her?

Restlessly, she got up from the table and opened the door to look out. The portal was flung back against the interior cabin wall with the force of the wind. It took everything Rose could muster to be able to close it again. She leaned back against it, her breathing ragged.

What would happen to the animals? They were safe in the barn, but Ward had forbidden her to go to them if there were a storm. Not that she was crazy enough to do so anyway.

She wandered restlessly around the cabin, not able to settle to doing anything. Even little Alicia's doll that she had started lay forgotten on the bed.

When darkness came, Ward still had not returned. It seemed the hands of the clock on the mantle ticked slowly by, dragging each hour to its fullest.

Supper sat untouched on the table. It had been something to occupy her time, and at least she had the hope that Ward would be home soon and hungry. But he hadn't come.

Finally, Rose could take the strain no longer and flinging herself to her knees beside the bed she began to pray loudly, trying to block out the sound of the wind. Before long, her voice turned hoarse with the exertion and trying to suppress her tears. Giving in to the inevitable, she allowed the tears to come. Great, wracking sobs tore at her body.

Suddenly, the door flung open and Rose sat staring at what seemed like a huge, hulking polar bear.

Rose came quickly to her feet and was across the room, flinging herself into her husband's arms.

Chapter 6

Rose glanced periodically at her husband thawing in front of the fire as she walked over to get him dry clothes and a blanket. Steam rose from his wet clothes as he tried to huddle closer for warmth, a hot cup of tea clutched in his shaking hands. She had been so glad to see him, so relieved that he was alive, that she had thrown herself into his arms.

She worried about that now. Had she given away her feelings with that action? She certainly hoped not, because although she may have discovered her own love for him, he had shown nothing that would give her hope that he felt the same. Hadn't he told her that his heart was dead?

"How did you ever manage to get home in this blizzard?"

He looked at her briefly, his teeth still chattering as he took off his wet outer clothes. "I just decided to let the horses have their head. Animals have a pretty keen sense of direction, even in a storm. I was hoping they would find their way home, and they did."

Bless Old Blue and Big Ben. She would give them an extra portion of oats to show her appreciation.

Rose handed Ward his nightclothes. "Put these on and get into bed," she scolded. "We'll be doing good if you don't catch pneumonia."

She turned her back as he fumbled out of his heavy, wet clothes and into his dry night things.

"Where's the blankets for my pallet?"

Not looking at him, Rose began laying his wet clothes over the chair to dry. "You're not sleeping on the floor. I'll not have you catching a chill."

The room grew so silent, she could hear the logs pop in the fireplace. When she finally turned his way, he was staring at her somberly. "Just what are you saying, Rose? 'Cause I'll have you know that I won't allow *you* to sleep on the floor."

She continued to flit about the cabin, straightening things here, fixing things there. Her face was the color of a ripe apple when she told him, "I figured as much. I'm willing to share the bed."

Although she couldn't see him, Rose could feel his eyes upon her back. His stillness reminded her of a cougar she had seen once, just before it had lunged at his prey.

Ward hesitated. Fatigue and confusion crossed his face. Without saying anything, he finally climbed into the bed. "Are you coming?"

Shaking her head, Rose picked up Alicia's doll. "No, not yet. I think I'll work on this for a while."

She wasn't fooling him and she knew it, but there was no way she could crawl into that bed next to him right now. The way she was feeling. . .

Sighing, Ward cuddled down under the covers. He appreciated Rose's concern, but this was a volatile situation. Could they ever go back to the way things had been after sleeping together? Even if nothing happened, it was still sure to change things. Still, things couldn't continue the way they had been, either. He thought he could sense a subtle change in Rose's attitude towards him, but his mind was too foggy with fatigue that he couldn't even begin to figure it out now.

There were many times in the last couple of days that he had longed to be in this bed, but he hadn't imagined it being this way. In his dreams he had imagined himself telling Rose of his love for her and her throwing her arms around him and telling him she felt the same way.

Well, she had certainly thrown her arms around him, but dealing with her sobs was not part of his fantasy. Nor was having her order him to bed as though he were a child. If he were a betting man, he'd wager she'd sit up all night in that chair by the fire just so she wouldn't have to share his bed.

He considered going to her now and telling her how he felt, but his eyes were already becoming heavy, his body succumbing to its ordeal. Besides, she had offered to share the bed with him, nothing more.

～

Before long, Rose could hear Ward's soft snores. The poor man was exhausted. The doll lay forgotten on her lap as she watched him sleep.

Getting up, she crossed to his side and stood observing him, her eyes tender with the love she felt. Reaching out, she pushed the dark hair from his forehead, bending and placing a kiss there.

He was definitely out. Nothing, including an earthquake, would wake him now. Feeling safe, she changed into her own nightclothes and blowing out the lamp, crawled into bed next to him.

For a long time she lay tense, listening to him breathe. Finally, she was able to relax and turning, she curled herself against his side, determined to share with him her body heat. The fear of pneumonia was never far from her mind.

Eventually, with an exhausted sigh, she too succumbed to sleep.

A thumping on the door brought them both wide awake. Ward tried to scramble across Rose just as she was trying to get from the bed. They wound up in a tangle of arms and legs. Ward propped himself up with his arms and gazed down into Rose's still sleep-laden eyes. A smile tugged at his lips and before they knew it, both were filled with paroxysms of mirth.

He quickly kissed her lips before climbing from the bed and opening the door a crack.

"Morning, Ward." Adam's voice sounded loud and clear in the bright morning sunlight slitting through the opened door. "Sorry I'm late, but there are some pretty big drifts out here."

Surprised, Ward hastened to assure him. "I'll be right with you."

Rose hustled out of bed once the door was closed.

"You can't go out today! You need to rest. Stay in bed."

Sitting on the chair pulling on his boots, he threw her a wicked grin. "What are you suggesting, Mrs. Taylor?"

Her face colored hotly and she began stammering in her confusion. "I. . .I didn't mean—"

Taking pity on her, he stood up and crossed to her side. "I was only teasing. I'll be back later. This should be our last load of logs and then we can start on the bedrooms."

The look he gave her was searching in its intensity, but Rose was too distraught to notice. Was he that anxious to have the bedrooms done that he would be willing to risk his health? Surely Adam would understand if he knew the situation. She lifted a hand to her temple, rubbing against a fast-approaching headache.

Bundling into his coat, Ward strode to the door. "See you later. I'll take care of the animals before I leave."

The door closed behind him.

For the next several hours Rose gave herself a good talking to. As she embroidered tiny even stitches to make the doll's mouth, she lectured herself on being a fool. When she began sewing scraps together to make a small quilt for the cradle, she admonished herself to be more careful to hide her feelings in the future.

It was only as she was sewing together some old pieces of leather for a musket case for Andrew that she stopped to think about that brief kiss this morning. She felt warmth creeping into her cheeks as she wondered what would have happened if Adam had not come this morning and they would have awakened on their own.

Was it possible that Ward might harbor some slight feeling for her? As impossible as it seemed, that little bud of hope refused to die. Such thoughts had her feeling as prickly as her pincushion by the time Ward was due home.

When Ward came in that evening, he carried a small tree he had brought from the river. "How's this for a Christmas tree?"

Rose's eyes lit up, and forgotten were those moments from this morning that had caused her such worry all day long. "Oh, Ward. What a great idea!"

He grinned back at her, tired lines radiating from his eyes. "It's the reason I insisted on going today. I wasn't sure when I'd get another chance."

Rose frowned as she looked about the room. Although the room was large enough, there really was very little furniture and the tree was so small it would need to be situated on a table. If they used the table in the kitchen area, they would have no place to eat.

"I was thinking," Ward suggested, "that maybe I could bring in that table of yours from the barn. Since it's larger than this one, we could move this one to the corner for the tree and then use yours for eating. It will give us more eating room when the Comptons come for Christmas."

Gripping her hands together, Rose placed the nails from her two index fingers against her teeth. Squinting her eyes, she tried to "see" how things would look in her mind's eye. "That'll work."

They shifted the table to the corner and Rose found a bowl for the tree. Laying the tree on the floor,

Ward took the bowl and headed for the door. "I'll get some dirt from the barn. Outside's too frozen. It would take me all day just to chip out enough dirt to fill this bowl."

When he came back, Rose helped him move the table and fix the small tree. They found themselves giggling like children when the determined thing tipped first one way and then another.

Finally, Ward leaned back sighing. "We need something to wrap around the base for support."

They both searched the cabin with their eyes. When Ward lifted an eyebrow at Rose, she just shrugged. "I don't know. What do you suggest?"

"I have some burlap in the barn. We could use that."

Rose wrinkled her nose. "I don't think so. The whole cabin would soon smell like the barn." She thought a minute and then her eyes lit up. "I know. Look in my trunk there by the bed. There's an old white blanket. We could use that, then it would look like snow."

Ward rummaged through the chest while Rose held the tree steady. It was a moment before Rose realized just how quiet the room had become. Turning to see where the problem lay, she found Ward holding her memory quilt across his lap. His eyes went to hers.

"This is beautiful. Why don't you use it?"

The color that had drained from her face now came rushing back. She opened her mouth to explain, but no words would come.

Ward crossed the room to her side, the white blanket clutched in his hands. He handed it to her without comment. Together they wrapped it securely around the base of the little tree.

"That should hold it," Ward told her.

She agreed, and though it was nothing like the pine trees back home, still it would do. She stepped back to get the full effect, smiling her pleasure. Ward was such a thoughtful man. Why had she never seen that before?

"It looks great. I'll decorate it tomorrow."

Smiling, Ward told her, "I'll help."

Rose turned to him in surprise. "That's right, you're finished chopping trees. Aren't you and Adam going to start building tomorrow?"

The look he settled on her was disturbing in its intensity. "I'm in no hurry," he told her quietly.

Unsure what to make of his attitude, Rose decided to leave him to his own thoughts and go fix supper. Ward's fingers closed softly but inexorably around her wrist when she turned away. "Tell me about the quilt," he commanded softly. "It upset you to see it. Why?"

Rose's eyes met his and she found herself unable to look away. She began to tell him of the quilt without quite realizing what she was saying. His nearness was doing funny things to her insides.

When he suddenly released her, she felt curiously bereft. He returned to the chest and pulled the quilt from it. Laying it across the bed, he motioned for Rose to come to him. Reluctantly, she moved to his side.

Ward motioned to the spread. "Tell me about the material."

Uncertain as to his reasons for wanting to know,

Rose still found herself telling him little stories about the various pieces. He laughed with her over her tales, and grew somber when she told him of the piece that was from the last dress her mother wore before she died.

He gently folded the covering and replaced it in its position in the chest. When he looked her way, his face was solemn. "Perhaps you will use it one day, perhaps not, but it's great that you have so many memories. What a unique way of making sure that those memories are around for a long time."

Ward was silent throughout supper, his thoughts far away. Rose assumed that in sharing her own memories, she had resurrected his own recollections of Elise. She picked at her own meal, pushing the stew around on her plate.

After washing the dishes, Rose decided to search through her things and see what she could use to decorate the tree. She hadn't much, but she had a lot of ingenuity.

Ward settled himself beside the fire to put the finishing touches to Andrew's gun. Although it wouldn't actually shoot, Rose knew the boy would be thrilled with it.

Taking out some scraps of material, Rose held them against the tree. Their bright colors added a bit of cheer to the drab interior. Yes, she would tie various colors of bows to the branches. That would be a start.

"Ward?"

"Hmm?"

Rose watched as he expertly smoothed the gun barrel with a piece of sandpaper.

"We don't have a gift for Alice and Adam."

He looked up at her then. "I'm sure they won't expect one." He went back to sanding. "If I'd thought about it, I would have picked up something in Yankton."

"Why *did* you go to Yankton?"

Without looking up he answered her. "I needed some supplies."

Rose had no idea what he could have possibly needed, but then she knew very little about the running of his farm. Shrugging, she sat down to cut some of her scraps into small enough strips to use as bows.

Although Ward said nothing, Rose could see the tired droop of his shoulders. He had battled a blizzard half the night and then rose at first light to go finish chopping logs for their cabin. It was obviously catching up with him, but for some reason he seemed reluctant to go to bed.

Rose put her things away and began to prepare herself for bed. After brushing her hair its required one hundred strokes, she crawled beneath the covers. Ward still sat next to the fire working on the gun.

"Aren't you coming?" Rose asked him.

She could see him swallow hard before shaking his head. "Not just yet. I'm almost finished here."

Rose lifted herself on one elbow. "Andrew will love that. And Alicia will love her cradle. You do beautiful work, Ward."

"Thanks."

The one clipped syllable brought a frown to Rose's face. Ward seemed almost like a stranger tonight. Cold. Aloof. Like he had been before their marriage.

Sliding back under the covers, Rose turned her back on him, feeling unreasonably hurt.

It was some time later before Ward banked the fire and prepared himself for bed. Rose pretended to be asleep, waiting to see if he would take up his pallet on the floor again. She thought she would die if he did, thinking that he would be rejecting what she had so shyly offered.

Ward blew out the lantern and Rose held her breath until suddenly she felt the bed dip as Ward climbed in beside her. He lay staring up at the ceiling for a long time before finally he rolled towards Rose's back.

Wrapping one strong arm around her waist, Ward pulled her back against his chest. He made no move to do anything else and Rose sighed with relief when after several moments she heard his even breathing. Feeling safe for the night, she allowed herself to relax back against his body and even in his sleep, he cuddled her close.

Goodness only knew how they were going to handle this situation in the morning.

Chapter 7

The morning light didn't penetrate the dingy interior of the cabin, so it was late when Rose opened her eyes. Sometime in the night she had curled herself into Ward's arms and now felt her face flame with color.

She made a move to get up, only to find herself pulled back and Ward's handsome face grinning down into her own.

"Where you going?"

"I. . .I have to fix breakfast."

He shook his head slowly and a lone curl dropped tantalizingly down across his forehead. "Not yet. There's something we need to discuss."

Feeling her heart begin to pound, Rose swallowed hard. "What?"

Ward stared down into her blue eyes as he traced a finger across Rose's flaming cheek, his eyes dark and serious. "Rose, I think I'm in love with you."

He waited for her reaction, and a long moment passed as Rose tried to believe her ears.

"What. . .what did you just say?" Her voice came out as little more than a croak.

"I said that I think I'm in love with you. I guess I

have been for some time, only I didn't realize it."

Rose could only stare up at him, stunned into a lack of speech. Ward frowned.

"Well, say something."

"I. . .I think I love you, too."

The frown eased from his features. "You're not sure?"

"You're not, either?"

Ward hesitated. "I've only had one experience with love, Rose, and it was nothing like this. I'm beginning to believe there are different kinds of loving between a man and a woman."

Rose could only nod.

"I want to be with you," he continued. "And when I'm not I find myself thinking about you. You're kind and loving, stubborn and proud. You make me feel. . .strong."

Rose knew he was having trouble putting his thoughts into words. For Ward, actions would speak more loudly than any words he could ever hope to utter. She smiled in understanding and he kissed her softly on her lips.

The moment his lips touched hers, Rose felt all her doubts vanish. She would gladly give her life for this man, and she knew without any more uncertainties that she loved him with her entire being.

Wrapping her arms around his neck, she tried to show him of her love in the oldest way known to women.

⌒‿⌒

Christmas day dawned bright and clear. Much of the snow had disappeared from the area, blown by the ever-present winds.

251

There was a spring in Rose's step as she set about making the cabin ready for their guests. She and Ward had spent the last several days getting to know one another better, and her love for him grew daily. She didn't think it was possible to love a man as much as she loved Ward. As they went about their duties, they found themselves eager to be together, to touch.

Ward had been hunting and had brought home a deer for their Christmas dinner. Now it roasted over the open fire as Rose prepared the vegetables.

Ward came in the door, his eyes searching for and quickly finding Rose. Setting down the crate that he carried, he smiled and held out his hand to her and she quickly went to him. He wrapped his arms about her and kissed her lightly on her nose.

"Before company gets here, I have something for you. A Christmas present."

Surprised, Rose could only stammer. "You shouldn't have. Oh, Ward, I didn't get you anything."

"You've given me the greatest gift a man could ask for. Your love."

Rose wrapped her arms around his neck and smiled. "You say the nicest things."

His return smile was wry. "Not always."

Rose's eyes began to glow. "What do you have for me?"

"You mean besides me?"

"Ward!"

He grinned, turning her loose so that he could lift the crate and carry it to the table. Using his hammer, he pried the top from the box and then moved aside so Rose could see what was inside.

Pushing back the paper, Rose found the crate filled with books. Her eyes grew wide with excitement. "Oh, Ward!"

She pulled out the first book and turned it gently in her hands. "Charles Dickens. I love Dickens! How did you know?"

"I think you can just about recite *A Christmas Carol*. I thought you might like something else."

"I've never read *The Cricket on the Hearth*, though I have heard of it." She rummaged in the crate again. "Alexandre Dumas' *The Three Musketeers*. You should like that," she told him.

"I will if you read it to me."

Rose wrinkled her nose at him, but her attention was more on the jewels she was uncovering in the crate. Not since her move from the city had she seen so many books. She pulled the last one from the box and set it with the others. "I heard about Louisa May Alcott before we left Boston. I don't know where you were able to find all of these books, but I thank you with all of my heart."

Ward wrapped her back in his arms. "You're welcome. Now thank me properly."

Grinning, Rose reached up and kissed his chin.

Ward shook his head. "Nope, that won't do it."

Reaching up again, Rose kissed his cheek.

He shook his head again. "Nope. Wrong again. I guess I'll just have to take the books back."

Rose tried to push away. "Never!"

One dark eyebrow winged its way upward. "I'm waiting, then."

Rose sighed. "Well, if I must," she teased.

She would have given him a peck on the lips, but Ward captured her lips with his own and suddenly, all humor fled for Rose. She kissed him back with abandon, wondering at herself and her ability to lose her restraint with a man that just a few short weeks ago she hadn't even thought she liked.

Ward finally pulled away, his voice husky. "Enjoy your present, Rose. I'm glad it pleases you."

He took the now empty crate and made his way back outside to break it into kindling for the fire.

Rose picked up the copy of *Little Women* and hugged it to her, her eyes sparkling. What a wonderful gift. If only she had something as nice to give Alice.

She went to her chest and rummaged through it, sighing when she found nothing suitable to give as a gift. Her eyes lighted on the quilt, and she rubbed the cover softly, thinking how happy her papa and mama would be for her.

With a determined sparkle in her eye, Rose quickly pulled the quilt from the trunk holding it up to the light. Firmly, she blanked her mind and refused the memories access as they tried to rush upon her.

She took the paper that the books had been wrapped in and some string, and quickly wrapped the quilt and placed it with the other gifts under the tree.

If only she had something she could give Ward. Remembering how he said he was happy with her love brought a flush to her face. Next year, maybe she could give Ward a son. The thought pleased her.

The Comptons arrived shortly thereafter. The children oohed and aahed over the tree, their eyes growing large at the sight of the presents under it.

Rose exclaimed over Alicia and Andrew's coats. Alice's face flooded with color. "I hope you don't mind, Rose," she stated quietly. "The coat you brought for Andrew was too big for him, so I took it and made it into two, one for Andrew and one for Alicia."

"What a good idea. And you've done it so beautifully. You must be a wonderful seamstress."

Alice shrugged, her head ducked shyly.

After everyone was in the cabin it suddenly seemed a lot smaller, but no one seemed to mind. Children and adults alike were willing to overlook the cramped confines of the small structure just for the joy of being together.

It was a happy time for everyone. The roast deer was devoured and pronounced a success. Squash, potatoes, corn cakes, boiled eggs, cake, and pie were consumed until everyone declared they hadn't feasted so well in years.

Ward announced that it was time for everyone to open their gifts, and Rose could see how relieved Alice was that she had been able to contribute. She handed Rose a small package wrapped in brown wrap.

"Oh, Alice. You shouldn't have."

Alice's face filled with color and she dipped her head shyly. "It's not much."

Rose exclaimed over the beauty of the fine stitching Alice had used to turn an old sheet into a beautiful tablecloth.

Ward handed the twins their presents and with a small smile watched them rip them open.

Alicia squealed with delight. "A baby! A baby, Mommy! Look!"

Adam's eyes found Rose's and in their shimmering brown depths she read his thanks.

"Wow!" Andrew pealed. "A gun! My very own gun!"

"I hope it's all right?" Ward questioned Alice.

She only nodded, her own eyes glimmering with unshed tears.

Finally, Rose handed her package to Alice. "For you and Adam."

Ward glanced at Rose in surprise, watching as Alice unwrapped her gift. Alice sucked in her breath, her eyes going wide. She pulled the quilt from its wrap and Ward quickly rose to his feet, his protest checked on his lips.

The tears in Rose's eyes matched those of the other woman as both embraced. "Oh, thank you, Rose. It's beautiful. Thank you so much."

The rest of the day was pleasant and Rose watched the Comptons climb into their wagon with a warm feeling of having done what was right. Papa would have wanted her to do just what she had done.

After their guests drove away, Ward followed Rose into the cabin. He pulled her gently into his arms. "Why did you do it?"

She sniffled into his chest. "Papa would have wanted it. The quilt was doing no one any good sitting in that chest. The Comptons needed it."

Ward rested his chin on her head, staring at the ceiling. "But your memories."

"I'll always have my memories," she told him. "And with you, I'll start to make new memories."

Ward sighed and Rose finally pulled away.

"Can we read the Christmas story now? That was always my favorite part of Christmas with Papa, when he would read the Christmas story from the Bible."

She handed Ward her Bible and waited while he settled himself in his chair. She curled at his feet prepared to listen.

At first, Ward's voice came out hesitantly, but as the story progressed it grew stronger with the feelings the story inspired. Rose wiped the tears from her eyes when he finished.

"I never get tired of hearing it. How God sent His only Son to die for people who openly mocked and ridiculed Him."

Ward was quiet for a long while. "He did it for the same reasons you gave the Comptons your special quilt. They needed it, and He loved them enough to sacrifice that which was most precious to Him. That's what makes a true sacrifice."

Rose climbed up onto Ward's lap, laying her head on his shoulder.

Ward's voice was husky when he nuzzled her ear. "Just like you gave me a gift of your love, so God gave us a gift of His love. I've forgotten that. I've lived my life the last several years without Him, but not anymore."

He pulled her face back so he could look into her eyes. "When I saw the sacrifice you were willing to make, knowing how much that quilt meant to you, I wanted so much to say something. To take it back. But it wasn't mine to deny."

"Just like sometimes I wish I could take back God's sacrifice. Make it never have happened. But then, the world would have been condemned to an eternity without God. I can't imagine a life without God," Rose told him.

"I can't imagine a life without you," Ward answered back.

Rose sighed. "I am so thankful that God brought you into my life."

"That makes two of us, because if not for your unshakable faith, I don't know if I would have ever realized just how much I needed God. How much I needed you. I've been selfish."

He kissed her with all of the love stored in his heart and Rose returned the kiss in kind. For a long time the only sound in the cabin was the soft murmuring of words of love.

Later, Rose went with Ward to feed the animals. A million shimmering lights glimmered from the dark sky above. As they watched, hand in hand, a shooting star left a fiery path across the sky and disappeared in an instant.

Just like that star so long ago had led the wise men to the Savior, so God had led Ward and Rose to each other.

Rose continued to stare at the night sky. She had found unexpected happiness after adversity. She had lost one precious man, and found another. She smiled slowly and Ward had to bend close to hear her say, "Thank You, Father. Thank you, Papa."

Darlene Mindrup

Darlene is a full-time homemaker and home school teacher. A "radical feminist" turned "radical Christian," she lives in Arizona with her husband and two children. Darlene has also written several novels for Barbour Publishing's **Heartsong Presents** line, including *The Eagle and the Lamb, Edge of Destiny, The Rising Son,* and *A Light Within.* She believes "romance is for everyone, not just the young and beautiful."

Honor of the
Big Snows

Colleen L. Reece

Chapter 1

*Be of good courage, and he shall strengthen your heart,
all ye that hope in the LORD.* (Psalm 31:24)

A gentle touch on Caitlin O'Rourke's shoulder roused her from the uneasy doze into which she had fallen. Janet McLachlan, whom Caitlin had loved as a second mother ever since the good woman moved into the thatched cottage next to Caitlin's home near Dublin, turned toward the bedroom door. A toil-worn hand beckoned the girl to follow.

Sixteen-year-old Caitlin glanced from the Scots-woman's deeply lined face to the still figure lying on a narrow cot. Dared she leave her beloved mother, even to obey Janet? Dr. Shannon had admitted the night before any breath might well be Catherine's last. "I can do no more." He had sighed. "Faith, and it surprises me she's been for stayin' with us this long."

Something in Janet's faded, compassionate eyes told Caitlin she must heed the summons. She rose from her cramped position on the floor between her mother's cot and her own. Her muscles screamed in protest at the hours of keeping vigil. She glanced at the open window. Morning had tiptoed into the room.

White lace curtains, a carefully mended remnant of better days, hung straight and still.

Another anxious look at her mother showed she hadn't stirred. Caitlin crossed the rude but well-scrubbed room on reluctant feet. She didn't speak until she and Janet reached the slightly larger room that served as kitchen, dining room, and living area. A cot stood near the fireplace hearth, bedclothes tumbled. Ever since Catherine fell ill, Janet and Caitlin had taken turns occupying it and the girl's cot in the other room.

"Ye dinna rest on your cot, lassie," Janet said in a low tone.

The understanding and compassion in the old woman's face brought a waterfall from Caitlin's clear blue-gray eyes. "I couldn't."

"I ken." Janet's rough hand smoothed the tangled braid of crow-black hair back from the girl's white forehead.

Caitlin had long since learned *ken* was Scot for *know*. She slipped to her knees and impulsively buried her tired head in Janet's apron. Hot tears came, the first she had allowed herself to shed during her mother's long illness. She fingered the thin, gold band on her right hand. If only Mickey were here! If only he hadn't sailed to America before Mother took ill. As yet, no word had come concerning his whereabouts. She must bear this sorrow alone. Nay, never alone. Did she not have Janet and the Heavenly Father to comfort her?

The old woman made no attempt to stop the torrent. She simply held the girl and crooned, "There, bairn. Don't ye fret. The Good Father knows your heartache. Dinna ye ken how His own heart ached when He lost His Son?"

The weary girl gradually quieted. The feeling of peace Janet's strong faith always brought stole over her. At last she rose and stared at her friend through drenched black lashes. Janet would not have torn her away from her mother's bedside without good reason.

"Sit down, lassie. I have that which must be said to ye." Janet led her to a chair. Her tone and the look in her eyes warned Caitlin. The girl felt no surprise when she continued. "Dinna try to keep your mother with ye." Kindliness laced Janet's voice, but did not detract from its firmness. "She is wearyin' for Home. For your father and our Heavenly Father. The greatest gift is to let her go."

Caitlin bowed her head. "I know."

"The doctor says she can hear, even though she canna speak," Janet reminded in her rich brogue. "Tell her it's all right to go Home."

A wellspring of strength Caitlin didn't know she possessed brought her to her feet. "Come with me, Janet," she pleaded.

The two who loved gentle Catherine quietly entered the bedroom. Caitlin took a deep breath, whispered a prayer, and knelt beside her mother. "Da is waiting," she said. "So is Baby Paddy. Don't fret. I'll be comin' soon."

Through blinding tears, Caitlin saw her mother's face relax. A tiny twitch that could have been a smile crept over the waxen features. The girl pressed Catherine's fingers, nearly transparent from the long illness. Joy shot through her. Had a slight pressure returned her clasp? Surely she couldn't have imagined it!

To her amazement, her mother's thin, blue lids opened and she looked lovingly at Caitlin. She whispered something, and Caitlin bent close to her mother's face.

"What did you say, Mother?"

"Mickey. . ." The whisper was so faint that Caitlin almost thought she had imagined it, but then her mother spoke again. "Promise me that you and he will be together again."

Tears sprang to Caitlin's eyes. "I promise, Mother."

"Never give up on him, child. . ." She gasped for breath. "Remember. . .love endures all things. . . Promise. . ."

"I promise. I won't give up on him." The tears poured out of Caitlin's eyes as she pressed a kiss to her mother's pale, thin face. A moment later, her mother's hand went limp. A slight breeze stirred the curtains, then all grew still. Sunlight streamed on the wasted face, giving it a glory look Caitlin knew she would never forget.

"Come." Once more Janet's faithful hand touched her charge's shoulder.

Caitlin stumbled to her feet. No need for silence now. She suffered Janet to lead her to the other room. She automatically accepted the cup of strong tea the Scotswoman brewed. She even managed to eat a bit of dark bread and Scotch broth Janet had ready in a black kettle that hung on a crane in the fireplace. Neither did she protest when the loving woman put fresh sheets on the cot near the hearth and tucked her in. Waves of fatigue threatened to drown her. The last thing she remembered was the fragrance of heather-scented sheets.

Caitlin flitted through the days before and after the funeral like a forlorn, black-clad ghost. "Her body and spirit need time to rest," she overheard the doctor tell Janet McLachlan. "She is wearied to the point of sickness by her loss." Caitlin knew in her heart he was right. She gratefully accepted Janet's ministrations. Her mind told her the sickness in her soul would end sometime, although her heart denied it.

"Bide a time," Janet advised. "And don't wurra."

Unfortunately, Caitlin's biding time shattered into a million pieces the next morning. An unpleasant-looking stranger rode a fine horse into the bit of a yard. He dismounted, strode to the door, and pounded with a heavy fist. "I've come to take possession," he bellowed when Janet flung wide the door.

"And ye would be who?" she snapped.

Caitlin's Irish eyes opened wide. She had never heard the Scotswoman speak so, even to a fishmonger who once tried to cheat her.

"Owner of this property." He gave a disparaging glance at the humble cottage.

Janet ruffled up like an angry turkey gobbler. "Be gone with ye afore I call the authorities." She grabbed the broom Caitlin had been using to sweep the earthen floor and brandished it like a sword.

The stranger's face turned ugly. "Old woman, I have

papers here to show ownership." He snatched a bundle from his pocket and thrust it at her. "If 'twere not out of the goodness of me heart, the woman and child would have been turned out long ago. Mickey O'Rourke owed me."

Janet turned red and speechless with rage. She raised her broom, as if to sweep the unpleasant man out of the house and out of their lives.

Caitlin shook off her apathy, took the broom, and stood it against the house. "I'll fetch Dr. Shannon, Janet. He can tell us what to do." She tore down the path as fast as she could run. Wild thoughts kept time with her racing feet. What if it were true? Where would she go? Janet could not take her. She barely had enough to care for herself.

An upsetting hour followed. Mickey O'Rourke had borrowed heavily from the landowner and repaid nothing before he had left for the New World. The cottage belonged to the irate man, who looked Caitlin over, raised a heavy eyebrow, and licked his thick lips. "I might be persuaded to let you stay, for a consideration," he told her. An evil leer followed his remark.

Caitlin had no idea what he meant, but she hated the way his gaze traveled from her stubby, worn shoes to the smoothly coiled braid crowning her head.

The doctor bounded from his chair like an angry parent. "That will be quite all from you, sir! You will be for gettin' no considerations from this innocent colleen who is pure as her name."

The man sneered. "Then the wench can get out. Now."

Dr. Shannon stood his ground. "Make good that threat and I'll see to it every inhabitant in Dublin hears of your black heart, you spalpeen."

The stranger looked so fierce Caitlin feared he would force her out of the cottage within the hour. But after a long and insolent stare into the doctor's granite-like face, he uttered a rude oath. "I'll be back in three days. See she is gone." He turned on his heel, and marched out.

Janet snorted. "A fine gentleman, he is not." Worry clouded her brow. "Doctor, what's to become of the lassie? I'm that ashamed I canna take her."

The doctor smiled. "Trust in our Heavenly Father and give me a little time."

❧

Before night fell, Caitlin had packed what the Scotswoman called the girl's "bit pieces" in an old-fashioned trunk. Handwork. Some pictures. A few precious childhood mementos. Clothing, hers and Catherine's. "I'll be for needin' them to make over for myself," Caitlin said with a wan smile. Janet's eyes overflowed and Caitlin wished she had not spoken. No matter how much her old friend longed to take care of her, it was impossible.

"I wonder why ye have not heard from Mickey," Janet said.

Caitlin turned her honest gaze toward her friend. "Mickey is not much for writin' letters. Besides, it could be weeks before my message about Mother reaches him." She raised her chin and blinked hard. Soon she would keep her promise to her mother and be reunited with Mickey, but she needed Mickey's help. "I know he loves me and will send for me when he receives word. Until then, I'm strong and must make my own way." She didn't add the taunting question *how?* that was beating in her brain. "God has promised to provide."

" 'Be of good courage, and he shall strengthen your heart, all ye that hope in the Lord,' " Janet quoted. "Now let's have a bit of a prayer and get to our wee beds. Things always look blackest at night."

Comforted as much by the old woman's presence as the prayer, Caitlin obeyed. Just before she fell asleep, a startling thought came. What if there were no work for her in Dublin? Suppose she had to go elsewhere? Could she stand to lose Janet, as well as her mother?

Her heart longed more than ever to be reunited with Mickey—and most important of all, she must keep her last promise to her mother. But what if it was a long time before Mickey could send for her. Although stories said the streets of America were lined with gold, she doubted it.

A daring idea teased at Caitlin's mind. She scorned it as impractical. It returned with an insistence she couldn't ignore. Her heart pounded in the silent darkness, broken only by Janet's even breathing. "I'll find work and save all I can toward passage to America," she vowed in a whisper. "It will shorten the weeks and months. No matter how long it takes, I'll follow Mickey to the land everyone says holds great opportunity for those willing to work hard."

A second, even bolder idea dawned. If Mickey sent passage money for her, why not use what she earned and take Janet with her? Her grief lessened at the exciting prospect. Young, filled with dreams, she slept.

Early the next morning, Caitlin bubbled over with the plans she had made in the dark night hours.

Janet merely nodded. "Och, 'twould be nice," she said in a reserved tone.

Disappointment filled the eager girl. She wanted to question her faithful friend, to demand the reason for her lack of enthusiasm. Yet something about Janet's dignity stilled Caitlin's questions. She felt a door had closed between them. It would not be proper to demand entrance to the other's secret chamber.

"It doesn't mean I'm giving up my plan, though," she muttered to herself when Janet moved out of hearing. "I'll say no more, but someday . . ." Caitlin lost herself in a daydream of that someday. She pictured the Scotswoman she loved and herself standing side by side at the rail of a ship heading west from the British Isles to the wonderful land of America.

The arrival of Dr. Shannon interrupted her pleasant plans. His broad smile when he stepped inside the thatched cottage heralded good news. "I contacted some former patients and friends. It paid off," he exulted. "Caitlin, if you're willing to be a scullery maid, I have a job for you. The work will be hard, but you're used to that. You'll be given room, board, and a bit to put by."

Janet frowned. "Ye approve of the house where she's to be?"

Dr. Shannon named a prominent and wealthy Dublin landowner. "He's a hard man and his wife has sharp eyes, but no harm will come to our colleen." He bent a keen gaze on Caitlin. "I'm to take you today, if you can be ready."

She gasped and glanced around the cottage. Her trunk stood ready and the room had taken on a foreign look, perhaps because she knew it was no longer hers. "As soon as I get my bonnet and mitts."

A few moments later, the three walked out the door for the last time. Caitlin shed a few tears on Janet McLachlan's shoulder. Yet the knowledge of what she planned to do dimmed some of her sadness.

"Send word when ye are settled down," Janet whispered.

"I promise." Caitlin kissed her and climbed into Dr. Shannon's buggy. He took the reins. Part of Caitlin wanted to urge the horse forward. The other part longed to leap from the buggy. Instead, she waved until Janet dwindled to a speck. Then she turned toward an unknown future—and someday, Mickey. She would keep her promise to her mother no matter what.

Chapter 2

What shall we then say to these things? If God be for us,
who can be against us? (Romans 8:31)

For two long years, Caitlin O'Rourke drudged in
the kitchen of the wealthy Dublin landowner.
For two long years, she was constantly reminded
of why he was so rich. The wage he paid those who
served him came to little more than nothing. His wife
proved even harsher. When the woman died a year after
the girl began service, Caitlin felt guilty that all she
could feel was relief.

Yet she never relinquished her dream. She saved
every penny possible. She accepted the hand-me-
downs her mistress scornfully passed on and wore them
ragged. The few decent garments she owned must be
safely kept in her trunk against the day when she sailed
to America and Mickey. Her love for him continued
steady, even though his letters were infrequent and eva-
sive. She never forgot what she had promised her
mother on her deathbed.

At the end of the second year, everything changed.
The master of the house hied himself to London and
brought home a new, younger and prettier wife than

the first. Near in age to the scullery maid, blond Priscilla immediately fancied Caitlin and begged for the Irish girl to become her personal servant. Her doting, fathoms-in-love husband agreed.

A new era began for Caitlin. She continued to be treated as a servant when guests were present, but she and her new mistress formed a solid, private friendship. They giggled together like two young girls. Priscilla delighted in giving Caitlin presents: scarcely worn clothing, now and then pieces of money. She taught her new maid-companion proper English and introduced her to good literature. By the end of the first year with Priscilla, except when she was excited, Caitlin had dropped most of her Irish brogue and colloquialisms.

Priscilla also considered her friend's desire to sail to America the height of adventure. "I'm fond of Reginald, of course," she always added in their discussions. "He's good to me and adores me, but I'm glad he doesn't expect me to travel to the ends of the earth to be with him." She looked at Caitlin curiously. "You can hardly wait, can you?"

"Waiting is hard," Caitlin confessed. She twisted the thin, gold ring she always wore. "There is no one like Mickey in the whole world."

Months later, Caitlin learned that Mickey had left the United States and headed into the far north of Canada and Alaska to seek his fortune.

"Will you actually follow him to that barren part of the world?" Priscilla demanded. "Why not ask him to come back here? I'm sure Reginald could find a job for him." She patted her rounding stomach and looked wistful. "I hate to think you'll leave me. If you stay, you can be nanny to my children. I want at least four and will see to it Reginald increases your wage."

Caitlin's heart gave a great leap. How wonderful to stay here with the mistress she loved! "I'll write and ask Mickey," she promised.

"Send your letter out in the next post," Priscilla urged. "That way, we'll hear all the sooner."

Alas for their girlish hopes. The ecstatic letter came back marked PARTY UNKNOWN. Anxious weeks limped into months before a scrawled missive with a blurry Canadian postmark arrived.

In the meantime, Priscilla's first child, a lusty boy who resembled his father, had kicked his way into the household and taken over as king! Reginald Junior's parents adored him. Caitlin loved him with all the pent-up mother love stored inside her. When he grew old enough to talk, he called her Mum, the same as Priscilla, who bore no resentment.

"I'll have my hands full with the new one," she confessed, laying a loving hand on her body that housed another soon-to-be-born child.

Mickey continued to sound vague about Caitlin's crossing the sea. Neither did he send money. In the privacy of her room, the girl shed hot tears. How could he treat her so? Anger gave way to concern. Were there things Mickey held back? Had he changed in the rough world to which he'd gone with such high hopes? *"Love endures all things,"* she reminded herself, and she remembered again her promise to her mother.

Fear gave way to determination, bolstered by prayer. Regardless of Mickey's lackadaisical attitude, she intended to follow him. A little more than a year remained before her twenty-first birthday. By then, she would have more than enough passage money.

Caitlin's blue-gray eyes misted. The voyage she had envisioned with Janet McLachlan would never be. Caitlin's dear friend had taken her own voyage and gone "Home" the previous year. Janet had known she would soon be leaving this world, and that was why she had not encouraged Caitlin to dream that the two of them would travel together to America. Her last words to Dr. Shannon, who bore the sad news to Caitlin, had been for the girl she loved. "Tell the bairn, 'If God be for us, who can be against us?' and not to fret. Och. Catherine and I'll be waitin' for her when she comes."

The saddened girl clung to the words. In spite of Priscilla's friendship, the mistress of the house wasn't her own folks. Mickey was the only one left who belonged to her. The thought gave small comfort. Much as she loved Mickey, she knew she could not depend on him.

Mother had known, too. Never one to criticize, she once warned her only daughter, "Don't be for relyin' too much on the lad. He's older than you in years, but not yet a real man. God willing, one day something will be for bringin' it about. Until then, you must be the strong one, colleen." And then she repeated that same verse from First Corinthians thirteen that she had quoted on her deathbed: " 'Love endures all things.' "

Now Caitlin fell to her knees beside her bed. "I

don't feel strong." Her voice sounded loud in her quiet room. "Dear Lord, please help me to endure."

Like a ghost from the past came the verse Janet had given her, the only possession of value the old Scotswoman had to bequeath. Lighter hearted than she had been for months, Caitlin rose feeling blessed. She slipped into a clean apron and ran to find Priscilla. It was only fair to tell her immediately what her maid-companion-nanny had in mind.

Priscilla acted according to form. "Dear me! How will I ever get along without you?" was her first dismayed reaction. Then she clasped her hands and laughed. "It is so exciting! Won't you be frightened to cross the ocean alone?"

Janet's favorite verse came to Caitlin's lips. " 'If God be for us, who can be against us?' " she quietly asked.

"I do admire you, even though I wouldn't be you for the world," Priscilla frankly stated. She quickly glanced at Reginald Junior contentedly playing on a rug nearby, then at her swollen body. "If my baby is a girl, I'm going to name her Caitlin Rose. Caitlin for pure, and Rose for the flower. Isn't that pretty?"

Caitlin blinked and swallowed hard. "Yes, but what will the master say?"

Astonishment raised Priscilla's curved brows and set her blue eyes sparkling. "Caitlin O'Rourke, you've been with us all this time and haven't discovered whatever I want is law with him?" She sounded both smug and incredulous. The next instant a bright drop fell to her lacy gown. "Besides, the name will be all I'll have of you once you're gone. I feel as if I were losing a sister.

It's so far away I'll never see you again."

"You don't know that. Now that we are nearing the 1900s, shipbuilders are building faster and better ships than ever. One day you and Reginald may come visit, or Mickey and I may come back to Ireland." She wondered why she didn't say *come home*. Had she unknowingly begun to separate herself from the land of her birth? Was it an unconscious way of dealing with the sorrow that would surely come when she said farewell to Ireland and all it stood for in her life?

Priscilla's drooping lips failed to curve into her usual sunny smile. She looked so desolate, Caitlin's tender heart longed to promise she wouldn't leave. She could not. She lapsed into brogue. "Mickey is for needin' me, too, even though he doesn't seem to want to admit it," she whispered.

"I know and I'm a selfish pig." Priscilla impatiently brushed away the telltale drop and donned a brilliant smile. "Anyway, it's a long time until your twenty-first birthday. Perhaps you'll change your mind."

Caitlin started to shake her head, then stopped. Strongly as she felt about following Mickey, God might have another plan in store for her. Why destroy the last shred of Priscilla's hope until the time came?

～ ～

Five years after Caitlin's mother died, the girl who had become a young woman asked her master to book passage for her on a sailing ship to America. When a short time before her birthday she drew from her reticule the money she had so carefully saved, she felt homeless.

America and Canada loomed in her future like mountains beyond shifting fog. Ireland would always be part of her—yet Caitlin no longer felt part of it. Her body remained, but her heart and mind had already traveled the wide ocean to a distant land.

With every day, the feeling increased. Priscilla and her family clung to the girl who had once been their scullery maid. Reginald Junior and Caitlin Rose wailed at the thought of her leaving them. Colin, the newest baby, joined in their howling without knowing why. Only the increasing feeling Mickey desperately needed her kept Caitlin steady to her course.

"It has been months since you heard from him," Priscilla pointed out just before time for her maid-companion-nanny to sail.

Caitlin sighed. Her eyes shadowed. "I know, but I must go." She laid a hand over her heart. "I must honor the vows that I have made."

Priscilla put her arms around Caitlin and choked out, "I'll never forget you."

"Nor I you." Caitlin's mouth quivered. "No matter where I go, you'll always be my best friend."

"You are bound for a wild land, filled with rough men," Priscilla reminded.

"I know." Caitlin lapsed into brogue. "If anyone is for annoyin' me, I'll give the spalpeen the back of me hand." She clenched her fingers, taking comfort from the smoothness of the thin, gold band she wore day and night.

"Then Godspeed, my Irish colleen."

"And the Lord's blessin' upon you, my English rose."

Caitlin tore herself free from Priscilla's embrace and hurried to the carriage her master had considerately provided to take her to the dock. She had refused to allow the family to see her off. It would be more than she could bear.

She looked back from the shelter of the carriage. Autumn sun laid a golden sheen over the stately house that had come to be home. Doubt attacked Caitlin. Was she mad to leave those she loved, all for the sake of vows made long ago? To follow a will-o'-the-wisp feeling of the heart? Her mouth flew open. She would call out to the carriage driver, forsake her journey, and stay in Dublin.

A heartbeat later, the wild desire subsided. Somewhere, thousands of miles away, a young man named Mickey O'Rourke needed her. She knew it as well as if he had proclaimed it from the church steeple or rung bells to call her to his side. To deny that call was to deny herself. No, she would honor the promises she had made.

"Ready, miss?" the driver asked, respectfully touching his cap.

"That I be."

"Verrry well." He rolled the *r*, sounding so much like Mickey a rush of tears threatened all Caitlin's courage. The horse started. The carriage wheels turned in a squeaking dirge. Every block took her farther from Priscilla.

"Yet every block is for carryin' me closer to Mickey," Caitlin comforted herself in a whisper.

At last they reached the ship. Never had the neophyte traveler been so close to such a structure. What a miracle of God for men to create ships that safely sailed the oceans! Heart pounding, red banners flying in her smooth cheeks, Caitlin boarded. To her amazement, her quarters were not at all what she expected.

The driver, who had helped carry her goods aboard, laughed. "Mr. Reginald was for makin' sure you had better," he told the amazed girl. "He said as how faithfulness needs rewardin'."

Caitlin looked around the small, single cabin. Utilitarian, yet nevertheless comfortable. Best of all was not having an unknown roommate or roommates to contend with on the long journey. "Tell him thank you," she whispered.

"That I will. Is there anything more I can be for doin' afore I go?"

A warning whistle blew. Concern filled her. "No, thank you. Oh, hurry, or you'll be on board when we sail!"

He grinned cheerfully. "Wouldn't mind, if 'tweren't for me wife." He touched his cap again and went topside.

Caitlin followed, afraid he would indeed be carried away. Along with hundreds of others, she hurried on deck for the moment of embarkation. A large man considerately made room for her at the rail. The waving hands on board and on the shore left her feeling more alone than she had ever been in her life. Not one person among all those gathered to see the ship off cared whether she sailed or stayed. Nay, one did. The carriage driver had raced down the gangplank, somehow located her in the crowd, and stood waving his cap above his head.

The humble servant's kindness warmed Caitlin's lonely heart. She snatched a handkerchief from her reticule and waved it with the others fluttering in the slight breeze. "Farewell," she called.

"Godspeed," floated over the water.

Caitlin couldn't tell from whence it came. It really didn't matter. "Godspeed," she shouted back. Heart too full to say more, she waved her handkerchief until Ireland disappeared behind her in the morning mists and only the gray ocean and even grayer sky lay ahead.

Chapter 3

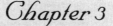

Maintiens le droit: Maintain the right.
Code of the North-West Mounted Police

Only Sergeant Angus Mackenzie's closest friends saw past his Scotch granite exterior. The single clue to softness lay in his steady gray eyes. They half closed in the presence of danger, but also twinkled merrily and lightened his otherwise dour Scot face on occasion.

Among those friends, few if any suspected the chivalry buried beneath the short, tight-fitting scarlet tunic that set him apart as a member of the North-West Mounted Police and struck fear into wrongdoers. Sandy hair topped a six-foot frame. Long, solitary chases across the treacherous north that smiled one moment and betrayed the unwary the next had stripped away fat and strengthened sinew. By age thirty-one, Sergeant Mackenzie had earned the respect of both the law and the lawbreakers he pursued.

Early in Angus' career, a rookie wondered how Mackenzie always brought in his quarry. Inspector Hardesty's response became legendary. He grunted, then barked, "He sticks to trails like a Scotch thistle.

Bloodhounds sometimes turn back. Mackenzie does not." Pride puffed the inspector's cheeks, but he hastily deflated them. Discipline prevented his admitting Angus Mackenzie had stolen into the officer's crusty heart and become the son he never had.

The parents who emigrated from the moors of Scotland to the United States, then Canada before their son's birth, chose well when they selected the Scottish Gaelic name Angus. Its meaning—unique choice; one strength—fit the strapping lad as none other could have done.

After his parents' untimely deaths, the boy Angus earned his keep through backbreaking work. He studied every spare moment. When he reached the age of eligibility, Angus presented himself as a candidate for the North-West Mounted Police. He easily passed every required test they offered, and became part of the Law of the North.

Love for the Force and his country filled Angus. He never tired of the protean land. Neither did he trust it. A hundred times an inner warning caused him to pause on the crest of a hill, or halt the onward rush of his dog team with a sharp call to Yukon, the Siberian husky-wolf who led the pack. Always he discovered danger. Always he thanked God in his simple way for deliverance.

Unlike many who tramped the northland, Angus treated his dogs well. They loved him to the point of sacrificing themselves should the need arise, especially Yukon, largest and greatest, as his name indicated. Gray and white with black facial markings, the splendid dog had more than once held men at bay while Angus dealt with their fellows. When duty ended, he wagged his tail, licked his master's hand, and curled into a ball of contentment beside the Scotsman.

On the few occasions Angus' weary feet lagged in their duty, he bolstered himself by remembering his swearing into the Force. Simply repeating, "*Maintiens le droit:* Maintain the right" bound him to duty with invisible, unbreakable chains. Yet Angus had another code. Although not from the Auld Book (Bible) he always carried, it had burned into his imagination when he first read of King Arthur and his knights. Oh, to have lived in the days of chivalry! What joy to have ridden out with one like Sir Galahad, adopting his motto, "Live pure, right wrong, and follow the King."

Angus' heart never ceased to pound when he recalled those words. He vowed at a young age that Sir Galahad's charge would be his own, with one important exception. Aye, he would live pure and right wrong. But his King was no British monarch. Almighty God, King of earth and heaven, had ruled the Mackenzie household for generations. He and He alone would Angus follow.

Angus had made that clear to Inspector Hardesty when he first approached him at Prince Albert. "I will uphold the law with my life unless it denies a Higher Law," he stated. The Scottish burr that softened his voice in moments of high emotion became more pronounced. "I canna promise tae do more."

Hardesty's brows raised in interrogation points. Never had a candidate dared qualify the vows necessary to enter the Force. He started to dismiss the stripling

upstart who stood before him. Something in Angus'
steady gray gaze robbed him of words. The inspector's
hand shot out of its own volition. "Agreed." He laughed.
"God forbid such a time ever comes! I see no reason it
will. We who uphold the laws of Canada and our queen
also recognize a Higher Power." He gripped the hand
whose strength promised faithfulness to the death.

"Verry weel. I will serve."

Nothing more was said between them at the time,
but Inspector Hardesty secretly petitioned the God
they both believed controlled the world and all in it,
*May the day never come when Angus Mackenzie must
choose between duty to an earthly tribunal and Thee.*

Passing years brought promotion to sergeancy. Angus
proudly wore the three-bar gold chevrons with their
crown. He became more manly with every fleeting
month. His chiseled face would never be considered
handsome, yet Angus Mackenzie's incredible gray eyes
saved him from plainness.

In time, Inspector Hardesty became Superintendent
Hardesty, graying in the service of queen and country.
The unspoken bond between Angus and him forged
into a steel chain without a single weak link. Neither
married. Angus suspected a lost, perhaps unrequited
love in his superintendent's past, although Hardesty
never referred to such a thing. As for himself—his
response to the idea was a ringing laugh that brought an
answering chorus of howls from Yukon and the team.

He was still smiling at the idea one afternoon when

they mushed their way to headquarters in response to a message from Hardesty. *Pack for a long journey and be ready to leave Prince Albert immediately,* read the familiar scrawl in the sealed envelope.

With the ease of obeying many such orders, Angus accomplished his task in an incredibly short time. What perverse imp had set him to wondering about his superintendent's marital status he couldn't say. He laughed again. "Should I want a lassie, where would I find one?" he demanded.

Yukon pricked his ears, cocked his head to one side, and gave a short bark.

Angus grinned. "Fine lot of help you are. You know as well as I do the closest thing to a white woman is the factor's wife at Lac Bain." Wistfulness softened his gray eyes. It would be good to see a white woman. Sometimes he stared at his mother's picture, wondering. It didn't seem likely God had such love and joy as he had observed between his parents in store for Angus Mackenzie.

The smile left his lips. He would settle for no less. Some of his fellow officers had married dusky Cree and Chippewa maidens or half-French girls and found happiness. Now and then, one disgraced the Force and hastily departed after transgressing the honor of the big snows, the unwritten law that protected girls and women from men's evil designs. That cardinal northern sin was secondary only to the law of the cache. Anyone who stole another man's provisions sentenced that man to death and faced the same punishment when apprehended. Those who broke the northern code of chivalry wisely fled for their lives or were summarily meted out justice by either the law or outraged families.

"I just haven't seen a lassie I care to call mine," Angus admitted. He ignored the tiny flames of envy he experienced when visiting in friends' cabins where love reigned. So far, they hadn't leaped high enough to make him consider leaving the Force. Angus had long since accepted others might justify long absences from their wives in the name of duty, but he could not. Should he take a wife, he would not leave her alone for weeks and months.

Having settled the question in his mind for at least the hundredth time, he paused beside headquarters and drank in the cloudless night. Scattered lights like empty yellow eyes marked the last outpost of civilization. A billion matching stars hung in the freezing sky. He shivered. Not the best time to take the trail. Yet the challenge of the unknown sent red blood coursing through his body.

He had fought the North a dozen, nay, a hundred times before, and won. God willing, he would do it again. If not—Angus shrugged. An unmarked, wilderness grave (should anyone be present to dig it) held no fear, just a sense of loneliness. Hardesty would mourn him, along with a few others. Those outside the law would rejoice in knowing his relentless step haunted them no more. His name would go down in the annals of northern history as one who did his duty.

"Live pure, right wrong, and follow the King," he muttered. A verse from the Auld Book came to mind, Paul's words to Timothy. " 'I have fought a good fight,

I have finished my course, I have kept the faith,'" Angus quoted to the brooding night. "What better epitaph could any honorable man ask, than to lie at rest knowing he did his best?"

A grim smile lifted his lips. Hardesty would not like to be kept waiting while he planned his demise! Angus raised his heavily mittened hand and rapped on the door.

"Enter."

Angus pushed the door open and stepped inside. The change from dark gloom into a warm, brightly lamp-lit room made him blink.

Superintendent Hardesty sat behind a battered desk piled high with papers and other paraphernalia. "Get out of your coat," he ordered. "This is going to take some time. You'll roast in here."

Something about the superintendent caught Angus' attention. He seldom saw such reluctance in the keen eyes that stared at him as if their owner's thoughts had strayed far afield. Sergeant Mackenzie's spine tingled. Only an assignment of the greatest urgency would cause Hardesty to start one of his men on a quest on such an icy night.

"Yes, sir." Angus shed the warmly lined parka, stripped his gloves from his hands, and breathed in warm air.

Hardesty motioned him to a chair. "I suppose you're wondering what this is all about." His stare never wavered.

"I am, sir."

"One word. O'Rourke." Hardesty's mouth twisted.

Angus felt his body jerk. He lapsed into brogue. "O'Rourke? Impossible! Och, he couldn't be abroad again so soon. Dinna ye detail Sergeant Smith and Corporal Halloran to deliver him to Regina just a few days ago?"

"I did." Hardesty's terrier-bright gaze never left Angus' face. "They just stumbled in, half-frozen. O'Rourke escaped not a hundred miles from here!" His jaw set and his hands clenched into fists. "It's a wonder they made it back."

"How did their prisoner escape?" The question cracked like a pistol shot. "Sir," Angus belatedly added.

Hardesty snorted and an unwilling admiration crept into his flintlike eyes. "Irish blarney, pure and simple. The lad—for despite his twenty-five years, he has the appearance of one—waited until Sergeant Smith was busy feeding the dogs. Then he asked Corporal Halloran in a pitiful voice if he wouldn't remove the shackles so he could walk a bit and 'be for warmin' meself' against the cold night. I'd be for doin' the same for you, if we were in each other's place,' O'Rourke added."

Angus felt a premonitory chill feather along his veins.

"Halloran felt sorry for his prisoner. That sympathy cost him dearly. When he bent to loosen the shackles, O'Rourke clipped him a blow with his manacled hands. According to Sergeant Smith, Corporal Halloran dropped without a sound. The first inkling Smith had of trouble was when he turned and discovered himself looking into the muzzle of Halloran's service revolver.

290

" 'Shure, and it's sorry I'm bein' for inconveniencin' you,' O'Rourke said. 'But I'll be needin' the team.' "

"Smith reached for his revolver but O'Rourke turned Halloran's gun on the downed corporal. 'Don't be for makin' me kill him or you,' he told Smith. The sergeant said he'd be hanged if the prisoner didn't sound cheerful as morning!"

Angus couldn't help admiring the Irishman's pluck, even while scorning anyone who ran afoul of the law and put himself in such a position.

"You have to hand it to O'Rourke. He forced Smith to free his hands, took the team and most of the provisions. He left enough so Smith and Halloran could make it back here." Hardesty shook his head. "Funny chap. After disarming Smith, he threw the bullets in the snow along with Smith's revolver. 'I thank you,' he said, and headed off with the dog sled and team, leaving my men staring after him." Hardesty's fingers drummed on the old desk. "He must have known leaving them alive meant less time before we took the trail."

"So O'Rourke hasn't added murder to stealing," Angus remarked. He leaned forward. "Which direction did he go?"

"Due north."

Angus felt the color leave his face. He leaped from his chair and protested, "Is the man mad? He would have to pass within a few miles of here!"

"I know." Hardesty's eyes gleamed in the lamplight. His fist crashed to the desk. "Can you see why I want you to start out now? With luck, and if he stayed on course, you can overtake O'Rourke soon. Your team is fresh and Yukon is the best lead sled dog in all of the Northwest Territories." He rose in such haste his chair turned over with a crash. "Bring in your man, sergeant. The honor of all of us here at Prince Albert is at stake."

"I shall." Iron hands gripped, then Angus Mackenzie strode out into the night.

Chapter 4

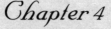

When I consider thy heavens, the work of thy fingers,
the moon and the stars, which thou hast ordained;
What is man, that thou art mindful of him?
and the son of man, that thou visitest him?
For thou hast made him a little lower than the angels,
and hast crowned him with glory and honour.
(Psalm 8:3–5)

Angus Mackenzie paused at the top of the great ridge above Prince Albert and surveyed his surroundings. Light from numberless stars shone down on him. His blue breeches with their yellow stripes were tucked into black boots. His short brown working tunic fit snugly under the parka designed to repel temperatures far below zero. His scarlet tunic was reserved for dress apparel, the color chosen for a reason. British soldiers had preceded the Mounted Police in Canada and earned the respect of the Indians, who viewed their scarlet coats as a symbol of fair dealing and justice.

Angus breathed deeply of the night air through a thin silk kerchief tied over his nose and mouth. He pulled a furry hat closer over his ears. The beauty of the night didn't protect him from the chance of frostbite. He had seen men lose fingers, toes, even parts of their noses because they failed to estimate the depth of cold.

What a night, one to remember forever! Half a mile below, the scattered lights of Prince Albert came down to the winding Saskatchewan River, sluggish with ice in the snow-smothered wilderness. Soon the frozen surface and all the waterways that provided entrance to far reaches would be thick enough to bear a man's weight and that of his dogs.

Angus turned and faced north, the way he must go. White gloom reached a thousand miles ahead of him, all the way to the Arctic Sea. A mysterious whispering accompanied great flashes of the aurora borealis, that wondrous and unforgettable sight. The Scotsman flung back his head and softly quoted, " 'When I consider thy heavens, the work of thy fingers, the moon and the stars, which thou hast ordained; What is man, that thou art mindful of him? and the son of man, that thou visitest him? For thou hast made him a little lower than the angels, and hast crowned him with glory and honour.' "

Dwarfed by the magnificent night, the balsam and spruce trees stretching into the sky like great arms reaching for their beloved, Angus heard a chilling wail coming from the north. He had heard the same sound from the throats of Indian dogs when their masters lay newly dead in teepees. Yet a different note told his wilderness-trained ears that no dog made it. A distant, answering cry confirmed his suspicions. His blood ran cold. Had O'Rourke met with misfortune so soon?

Did he even now lie injured, at the mercy of wolves?

"Och, man, what are ye thinking?" Angus admonished himself. "Wolves don't attack humans except in times of famine." His scolding brought little comfort. Winter had swooped down early this year, like a great eagle plummeting toward his prey. With it came a strange sickness. It swept through plains and forest, leaving behind death and carnage among the animals. Despite known fact and superstition, no one could predict what a starving wolf pack might do to survive.

Angus shook himself and called to his dogs. A good 150 miles lay between Prince Albert and Lac La Ronge. Surely he would overtake Mickey O'Rourke long before then. If not, he would go on. His mouth set in grim lines. More than twice that distance lay between Lac La Ronge and Fond du Lac, on Lake Athabasca. God forbid he should have to go on. Even an intrepid Mackenzie soul recognized the folly of tracking a man farther. Only fools or the hunted tackled the grueling journey to Fort Smith, Fort Resolution, and Great Slave Lake this time of year.

Angus chuckled and the dogs pricked up their ears. "Well, O'Rourke is hunted and I'm a bit o' a fool at times," he admitted. He bowed his head. "Father, I thank Thee for Thy care." Memory of the bright-faced young Irishman who had broken the law and must pay, yet smiled even while in chains, caused Angus to add, "And I thank Ye for watching over the lad, as well."

A moment later, he gave a shout. A wild barking followed and the journey began. Angus ran lightly, in spite of his size. One hand rested gently on the gee-pole.

The crust of the snow offered perfect traveling conditions. *How far ahead is O'Rourke,* Angus wondered. Would he come up to him before they reached the scattered huts that those of the North depended on for life? A dozen times, he and his team had staggered into a rude structure just in time to escape death. On other less fortunate occasions, he had dug snow caves and waited out the raging storms.

In spite of every adversity known to humanity lurking ahead, Angus exulted in the chase. *"Maintiens le droit,"* he told the dancing heavens. "Maintain the right!" He longed to shout, to praise his Creator for the glorious night.

Yet caution prevented an outburst. At this point, he had no way of knowing how close he was to O'Rourke. He had picked up the Irishman's trail, but the heavily frozen snow kept secret when it had been made. The lawbreaker could be a mile away or fifty. All Angus knew was that somewhere ahead he would find the man who had the audacity to consider himself above the law. When he did, he would take O'Rourke captive, according to his duty and the law he had sworn to uphold.

A niggling feeling crept into Sergeant Mackenzie's running body. In all the years he had served as a member of the North-West Mounted Police, he had taken Exodus 20:13—*Thou shalt not kill*—literally. At times his service revolver spoke sharply, but only to subdue a prisoner. Even the hardest outcasts from the law lost their fight when their arms hung limp and useless.

Angus hated that part of his job. He made peace

with himself and with his God by reasoning only thus would countless other lives be spared. Never did he begin a quest without a prayer to avoid bloodshed. Never had God let him down. Ways of escape nothing short of miraculous opened before him, and he rejoiced. Now he halted his dogs for a short rest and repeated his prayer. At peace once more, he went on.

Fewer miles ahead than Mickey O'Rourke cared to consider, the hunted man's lips also moved in prayer. "God forgive me," he brokenly whispered, increasing his pace. "I could have been for killin' a man tonight. Why did I ever leave Ireland—and Caitlin?"

A vision of the girl's sweet face rose to haunt him. How shabbily he had treated her, the only one in the world who truly loved him! A lump rose to his throat. He slowed, weary of it all, longing to turn back. What kind of existence was this, running, always running? Who would have dreamed he would ever become a friendless fugitive, halfway past the borders of nowhere?

The northern lights sang above him, mocking, uncaring. Mickey halted his tired team, the same team he had stolen from Sergeant Smith and Corporal Halloran. Regret filled the Irish eyes made for smiling. "God be merciful to me, a sinner," Mickey whispered. "I'll be for goin' back."

The next instant, his gloved hand crept inside his parka. Above the aurora borealis, he heard the crackle of paper. If only the stained letter with its many crossed out addresses had come sooner! "Or not at all," Mickey mumbled. How could he ignore the pleadings of a loving, faithful heart? A heart that had trusted and prayed for him for more than five long years?

Good intentions fled. Mickey called to his ill-gotten dog team and started on, feeling pursued not by the North-West Mounted Police, known for always getting their man, but a thousand howling devils. With every step, conscience—or God—whispered, "You cannot outrun the consequences. Because you have for saken the teachings learned at your mother's knee, you must pay the consequences. And you do not pay alone. Your actions will affect the lives of others as well." Mickey O'Rourke felt he would go mad from the agony in his heart and the remorse in his soul.

The twin regrets made him careless. For a single moment, they left him off guard against the gloating north that brooks no such inattention. It took full advantage. Lost in misery, Mickey failed to notice a shallow, snow-covered gully. Instinct warned the lead dog. He swerved sharply and avoided falling, but his mates tumbled over him and ended up in a furry, barking pile.

Their present master had no such warning. He plunged straight ahead and fell heavily, unconsciously twisting his body in an attempt to save himself. He could not. He landed hard, with his left arm beneath him, momentarily dazed. The frantic commotion of the dogs, still in their traces and struggling to their feet, roused him. If they panicked and left him here with only one good arm, they took with them all hope of escape.

Bruised and shaken, Mickey climbed from the gully

and quieted the team. Using his right hand and teeth, he managed to bind his left arm to his side, then climbed into the basket-sided sledge and burrowed into the blankets. For a craven moment, he wished he'd kept all of them, instead of leaving some for Smith and Halloran. A rueful grin crossed his face. He needed them far more than the two Mounted Policemen who by now must be safely back at Prince Albert. The pressing question was: could he make the journey in his condition?

"I must," Mickey decided. He set the jaw that had not known a razor's touch for many days. "Achin' arm and all." With a prayer he knew he had no right to ask and couldn't expect to be answered, Mickey ordered the dogs straight ahead, northward, ever northward.

His original plan had been to travel north for at least another day before doubling back. A twinge of his arm reminded him the mishap had changed everything. He soon turned the dogs west, then south, making a parallel track to the way he had come.

For a time luck seemed to be with him. A wicked wind rose out of the clear and starry sky. It carried a burden of snow, enough to hide Mickey's tracks from all but the keenest eyes. "I'm for hopin' they don't put Mackenzie on the trail," the fugitive muttered. "If they do, I'm a gone goose." Stories about the gimlet-eyed police sergeant swirled in his head. It would take every ounce of cunning a man possessed to elude that one!

A feeling of genuine regret swept over Mickey, along with another blast of icy, snow-filled air. If things had been different, he would have liked Mackenzie, whom he'd seen at Prince Albert. Sergeant Smith and Corporal

Halloran weren't bad micks, either. Even Superintendent Hardesty had treated his prisoner square.

Mickey shrugged. No use crying over spilt milk now. Not one of them would believe him innocent of the original charge of stealing mail. Even if they did, there was the little matter of helping himself to the Force's dog team, a crime not to be easily forgiven. Mickey could picture the superintendent's towering rage when he learned of the dirty trick the prisoner had played on Corporal Halloran. 'Twould almost be worth being captured to see Hardesty's expression!

"I must be goin' daft," Mickey told his team. "The last thing I'm for needin' is to be hauled up before Hardesty."

The storm didn't last long. Not long enough, Mickey knew. In only a matter of time whoever had been set on his trail would discover he'd been tricked. Fresh snow covered his tracks in the open, but not in places where he'd been forced to travel under the shelter of trees. Ironic. Somewhere along the way, he and the representatives of the law would pass, with scarcely a mile between them.

If only he could reach Saskatoon and then Regina before the long and relentless arm of the law reached out and plucked him like the Indian women picked berries in summer! Would God help him if he promised to turn himself in, once he got there?

"Faith, and I am daft for even thinkin' such a thing," Mickey muttered. He'd been taught far too well to believe he could make such a bargain with God. " 'Twould have been better for Caitlin if she'd given me

300

up as a bad cause," he admitted. "She wouldn't, though. She's the kind that sticks for better an' worse." A familiar thrust of guilt pierced his heart. Even God must know 'twas not for lack of either love or money that he'd not sent for her sooner. Only the false charge for which he couldn't prove himself innocent had stayed the hand that itched to write the words he knew she most longed to hear. His heart had nearly broken when he read her sad message so long ago: *Mother has gone "Home," as Janet calls it. I long to be with you.*

How many other letters had Caitlin sent that failed to reach him? Had more than chance brought him the one he now carried over his heart? Mickey shook his head. Only God could be for knowin' that and He wasn't tellin'.

Chapter 5

Greater love hath no man than this,
that a man lay down his life for his friends.
(John 15:13)

S ergeant Angus Mackenzie stared at the almost-obliterated trail beneath the sheltering arms of a great evergreen. Admiration tilted his firm lips. "Och, the lad knows this land," he muttered to Yukon. "So he's not headed for the north country after all. I wonder why? Let's find out." Angus turned the dogs south and west. Mickey O'Rourke must be Saskatoon-bound. Or would he veer off in another direction soon in another clever attempt to foil his pursuer?

Nay. Every telltale sign confirmed Angus' first suspicions. They also showed he was slowly gaining on his quarry. "O'Rourke must be getting low on provisions," Angus shrewdly observed. "He will stock up at Saskatoon." A frown wrinkled his forehead and he urged the team into a faster pace. If the hunted man once reached Saskatoon, his trail could lead anywhere. The Canadian Pacific Railway offered far faster transportation than a dog sled and a man's two good feet!

Angus grimaced. No one seeking an easy job enlisted

in the North-West Mounted Police. Should O'Rourke take himself for a railway trip, so would Angus Mackenzie.

North of Prince Albert, the wilderness policeman made a startling discovery. The due south trail he followed had suddenly taken a sharp western turn. He mulled it over in his mind. "Canny, the lad is," he admitted. Even though it added miles to the distance between Prince Albert and Saskatoon, the route was safer for a fugitive. Traveling on the eastern side of the Saskatchewan River increased the risk of detection by someone from Prince Albert.

The ability to mentally crawl inside others' skins and accurately predict their movements had always accounted for much of Angus Mackenzie's success. Now he laid out a reasonable road map as he traveled. "If I were O'Rourke, I'd do the same," he decided. "I'd follow the river to where it turns back northwest about thirty miles above Saskatoon and cross there." A wintry smile showed the gleam of strong white teeth. "Bridges are safer than crossing on the ice." He glanced at the ice-encased waterway. "Although in good conscience, it may be frozen enough now to bear the weight. If not, it will be in a few days."

Late one afternoon, Angus and his team came to the top of a slope that overlooked the Saskatchewan River. He stifled a shout of triumph. The dark shape of a sledge and dog team stood etched against the winter world on the bank of the river less than a half mile below him. Angus' farseeing gray eyes shone. They also quickly noted the drooping dog team, the figure slumped in the sledge. Everything about the scene spoke of a good fight, but a lost cause.

Commanding his dogs to stay, Angus began his silent stalk. If all went well, O'Rourke would be in handcuffs before he realized he was no longer alone.

Mickey's highly trained mind and body foiled Angus. Halfway through the other's approach, O'Rourke leaped from the sled and glanced back. He shifted his gaze. Right. Left. Back to the running figure, then ahead. With a shout of desperation that brought horror to the watching man, he drove the dogs straight ahead onto the broad, frozen expanse of the Saskatchewan River!

"Come back, O'Rourke! It's not safe," Angus bellowed.

Mickey paid no heed, but urged his dogs onward. Their toenails scrabbled on the ice as they fought for a foothold. A laugh floated back. "Faith, and an Irishman never turns back."

Where an outlaw led, the law must follow. "Yukon!" Angus shouted. The well-trained team raced down the slope to where he stood. Moments later, they hit the frozen river. Angus' heart thumped. Had even the sub-zero nights been enough to make safe their course? Concentrating on the fleeing man and team ahead, he forgot the unspanned gulf that lay between them. He forgot the law, his service revolver, everything except the danger they and their dogs shared. Faster than an avalanche, Sergeant Angus Mackenzie and fugitive Mickey O'Rourke became a united force, fighting the cruel North in order to survive.

Mickey and his team reached the middle of the river, then the far bank. They scrambled to safety. Caught up in their common bond, Angus uttered a loud cheer. O'Rourke halted his team and looked back. A horrid report sounded in Angus' ears. He ducked. Anger and disappointment filled him. He wouldn't have believed O'Rourke would fire at such a time. "Coward!" he bawled.

A second sharp crack came. A third. Above them Angus heard a high-pitched cry from the east bank of the Saskatchewan "Faster, man! Faster!"

Truth dawned, bringing with it fear more intense than any Angus Mackenzie had ever known. O'Rourke had not fired. The ice beneath his feet was cracking, too weak to hold him and his team. O'Rourke's crossing had weakened it.

A horrid, rending sound came. A gaping, black hole appeared at the travelers' feet. Yukon and his teammates' momentum carried them to safety in a mighty, flying leap. Angus sprang forward in a jump so high and wide it carried him to the far edge of the rapidly widening hole.

The ice gave way. Both hands flung upward, Angus crashed into the black depths of the frigid Saskatchewan River. *God, are Ye here?* he silently screamed, kicking his waterlogged feet in an attempt to keep near the surface.

Something yanked on his right arm. Angus felt it would be jerked from the socket. Had he hit a submerged log? Nay. A second terrible pulling brought him to the surface. Great cords stood out on the face of the man who lay belly down on the ice, long arm extended. Orders came through his beard when Angus tried to lunge forward. "Be for takin' it slowly."

"God be praised!" sneaked out through Angus' clattering teeth.

Inch by inch, every moment a menace to his own life, Mickey O'Rourke worked Angus free from the clutches of a river determined not to be cheated of its prey. By the time they reached shore, Angus felt he had turned into an icicle. He stripped off his clothing and rubbed his body until the skin burned, then slid into dry apparel. By the time he was clad, his quarry had built a fire and had boiled coffee. Angus gripped the tin cup. Never had anything smelled or tasted better. When he finished the last drop, he looked into his rescuer's face. He spoke only one word:

"Why?"

O'Rourke didn't pretend to misunderstand. He grinned and his Irish eyes lit up like the Canadian mountains at sunrise. "Only God's for knowin' and He isn't tellin'." A heartbeat later, Corporal Halloran's service revolver appeared in Mickey's steady hand. "I'll be troublin' you for the handcuffs," he said. The twinkle in his eyes deepened. "Unless of course, you're for givin' me your worrrd you won't try to escape." The rolling r's in no way detracted from the fact he meant exactly what he said.

Nothing on earth could keep back Angus' hearty laugh. He howled until tears rolled down his Scot face. "Och, ye know I canna do that." He ruefully extended both hands and added while Mickey manacled them, "So, 'tis farewell for now?"

The matching laughter in his captor's face died. "Aye, bad cess to it." O'Rourke straightened. "I could have been for likin' you, Mackenzie, if we weren't on opposite sides of the law."

Angus blinked and swallowed. "And I ye, lad."

"I'm for needin' a bit of a start," Mickey told him. He emptied Angus' service revolver and scattered the bullets in the snow. He unhitched the dog team, unrolled Angus' service tent, and piled the rest of the sled's provisions on it. He grinned through his beard. "You know this country well?"

"Aye," Angus agreed. *What now?* he wondered.

Mickey held up the key to the handcuffs. "I'll be leavin' it hid five miles southeast at a burned-out shack. The key will be under a log at the northwest corner. There's no reason for you to be shamed before all of Saskatoon." Mickey straightened and flung back his head. The merry twinkle returned to his blue-gray eyes. " 'Til we be for meetin' again. God willin', it won't be soon!"

Angus' eyes misted and his throat hurt. "Godspeed, lad, and thanks to ye."

With a cheerful wave of his hand, Mickey hit the trail. Angus watched until he vanished before beginning the clumsy task of repacking and getting the dogs back in traces. O'Rourke had chosen well his way of slowing his nemesis.

In the midst of trying to perform duties made mountainous by the handcuffs, Angus stopped short. "I wished him Godspeed," he marveled. "I wished Mickey O'Rourke, enemy of the government and the people, Godspeed!" Appalled by the lack of loyalty to his chosen profession, Angus stared at his manacled hands. He felt hot color rush into his face. How could he have forgotten Duty, which the law stood for in capital letters? What had caused him to utter those traitorous words?

Don't be a fool, a voice inside clamored. *The man risked his life to save you.*

Angus fell to his knees, pulled like the wishbone of a roasted prairie chicken. Broken words poured out, a verse learned long ago in a small church. " *'Greater love hath no man than this, that a man lay down his life for his friends.'* "

Friend? Angus winced. Another verse came to him, Matthew 5:44, and he quoted, "*'But I say unto you, Love your enemies, bless them that curse you, do good to them that hate you, and pray for them which despitefully use you, and persecute you. . . .'* "

Sergeant Angus Mackenzie was no friend to Mickey O'Rourke. Angus was the embodiment of the law, a tunic-clad enemy who hounded the Irishman in order to bring him to justice. Angus frowned. What had his deliverer said when asked why he would risk his life to save his stalker?

The answer came clear as when spoken. "Only God's for knowin' and He isn't tellin'." Angus had a feeling the words and the look on Mickey's face would haunt him for as long as he lived.

The thoughtful Scotsman finally took the trail on reluctant feet. How could he hunt down a man who had saved his life? On the other hand, how could he do otherwise? "*Maintiens le droit:* Maintain the right." He had pledged to defend the law with his life, unless it conflicted with a Higher Power. Did Mickey's act of heroism atone in small part for past sins? In Angus' eyes, aye. In God's? Perhaps. In the eyes of the law? Nay.

Angus shivered, in spite of the warm blood coursing through him as he ran. The law demanded the last full measure of payment for crimes, no matter how extreme the situation. Angus knew this only too well.

Early in his career, he had helped track down a man wanted for murder. It turned out the hunted had killed in defense of his wife; the dead man had been little better than a beast. But the law had no mercy. The fact remained: in spite of the extenuating circumstances, the beast lay dead at the accused's hand. His killer was tried, sentenced, and convicted to die. God alone knew how deeply Angus rejoiced when friends spirited the man away before the day set for his execution. Rumors floated back, saying he and his wife had fled to the United States to make a new life.

That same blind, inflexible justice would imprison O'Rourke. "Even Hardesty canna save the lad, should he know the truth," Angus brokenly said. "What should I do?"

By the time he reached the burned-out shack, he had considered and rejected a dozen ideas. If he disappeared, O'Rourke could be charged with murdering him. If he quit the Force, someone less sympathetic to the Irishman would take the trail. Thoroughly miserable, Angus still felt bound after finding the key and ridding himself of the handcuffs. He rubbed his wrists. What a terrible thing to be shackled, caught like a beast in a trap, and mercilessly held for judgment!

The miles between there and Saskatoon steadied Sergeant Mackenzie and he reached a decision. Hardesty had said the honor of the Force at Prince Albert was at stake. So was Angus' personal honor. The only thing he could do was complete the assignment he now hated, and then resign. The decision brought relief. He believed even O'Rourke would understand.

Angus discovered the man he sought was at an obscure hotel in Regina. When he reached it, he strode to Room 12 and thumped on the time-scarred door. "Open in the name of the law," he called, glad the chase was all but over.

A quick gasp came from inside.

"Open the door, O'Rourke," Angus thundered.

The door flew open. No grinning Irishman stood there, but a young woman, a girl with the sweetest eyes on earth. Her face was haloed by crow-black hair and her cheeks were highlighted with wild roses that quickly faded. Angus reeled. Surely he'd been given the wrong room number. "Who are you?" he choked out.

A slim, white hand with a thin gold band flew to the girl's throat. She stared at him with enormous, blue-gray eyes.

"Well?"

Color swept back into her cheeks, faint as the brogue in her voice. "I am Caitlin O'Rourke," she replied. "And you are for bein'. . . ?" A lift of silky brows completed her question—and Angus Mackenzie plunged deep into confusion.

Chapter 6

Woman's honor is nice as ermine.
It will not bear a soil. —John Dryden

Caitlin O'Rourke stared at the haggard-faced man who staggered back from the door as if dealt a mortal blow. Who was he? Why should he look at her so? She caught a glimpse of his service uniform. What had this steady-eyed North-West Mounted Policeman to do with her?

Swift realization came. Sickening. Terrifying. *Not you, Mickey.* Caitlin closed her eyes against the taunting voice in her heart. She barely heard the officer's reply to the question she had asked what felt like a lifetime ago.

"Sergeant Angus Mackenzie. I seek a man by name of Mickey O'Rourke."

Caitlin opened her eyes and gripped the door frame so tightly her fingers turned white and ached. She slipped into dialect. "He is not for bein' here."

"Where is he?" Angus barked, then his voice softened. "Begging pardon, lass, but O'Rourke is wanted by the law."

Caitlin's hands flew to her mouth to stifle a moan.

A hundred thoughts flashed through her churning brain. Foremost among them was her mother's voice:

Don't be for relyin' too much on the lad. He's older than you in years, but not yet a real man. God willing, one day something will be for bringin' it about. Until then, you must be the strong one, colleen. No matter what happened, Caitlin knew her mother would expect her to keep her vows, although many years had passed since she had made them. Even if Mickey proved to be unworthy of her loyalty. *After all,* she reminded herself, *love endures all things.*

She took a deep breath and whispered, "Why are you for seekin' him?"

Sergeant Mackenzie told her. His clipped words contrasted sharply with the pity in his expressive gray eyes. "Mail theft. Resisting arrest. Stealing a dog team, sled, and provisions to make his escape."

Caitlin cringed. The crimes meant years in gaol. "There is no mistake?"

"Nay." Angus shook his head. "As God is my witness, I wish there were!"

Caitlin straightened and stared at him, disbelieving her own ears. "You say that? You, who hunt Mickey O'Rourke like a beast in the forest?"

"Aye. He saved my life." Great drops of sweat sprang to Angus' forehead. "Even though it meant less time before another of the Force took his trail."

The agony in the uniformed officer's face filled Caitlin's heart with the same pity his watching eyes had held for her a few moments earlier. "Tell me."

He bowed his head, then looked straight into her

face. "I tracked O'Rourke to the frozen Saskatchewan. He and his team made it across and started on. I was not so lucky. I heard the ice crack a warning and saw O'Rourke halt in his flight." The harrowing moment showed in Angus' face.

"A deep, dark hole appeared. My dogs sprang to safety. I could not make it. The edges of the ice gave way and I plunged into the depths, kicking to stay near the surface, knowing once I was swept under the ice I could not find the hole."

Caitlin's lips parted with horror. She clasped her hands, never taking her gaze from the face contorted by memories.

"When I went in, I flung my arms in the air. Something pulled. I thought my shoulder would be torn from the socket. I looked into Irish eyes. O'Rourke held me. Inch by inch he worked me free, with the ice snapping like the flames of the fire he built to warm me and dry my clothes." A rueful grin crossed his craggy face. "Of course, he made sure I'd be delayed." Angus reported how Mickey had handcuffed him and dismantled his gear.

"And yet you hound him." Scorn underscored every word.

Dull red showed in Angus' cheeks. "I canna do else. 'Tis my duty." His shoulders sagged. " 'Twill be my last. Once completed, I will not hunt another."

Caitlin didn't understand what he meant. She didn't care. Something sang in her heart, heedless of the bleak future that lay ahead. Time enough later to consider what would become of the girl who had loved Mickey for so long. Now she rejoiced. Outside the law Mickey O'Rourke might be. Yet faced with the terrible choice of making good his escape at the expense of another's life, Mickey had thrown selfishness to the biting winter winds and saved his sworn enemy. At the risk of his own! Pride filled Caitlin's breast. Whatever lay ahead, she would thank God with her dying breath that Mickey had played a man's part.

Angus looked at her with misery in his eyes. "I have no choice but to ask ye where the lad is," he mumbled.

Caitlin slowly shook her head.

"Do ye not know or are ye not telling?"

She didn't move a muscle.

"How is it ye came to Regina?" Angus questioned.

For the third time Caitlin made no answer. Years of loyalty locked her lips against uttering one word that would betray Mickey. She had come too far for that. Respect for the law and the need to obey it whispered she must speak. Caitlin could not. One careless word, one admittance that after weeks and months she had at last received word to come to Regina would jeopardize Mickey's future. And hers. Caitlin O'Rourke would not, could not be the one to clang the iron bars of gaol behind the man she loved.

Steel replaced the pity in Sergeant Mackenzie's eyes. "If ye will not speak, I canna do aught but take ye to the authorities," he said heavily.

"May I be for gettin' my cloak, gloves, and bonnet?" she asked, trying to keep the tremble from her voice.

The dull red again rose in his face, but he only nodded. Caitlin had the feeling the call of Duty went against every ounce of Scottish chivalry in his strong frame. The feeling increased when he led her the short distance to a forbidding building and ushered her into the presence of a uniformed officer with eyes colder than the Irish sea. "Sir, this is Mrs. O'Rourke."

A nervous laugh escaped Caitlin as she watched the words change the man's expression. Her laughter died when the official's glacial glare bored into her. "How dare you laugh?" the man behind the desk bellowed. "Where is your lawbreaking husband?"

Caitlin maintained a stony silence.

"Speak, woman," he thundered. "Or I'll clap you in gaol until you do!"

She flung back her head and spoke for the first time since Angus had finished his recital of rescue from the watery grave. "So be it." She felt she had just signed her own death sentence. Yet what else could she do? *Nothing,* her wildly beating heart declared.

Angus Mackenzie protested on her behalf. "It's not fit for a lady, sir," he stated. "Let her stay in her room under guard. She refuses to speak, but it's that sure the hotel's where the lad is expecting to find her. We'll nab him." Caitlin threw him a tremulous smile of thanks, but Sergeant Mackenzie only ground his teeth in his frustration.

The interrogating officer didn't seem to notice the unwilling determination in his subordinate's manner. He grumbled and complained, but at last agreed to Angus' plan. In parting, he closed his right hand into an iron fist and slammed it onto his desk. His icicle gaze fastened on Caitlin. "You haven't heard the last of

316

this. If O'Rourke doesn't show up soon, you'll go on trial as an accomplice and be put away for shielding a wanted man."

Caitlin returned his look of hatred with a calm she hadn't believed possible. Her heart repeated, *So be it.* Never would she tell either him or anyone else what little she knew about Mickey.

Angus delivered her to her door after a second, silent walk. "Ye dinna ken how sorry I am," he told her. His honest eyes showed the struggle in his soul, and something else as well. Admiration? Respect? Something even deeper?

Caitlin impulsively laid her small, gloved hand in his. "I do," she said in a small voice. Now that she was away from the presence of the other officer, the stiffening in her spine began to crumble. She hastily excused herself and opened the door to Room 12. Angus remained on duty in the hall. Later another officer would relieve him.

Caitlin stepped inside the cheerless room and smiled weakly. At least it was better than being incarcerated. Her smile faded at the sound of a key creaking in the lock of her door, imprisoning her as surely as though she were in gaol. Panic swept over her. She raised slender hands, wanting to beat on the door, to plead with Angus Mackenzie to help her. For one insane moment, she considered using a woman's wiles to gain her freedom. If she had correctly interpreted the look in her captor's eyes, she might be able to. . .

Never! Caitlin blazed with anger at herself. No daughter of God dared make use of her womanhood to gain even desperately needed results. Her lashes lowered and touched her hot cheeks. Her hands flew to them. What disappointment, nay, disgust would spring to Angus Mackenzie's face should she so cheapen herself. Besides, no matter how much pain it caused the sergeant to carry out what he proclaimed would be his final duty, something in the firm lips showed he would be true to the law so long as he remained part of it. Her hand fell to her side. That law declared Mickey O'Rourke guilty until proven innocent. Neither sympathy nor dereliction of duty on the part of an officer could change that.

Caitlin stumbled to the narrow bed and fell to her knees beside it, trying to pray. Did she dare seek God's help while shielding Mickey? Oh, to be a child again in Ireland, with no such terrible decisions! Caitlin pressed her fists against her burning eyes. Why must life be so hard? Why hadn't she stayed in Dublin with Priscilla and her family instead of coming to this merciless land of ice, snow, and everlasting winter? Yet the thought of never seeing Mickey's eyes brighten when she ran to him, never hearing his merry whistle, left her desolate. Right or wrong, she had come. She would honor the promises she had made. Now she must pray that somehow God would have mercy on her, even while the law would not. She would add a prayer that He would forgive her for the temptation to be unworthy of her calling by attempting to use feminine wiles to sway Angus Mackenzie.

Hours later, Caitlin roused and made ready for bed. She had forced herself to stuff down the simple but surprisingly good supper Sergeant Mackenzie procured for her. She must not allow her strength to dwindle. Doing so meant the chance of giving way to weakness and reversing her decision to accept Mickey's punishment as her own rather than betray him. She fell into a heavy sleep and woke amazed at how much better she felt.

While she slept, it had begun to snow again. The storm continued for three days. Each day, Sergeant Angus Mackenzie escorted her to be questioned. She held her tongue until the third afternoon when the officer in charge thrust an enormous Bible in front of her and commanded, "Put your hand on it and swear to tell the truth, the whole truth, and nothing but the truth."

Caitlin heard Angus' quick intake of breath. She saw pity and regret in the faces of Sergeant Smith and Corporal Halloran, who had come to add their incriminating testimony to the list of sins Mickey O'Rourke had committed against the law. All their training could never stamp out what was called "the honor of the big snows," the North Country's unwritten code of gallantry for women.

Their unspoken compassion gave her courage to speak. Caitlin O'Rourke looked straight at the officer holding the Bible. She opened her mouth and spoke one word in clear tones that rang throughout the room and stunned those present.

"No."

A gasp turned her attention to Sergeant Mackenzie. She blinked, stared again. A poignant light had crept into his eyes, softening their gray into Scottish mist, with an expression that set Caitlin's heart afire. No man had ever given her such a look of devotion.

A boot heel scraped. The sound shattered the dramatic silence. The investigating officer rose in such haste his chair crashed to the floor. He towered over Caitlin like a grizzly bear over a rock rabbit. "Young woman, *what did you say?*"

Weary of the cat-and-mouse games he had used in his attempts to trick her, Caitlin reached into her last remaining store of strength and dredged up a blinding smile; a smile Mickey O'Rourke always said could charm birds out of the trees. Her courageous act in the face of disaster sent a low whisper of fresh sympathy through the unnaturally silent room.

For the space of a single heartbeat, even the examiner's hard lips softened with admiration for the plucky Irish girl. The next instant, he set them in a grim line, causing Caitlin to wonder if she had actually seen momentary weakening.

"Am I to understand you will not swear? Will not speak?" the investigator boomed, so loudly his voice rattled the windows.

The contrast between his voice and Caitlin's faint, "Sir, I cannot," made the listeners strain to hear her words.

"So be it, then." He unconsciously echoed her words of a few days before. "You have one more night to reconsider. Should you refuse to disclose your husband's whereabouts within twenty-four hours, you will be imprisoned. Sergeant Mackenzie, take her away."

He waved toward the door.

"Aye, sir."

Caitlin bowed to Sergeant Smith and Corporal Halloran. They hurriedly turned away, faces working. Did they have wives, mothers, sisters, who but for the grace of God could be standing in her place? Caitlin hoped they never would.

The investigating officer had detained them so long at the questioning, evening shadows mingled with the deepening snow. A short time before Angus and Caitlin reached the hotel, she stumbled in the darkness, blinded by the gloom and pent-up tears she could no longer hold back. Angus caught her before she fell.

For a few precious seconds, she rested in his arms, feeling she had found safe harbor after a long and perilous journey. Was it her imagination, or did Angus tighten his hold? Did he graze her cold-numbed cheek with his lips? The thought left her weak, and she clenched her fingers to keep from clinging to him.

A heartbeat later, a figure leaped out of the darkness. A single blow sent Sergeant Mackenzie reeling to the ground. A gloved hand covered the scream rushing from Caitlin's throat. Then strong arms caught her up and bore her away into the snow-clogged night.

Chapter 7

Better to die ten thousand deaths than wound
my honor. —Joseph Addison

When faith is lost, when honor dies,
the man is dead! —John Greenleaf Whittier

Angus Mackenzie shivered and opened his eyes. He passed a gloved hand before his eyes. Fear spurted. "Father, have I gone blind?" he whispered.

The terrifying thought and sound of his own voice brought him to full consciousness. A yellowish light in the dark shape of a nearby building reassured him; memory pounced like a mountain lion on unsuspecting prey. He had been escorting Caitlin O'Rourke to her hotel. Someone had struck from the shadows, a blow calculated to put him out of commission.

But not to kill.

The words rang in Angus' aching head. He struggled to his feet. "Lass?" he croaked. Only the sound of softly falling snow replied. It brought a sickening premonition that changed to certainty with the speed of a caribou.

Who but Mickey O'Rourke had reason to strike Sergeant Angus Mackenzie down? All others who hated him either lay in prison or were temporarily safe from his pursuit because of the weather.

His heart lurched. So his quest had not ended, but only begun. Now he must track down the two who had vanished in the night. His mind cleared. How long had he lain motionless? Angus strode toward the lighted window. Its dull glow showed less than half an inch of snow on his sleeve. He grunted. The O'Rourkes didn't have much of a head start, but former experiences with Mickey showed his cunning. If anyone could elude the law's long arm, it would be the Irishman.

Angus turned on his boot heel. He must report the incident and get on the trail. Why then did his steps slow as he approached the forbidding building he had left such a short time before? In spite of his throbbing head, his cool and calculating mind whispered a warning to do nothing until he considered well.

Memory of his own craven action stopped Angus short. He felt scorched with shame. Had the dim light revealed to O'Rourke the stolen caress? He had not planned on anything like that happening. Yet when his arms encircled Caitlin, a lifetime of longing swept through him. His defense against her sweetness had fallen like a child's cardboard sword, brandished high, then broken and tossed aside.

He prayed for forgiveness, then raised a booted foot to stride forward. Despair stopped him. Once he alerted the higher powers of the North-West Mounted Police, only God Himself could save the sweet-faced girl with starry eyes that gazed into a man's very soul. Angus knew the clang of prison doors, the grim walls that closed in on those they held. Sweat broke out on his forehead, in spite of the freezing air. "I canna send her there," he whispered. "She would fade and die like the grass in winter. Is there not another way, Father?"

Despondency overtook his heart and spirit. Then like the glimmer of a match in the Arctic gloom, an idea flared. It faded, almost died, leaped into flame. What if he didn't report the attack? The girl would slow O'Rourke down. Yukon and the rest of Angus' team were enjoying a well-deserved rest. Fresh and eager, they could surely overtake the fugitives. Could Angus make O'Rourke see what a terrible thing it was to involve Caitlin in his flight from the law?

"I canna help but try," Angus muttered. He grew aware of unpleasant dampness seeping through his heavy clothing. First, he must dry and warm himself, then prepare for what could be a long hard journey.

He smiled bitterly. Christmas loomed ahead, a season identified with peace on earth to men of goodwill. Where would he spend the holiday? In a snow cave of his own making? Lying quiet and eternally still beneath a blanket of winter white? O'Rourke's last action shouted his desperation. If he chose to use the service revolver in his possession, his pursuer's mission of mercy would be his last.

"The lass will not stand for it," Angus mumbled. Yet doubt assailed him. Perhaps O'Rourke had slipped word to her in spite of her guards' precautions. She might be up to her neck in the nefarious schemes.

Angus violently shook his head. The purity of her face, the refusal to speak when silence meant disaster to herself, rose in her defense.

Had it all been an act? The thought plunged into his heart like a long, slim blade. "Why should ye care? The lass is a married woman." Angus berated himself—and yet he did care. The first look from the girl's seemingly honest blue-gray Irish eyes had stirred him as nothing before. Growing admiration for her pluck increased the turmoil inside him, bringing with it all sorts of feelings he hadn't known he possessed.

Angus lengthened his stride, praying to get in and out of his quarters without being observed. His prayer was answered. Yet even while he discarded his wet uniform and rubbed down, an intangible something beat on the door of his heart, demanding to be recognized. That door flew wide, never again to be slammed shut. God help Sergeant Angus Mackenzie. He had irrevocably fallen in love with one who belonged to another, a lass who wore on her finger the symbol of her faithfulness to an enemy of the law.

From force of habit, Angus reached for a dry working tunic of brown. He stopped. Mickey O'Rourke could not help knowing how the Indians revered the Force's showier dress tunics. On this final quest, Sergeant Mackenzie would proudly wear scarlet. Superstition had nothing to do with his choice, but only his desire to be clothed in the brilliant color that conveyed fair dealing and justice.

Less than an hour after he regained consciousness, Angus harnessed his team and struck out from Regina.

He blessed the snow that had ceased and the great winter stars that shone with an unearthly light, making it possible for him to discern a faint sledge trail and tracks of a man and team heading north. No smaller tracks showed but that didn't matter. O'Rourke could have put Caitlin on the sled to avoid leaving evidence a woman traveled with him. There was small chance the trail belonged to another.

The trail veered a little west from Regina and turned north again. Angus' blood congealed. Was O'Rourke going back to Prince Albert by way of Lost Mountain Lake? More than two hundred desolate miles lay between the spot on which Angus stood and the tiny village on the Saskatchewan.

A mirthless laugh escaped Angus' grim lips. Only lawbreakers and North-West Mounted Police officers dared pit themselves against nature this time of year. He doggedly took up the trail again. With instinct and the North Star to guide him, he would follow until he either lost the trail or came upon Mickey O'Rourke and the girl who had entered Angus' unwilling Scottish heart.

The yearning inside his heart grew stronger with every mile. It would not, could not be denied. At the top of a barren slope, Angus halted and bowed his head, unable to contain his feelings. "Forgive me, Father," he cried to the night. "I love the lass—*and she the wife of another!*"

Tales of those who broke the honor of the big snows poured down on Angus' bowed head. How dared he admit such a thing? Did he not at this moment wear scarlet, symbol of fair dealing and justice? Anguish filled him. Far better if he were garbed in sackcloth and ashes.

A less honorable man than Sergeant Mackenzie would have compromised his soul by telling himself only God could ever know his deep and tender feelings. Angus' personal code of ethics denied him even that relief. It condemned his silent love for another man's woman. Whether his love remained unspoken or was shouted from the top of the world, it must be wrenched from his soul. So must the memory of the only kiss his lips would ever desire, a kiss stolen in a moment of weakness.

Angus raised his head to the cold, uncaring stars, but he spoke to One far beyond them. "Forgive me," he said again. "Help me be true." A few moments later, a measure of peace came. He called to Yukon and his team, then set his face toward the North.

Caitlin O'Rourke huddled in the basket-sided sled where Mickey had tucked her before they left Regina. She relived the horror of the moment when she heard a dull thud, followed by Sergeant Mackenzie crumpling to the ground. Sheer terror followed. A gloved hand covered her mouth and strong arms carried her away into the snowy night.

"Don't be for strugglin'," a voice warned in her ear. "It's Mickey."

Caitlin sagged in his arms. Never in her wildest imagination had she dreamed that after six long years, her first meeting with him would be like this. Fear choked off her voice. Were the stories she'd heard of his sins true? They must be, else Mickey would not have struck down Sergeant Mackenzie and spirited her away. Dear God, had Mickey killed the officer? Did the man whose gray eyes stirred her to the depths as no man had ever done before even now lie bleeding and helpless in the snow?

She realized then the incredible swiftness with which Angus had become so firmly woven into the fabric of her life. Realization descended like an avalanche. If Sergeant Mackenzie lay dead, life would stretch ahead of her like empty miles, colder and more barren than the windswept winter plains. And yet if he did live, she must still honor the vows she had made so long ago. To leave Mickey and make a new life with Sergeant Mackenzie would be to abandon her honor. She would never do that. She loved her Heavenly Father too much. She must refuse to even contemplate her feelings for Angus—but still, if only she knew that at least he was alive!

She started to cry out, to say they must go back. Mickey must have sensed her intention, for he whispered again. "Shh."

Her long-ago promises stilled Caitlin's protest. She kept silent until Mickey deposited her in the sled he had waiting a goodly distance from the scene of their encounter. "We can't leave him," she said in a low, but firm voice.

"I barely tapped him. Mackenzie will be on our trail all too soon."

The last shred of hope, the final struggle to have faith in Mickey died. "Then everything they said about you was true."

"Nay." Mickey tucked blankets more securely about her and dropped a kiss on her forehead.

Caitlin recoiled.

He jerked back from her. "I swear to you by all that's holy, Caitlin, I never stole! The man who robbed the mail stopped by my cabin while I was for bein' away. The thief took money from the letters, burned the envelopes in my stove, and disappeared. Traces of the envelopes remained. I came home to find the law accusin' me. I had no way to prove I was innocent."

Caitlin felt as though a hundred-pound weight had been lifted from her shoulders. "God be praised," she cried. Then a fresh black cloud overshadowed her joy. "But the other. Escaping from Sergeant Smith and Corporal Halloran."

"I had no choice," Mickey mumbled. "Tried and convicted, any chance of findin' the spalpeen whose shame I bore would be gone forever. 'Tis sorry I am for bein' forced to hit the corporal and now, the sergeant." Genuine regret in his voice cheered Caitlin. "I came to Regina the same day as Mackenzie, too late to save you. Ever since, I've prayed to know what to do. There's no one to be for lookin' after you, should I turn myself in. I'd be tried, convicted, and thrown into gaol. I have to track down the real thief. It's the only way. You can't stay in Regina. Can you stand a long, hard trail?" He laughed and it sounded like tears lurked just beneath the mirth. "Every man, woman, and child's tongue is a-clackin' about your refusal to speak."

Torn between love and duty, hope and despair, Caitlin responded to the earnestness in Mickey's voice. She whispered, "God willin' we'll find the man." A sense of urgency filled her. "Oh, Mickey, go quickly! May God forgive us if this is wrong."

"So be it." He called to the dogs. The sled slipped easily over the fresh snow. Soon it stopped coming down and the sky cleared.

Never had Caitlin seen such a night. The northern stars looked close enough to reach up and pick. Yet the beauty of the night, the excitement of being with Mickey again, and the bittersweet feelings of love for Angus Mackenzie could not withstand her need for sleep. Caitlin had slept little in all the time since she left Ireland. The creaking and groaning of the ship as she crossed the tempestuous Atlantic Ocean had left her wide awake and fearful. So had the prospect of the immigration examination at Ellis Island. Then came the long weeks of travel to the North country and finally, her arrival at Regina.

With wildly beating heart, she had flung wide the door of Room 12. Happiness and anticipation had changed to alarm when she faced the uniformed officer. Now she felt thankful for the shadows that hid her burning face. How could she ever tell Mickey how much that same officer had come to mean to her? Angus' chivalrous defense, his gracious escort, his thoughtfulness to his prisoner went far above and beyond duty. She wondered when she had first noticed the homage and something deeper in Sergeant Mackenzie's face. When had something within herself clamored to be recognized?

She pressed her lips together and shook her head. *Forgive me, dear Father. I will keep my vows, as I know You want me to.* Her heart longed for Angus, but she would never dishonor either her Heavenly Father or her mother's memory by breaking the promises she had made. "It can never be," she whispered. "It is disloyal to Mickey for me to even feel kindly toward his enemy. I must never let him know." Caitlin tried to turn her thoughts from Angus Mackenzie. Tormented by guilt, she found it impossible. He had crept unbidden into her heart. She might never see him again, but the memory of his honest gray eyes would haunt her forever. Over and over, her heart cried out in prayer that God would give her the courage to do what was right.

Days and nights passed, so many Caitlin lost track of time. She sometimes felt she and Mickey had been on the trail forever. Her years of hard work paid off. Each mile saw her more able to continue the journey to Mickey's old cabin. If only they could find an overlooked clue, something to clear his name. "I'll still have to pay for holding up Smith and Halloran." He grinned a lopsided grin. "With the luck o' the Irish, perhaps the law will remember if I hadn't been falsely accused, there'd have been no need for me to escape!"

They pressed onward, avoiding Prince Albert and continuing due north. Mickey's cabin lay tucked in a fold of the Wapawekka Hills, just north of Montreal Lake and roughly halfway between Prince Albert and Lac La Ronge. They reached it at dusk a few days before Christmas.

Mickey halted the dogs. Pointed. He grabbed Caitlin's arm and hissed, "Somethin's for bein' wrong. There's a light in the window."

Caitlin peered through the gloom, too numb to reply. The tiny, flickering light held no welcome. Instead, the relentless North had played another cruel trick. Even the cabin they'd counted on for safety and shelter had betrayed them. Through tear-dimmed eyes, the fugitives looked once more, turned, and went on.

Chapter 8

This above all: to thine own self be true,
And it must follow, as the night the day,
Thou canst not then be false to any man.
—William Shakespeare

Misfortune plagued Angus Mackenzie from the time he left Prince Albert, starting when Yukon cut his foot on a sharp piece of ice buried in the snow.

Angus halted the team and sprang to his lead dog's side. "What is it, boy?" He gently lifted the injured foot. "We'll let ye ride," he told Yukon. "Neither man nor beast should walk on such a foot." Angus cleaned the wound, then applied an evil-smelling salve and a bandage so the dog wouldn't lick off the medicine.

The team showed their dislike of change when Angus moved a strong husky into lead position. Even though they obeyed orders, their work lacked precision.

Angus laughed grimly. "Just enough to even the odds again," he muttered.

The dog cocked his head in the near-human expression that amused his master. "It's all right." Angus patted the powerful head. "We'll manage."

Miles north, more trouble befell them. It couldn't have come at a worse time. That very morning, Angus had spotted dark specks far ahead across the frozen plains. His heart leaped. Although Yukon still rode on the sledge like a king on a throne, they had made good time. Angus' service binoculars showed two persons and a dog team. A Scottish burr crept into Angus' voice when he told his dogs, "Och, it canna be other than them. They're making for O'Rourke's cabin."

In his eagerness to overtake his quarry, Sergeant Mackenzie made a near-fatal mistake. He leaped toward his sled, but miscalculated the distance. A snowy runner whacked his left leg. Heavy boots saved him from serious injury, but couldn't slow his forward rush. Numbed by the blow, Angus' leg buckled. He smashed into the sled and overturned it, left ankle beneath him.

Angus extricated himself and examined his ankle and leg. No breaks, but pain when he stood. "Clumsy fool! Move over, Yukon. Ye have a buddy."

In spite of the mishaps, Angus lost little time. Snow packs helped reduce the swelling in his ankle and he refused to stop at Prince Albert to have it examined. A few days before Christmas, he reached Mickey O'Rourke's wilderness cabin at the last gleam of twilight. A tiny, wavering light bravely shone from a window.

Angus thrilled. No sight was more welcome in the North. It mattered not whether the glow came from fireplace, stubby candle, or battered lamp. Lighted windows reached out to those who were law-abiding and lawbreakers alike.

But then his spirits sank. If only things were different! He closed his eyes and allowed himself to visualize Caitlin waiting inside the cabin. Smiling as only she could smile and waiting for him, not O'Rourke. The next moment, he brokenly whispered, "Forgive me, God."

He yanked his attention from the impossible dream to reality. How should he proceed? O'Rourke's foxlike ability to escape those who hounded him was legendary. Angus bade his dogs to stay and be still while he tested the wind. If O'Rourke's team caught his scent and howled, nothing on earth could keep Yukon and his mates from replying.

Closer and closer he crept. A frown turned his face craggier than ever. Were the fugitives so scornful of pursuit they had penned their dogs somewhere behind the cabin, instead of leaving them to sleep outside the front door where they would give warning of intruders? Surely they hadn't lost their team!

Angus reached the window beside the front door and peered inside. The light of a sullen, dying fire showed a prone form on the one rough bed the cabin afforded. Fear attacked. The motionless figure must be Mickey O'Rourke, but where was the lass? Was it a trap? Blankets piled to look like a man, while the O'Rourkes stood behind the door ready to ambush him?

Angus shook his head to clear it. Nay. No man could have heard his approach. Service revolver in hand, he reached a long arm and rapped, gaze still glued on the bed. "Open in the name of the law."

The bundled figure stirred. It started to sit up, then fell back.

Revolver ready, Angus pushed the door open with a mighty heave. The stench of sickness nearly overcame him, but Angus forced himself to approach the bed and look down. Dull eyes that proclaimed their owner had little time to live stared back at him from the wasted face of a stranger.

"Who are ye?" Angus demanded. "Why are ye in Mickey O'Rourke's cabin?"

"Water," the man pleaded. Talonlike fingers gripped Angus' arm. He felt in them the grip of death. He freed himself, flung fuel into the blackened fireplace, and threw aside his parka. His red tunic had an electrifying effect on the man. "Thank God you've come!" burst from the pallid lips. "I can't die until I—"

Angus cut him short by stepping outside and whistling for his dogs. Moments later, the sick man gulped a few swallows of the beef tea Angus prepared, then pushed the battered cup away. "I'll not last the night. Write down what I say."

Sergeant Mackenzie had heard many strange stories in his long and illustrious career. None affected him as did the words from the lips of the dying wretch who stayed alive by sheer will, long enough to confess his crimes. He barely managed to sign the confession before the pencil fell from his hands.

Angus checked for a pulse. None. He pulled a blanket over the dead man's face, folded the page and fitted it inside his waterproof matchbox. He hunkered down by the fire and stared into its heart, long arms clasped around his bent knees. After a time, Angus' head dropped to his arms and he slept, awakening from a dream so real it brought him to his feet in alarm. All his life he had discounted superstition. Now he couldn't help wondering if the dream held portent.

Angus' pulse pounded and he recalled every detail. Jagged white mountains slashed an electric blue sky. Thick evergreen branches drooped to the ground, heavy with their weight of snow. A small service tent stood to one side. A campfire burned brightly before it. His dog team waited in their traces, with Yukon in the lead position.

Angus saw himself by the fire, scarlet tunic and blue breeches a slash of color against the white world. A girl appeared. Long, black lashes framed troubled blue-gray eyes that called forth every ounce of chivalry he possessed. A smooth, crow-black, curving bang showed against the white fur lining of her deerskin parka. Short deerskin skirt, leggings, laced boots, and heavy fur-lined mittens had changed her from Irish colleen to Northern maiden.

"Why should I dream such a thing?" Angus burst out. "I've never seen the lass in trail clothes. There are no rugged mountain peaks closer than western Alberta." He concentrated, trying to fit Mickey O'Rourke into the dream. He could not. The look in the girl's eyes haunted him. Was the Irishman who risked his life to save his enemy in danger?

Father, he prayed, urgency gnawing at him like a mouse nibbling rawhide thongs. *Is it a sign? Will months or years pass before I come upon the O'Rourkes in a far place? Please. Dinna let it be so.*

Exhausted as much by mental turmoil as the long, hard journey, Angus again fell into an uneasy sleep. This time no oppressing dreams disturbed him. He awoke to a cheerless day and a renewed sense of urgency. He must overtake the O'Rourkes. Soon. Yet duty reminded him his work at the cabin was not ended. By the time he dug through the snow and into the frozen ground enough to make a shallow grave, he panted from exertion. He marked it with a rude cross in case anyone ever came seeking the dead man.

Angus harnessed his dogs and considered a drastic change of plan. Should he return to Prince Albert and make his report instead of going on? Wouldn't circumstances justify it? He sighed. Nay. He must be true to himself. He could not give up, especially now. He sighed again, signaled to Yukon who had proudly resumed his leadership, and headed north.

Unknown to Angus Mackenzie, the objects of his search had spent the night in a hastily constructed snow cave just a few miles from the cabin. After a rationed meal, the wanted man looked straight into Caitlin's eyes. "*Mavourneen,* I'm rememberin' Polonius' advice to Laertes in Shakespeare's *Hamlet.*"

Caitlin looked at him in surprise, wrinkled her brow, and softly quoted, " 'This above all: to thine own self be true, And it must follow, as the night the day—' "

" 'Thou canst not then be false to any man,' " Mickey finished for her. "We'll be goin' back tomorrow."

Caitlin sat paralyzed. "Back?"

"This is no life for us." Misery deepened his eyes to dark gray. "I'd decided to turn myself in once I saw you in Regina. When I learned the law had accused you, running seemed the only way. I've outwitted the law for months, but I can't outrun Mickey O'Rourke. Or God. He's been for trailin' me too long. 'Tis time I stopped and let Him catch me."

The low words brought such joy to Caitlin she could scarcely contain it. "It's been worth everything just to hear you say that," she choked out.

"Aye." He leaned forward and tenderly kissed her forehead. "Sleep. Tomorrow we turn south, like the wild geese in autumn."

I'll see Sergeant Mackenzie again, Caitlin thought. Rich color flowed into her smooth cheeks and she sternly gathered her wandering thoughts. She had no right to thrill at the prospect. Even though Mickey gave himself up, a barrier as wide as the plains of Saskatchewan lay between her and the gray-eyed officer.

Caitlin slept far beyond their usual starting time the next day. Mickey had decided they would spend Christmas at his cabin, so they didn't need an early start. "We may be for havin' Sergeant Mackenzie for a guest," he warned, eyes twinkling. "I'm sure 'twas him there last night. How he managed to get ahead of us, I'm not for knowin' but we'll soon find out."

Again Caitlin felt her heart flutter. Again she ordered herself to stop acting like a lovestruck heroine in a romance novel. How could her loyalty melt before the homage in a man's eyes or the brief touch of his lips? What would Mickey think? Again and again, she poured out her anguish and guilt and confusion to her loving Father in heaven, but still, Caitlin drooped. Being brave while Mickey watched her was hard enough. She couldn't keep it up when he turned his attention elsewhere.

They reached the cabin at noon. Mickey seemed in high spirits, but Caitlin's fell lower and lower. He flung wide the door. "Phew! Place needs a good airin'."

Caitlin's gaze followed his inquiring one around the cabin. She noted the tumbled blankets, dead ashes, the overpowering odor.

Mickey stiffened. "Something's wrong. Stay here." He bounded out.

When he appeared in the doorway, he looked sick and clutched the frame for support. "There's a freshly dug grave and a cross. Someone must have been lyin' in wait and mistook Sergeant Mackenzie for me."

Dead? The tall man who seemed almost invincible? Caitlin reeled in disbelief. The dammed-up feelings in her heart burst into a raging torrent. "Impossible!" A horrid thought came. She clasped her hands. "Father in heaven, help us! Mickey is sure to be blamed for the death of Sergeant Mackenzie!"

A quiet voice from behind Mickey cut into her cry. "Nay, lass."

Mickey whirled. His face shone with a radiance that made Caitlin's eyes gush. "Man, darlin', you're for bein' the most beautiful sight in the world!" He threw his arms around Angus in a great bear hug.

Red streaks mottled Angus' face. Shock followed

when Mickey added, "You've won, Mackenzie. Caitlin and I are goin' back to turn ourselves in."

A curious look crept into the watching gray eyes. Angus ignored Mickey's outstretched hands and turned to the girl. "Is it true?"

Caitlin licked dry lips and silently nodded.

"Sit down," Angus ordered. He turned to the fireplace and built a fire.

The girl sent Mickey an astonished look. There was no triumph in the carelessly kneeling officer. Was it a trick to see if Mickey would flee while the sergeant's back was turned?

Angus did not speak until flames shot high and the cabin warmed. Then he reached into his tunic and brought forth a waterproof match box. He extracted a folded paper and handed it to Caitlin. "Read the message aloud."

She took it, feeling they stood at a crossroads that would forever affect all three lives. The bold writing blurred, but Caitlin blinked and began to read.

"I'm afraid to die without confessing. I swear on my deathbed that Mickey O'Rourke told the truth. I stole the mail, burned the envelopes, and fled. I never heard anything more about it until a few weeks ago when I learned the Irishman had been arrested. Frostbite got my lungs, but I hung on. O'Rourke is innocent."

A nearly indecipherable signature followed.

Caitlin stared from the proof of Mickey's innocence to the tenderness in Angus Mackenzie's unguarded gaze. Her heart leaped like a frightened reindeer.

Mickey swept her into a wild Irish jig. "I'm for

thinkin' 'tis a fine Christmas present," he gasped, brogue thicker than ever. He whirled Caitlin back into a rude chair. "Sergeant Mackenzie, will you take my hand?"

"Gladly." Two strong hands met and clung. Angus added, "Laddie, ye aren't yet free. I never reported your striking me and I'll put in a good word, but the law must be satisfied concernin' Sergeant Smith and Corporal Halloran."

Mickey nodded and tightened his hold. Caitlin swallowed hard at the look that came into his face and the husky note in his voice when he asked, "Angus, will you be for lookin' after Caitlin while I'm in gaol?"

Hot blood rushed to her face. How dared Mickey ask such a thing?

Angus dropped O'Rourke's hand as if it were a hot coal. He fell back, face paler than the snowy land surrounding the cabin. "Nay, lad. I canna do that."

Caitlin winced as though he had struck her. Mickey took it more quietly. "I suppose it was too much to ask, but I know of no other man I'd trust to care for my sister."

"*Sister!*" Angus staggered. "Then I've not been guilty of lovin' another man's wife?" He snatched Caitlin's hand. "But the ring!"

"Our mother's," she faltered, unable to believe what she had just heard. "When she grew ill and thin, she feared it would fall from her finger. She placed it on my hand as a symbol of her love."

Angus shook his head in bewilderment. "Why did ye not speak when the investigator called ye

Mrs. O'Rourke?"

Mickey quickly said, "She knew 'twould go harder on a sister than a wife who held her tongue." He stared at Angus. "You mean all this time you—she—"

"She knew naught of my feelings," Angus confessed. "I swore before God neither of ye would ever know. I tried to tear her sweet face from my memory. As well try to forget the morning sun." He swallowed. "I'm not askin' anything until we learn your brother's fate, lass. Then I'll come callin'."

Caitlin longed to fling herself into the strong, scarlet-clad arms. She wanted to shout for joy, to rouse hibernating grizzly bears a thousand miles away with the gladsome news Sergeant Angus Mackenzie loved her and she loved him. But she would still be true to the long-ago promise she had made to her mother. Her love for her brother must endure even if he were in gaol, and one day he and she must be reunited. Nevertheless, the gray-eyed glance that had first stirred new emotions now shattered every barrier except Mickey's uncertain future. That hung over her love like a vulture above a feast and locked her lips. She would wait to see what the future brought for Mickey.

Yet she could not hide the light that sprang to her eyes. She dropped an old-fashioned curtsey. "You may call upon me, sir. But I must wait to see what happens with Mickey before I can make any new promises. You see, I promised our mother long ago that he and I would be together again." She knew love flowed from her telltale eyes. "I'm for thinkin', though, that your request is. . .well, 'tis a fine Christmas present," she added in an exact imitation of her brother, bringing healing laughter.

They celebrated Christmas together, and on December 26 started back down the long trail, stopping in Prince Albert to show Superintendent Hardesty the signed confession that unequivocally cleared Mickey O'Rourke of mail theft. Angus eloquently pleaded for leniency concerning Mickey's lesser offenses. He cited the Irishman's risking his life to save a member of the Force and added, "The team has been returned, sir. O'Rourke will pay for the provisions."

Hardesty grinned sourly and promised to do what he could. He turned his keen gaze from his sergeant to the pretty Irish colleen. "I can see she has captured you. Will you be resigning?"

Caitlin's own heart thundered. She had wondered that very thing. How could she bear knowing her husband relentlessly pursued men, some perhaps as innocent as her brother? The thought of anxiously waiting long weeks and months wondering if Angus would come home tore at her with wolverine claws.

"Aye." A misty look came into Angus' expressive eyes. "I promised God some time ago this would be my last trail."

Hardesty shook hands. "You've kept the faith, sergeant. I'll put through your discharge papers. May God smile on you." He wrote a recommendation that Mickey O'Rourke be given a full pardon, waved aside the Irishman's stammered thanks, and told Sergeant Smith when they had gone, "The North-West Mounted Police will never have another man like Mackenzie."

The remainder of the trip proved uneventful except Caitlin plunged deeper in love with every step. Each mile also made it harder to withstand the pleading in Angus' eyes. Caitlin held firm, wanting no bittersweet drop in her moment of supreme happiness. At last they reached Regina. They knelt beside Yukon and the team on the outskirts of town, asking their Heavenly Father to go with them. He would be beside them, no matter what happened.

Those prayers joined forces with Angus' stirring tale of rescue from a watery grave and Hardesty's recommendation. Mickey O'Rourke was pardoned and freed; Caitlin cleared of all charges. Unashamed tears stood in the Irishman's eyes when he gripped Angus' hand, yet his irrepressible sense of humor spilled over. "Just in time for a weddin', I'm thinkin'."

Caitlin fled, but Sergeant Mackenzie's long legs soon overtook her. "Lass?"

Memories of all they had shared swept through her. She raised her head and said clearly, "I love you, Angus. I always have, even when I could not love you and still keep the promises I'd made to my mother on her deathbed. Even when you were the enemy."

"I dinna think I was ever that," he whispered, catching her close to his beating heart. "Even when I tried to convince myself." His lips met hers.

Caitlin clung to him and returned their betrothal kiss with all her heart. Angus' magnificent struggle to be true to his God and the honor of the big snows had intensified her love for the rugged Scotsman until her heart could scarcely contain it. Like her, he would always keep his promises.

Caitlin looked deep into her beloved's eyes. Twin reflections of herself shone brightly—and the promise of many springs, summers, autumns, and winters together.

Colleen L. Reece

Colleen is a prolific writer with more than 100 books to
her credit. In addition to writing, Colleen teaches and
lectures in her home state of Washington. She loves to
travel and, at the same time, do research for her inspirational historical romances. Twice voted "Favorite
Author" in the annual **Heartsong Presents** readers'
poll, Colleen has an army of fans that continues to
grow, including younger readers who have enjoyed her
"Juli Scott Super Sleuth" series for girls aged nine to
fifteen.

If you enjoyed *Nostalgic Noel,*
then read:

Only You

A romantic collection of four
inspirational novellas including:

Interrupted Melody
Sally Laity

Reluctant Valentine
Loree Lough

Masquerade
Kathleen Yapp

Castaways
Debra White Smith